COUNTDOWN

A Selection of Recent Titles by Susan Rogers Cooper

The E J Pugh Mysteries

ONE, TWO, WHAT DID DADDY DO?
HICKORY DICKORY STALK
HOME AGAIN, HOME AGAIN
THERE WAS A LITTLE GIRL
A CROOKED LITTLE HOUSE
NOT IN MY BACK YARD
DON'T DRINK THE WATER
ROMANCED TO DEATH *
FULL CIRCLE *
DEAD WEIGHT *
GONE IN A FLASH *

The Milt Kovak Series

THE MAN IN THE GREEN CHEVY
HOUSTON IN THE REARVIEW MIRROR
OTHER PEOPLE'S HOUSES
CHASING AWAY THE DEVIL
DEAD MOON ON THE RISE
DOCTORS AND LAWYERS AND SUCH
LYING WONDERS
VEGAS NERVE
SHOTGUN WEDDING *
RUDE AWAKENING *
HUSBAND AND WIVES *
DARK WATERS *
COUNTDOWN *

* *available from Severn House*

COUNTDOWN

Susan Rogers Cooper

severn
House

This first world edition published 2014
in Great Britain and the USA by
SEVERN HOUSE PUBLISHERS LTD of
19 Cedar Road, Sutton, Surrey, England, SM2 5DA.

British Library Cataloguing in Publication Data

Cooper, Susan Rogers
  Countdown. – (A Milt Kovak mystery)
  1. Kovak, Milton (Fictitious character)–Fiction.
  2. Murder–Investigation–Fiction. 3. Hostage
  negotiations–Fiction. 4. Sheriffs–Oklahoma–Fiction.
  5. Detective and mystery stories.
  I. Title II. Series
  813.6-dc23

ISBN-13: 978-0-7278-8395-7 (cased)

All Severn House titles are printed on acid-free paper.

Severn House Publishers support the Forest Stewardship Council™ [FSC™],
the leading international forest certification organisation. All our titles that
are printed on FSC certified paper carry the FSC logo.

Typeset by Palimpsest Book Production Ltd.,
Falkirk, Stirlingshire, Scotland.
Printed and bound in Great Britain by
TJ International, Padstow, Cornwall.

For Evin, Tristan, Marian and Josey, with all my love

PROLOGUE

Eunice Blanton was not a happy woman. In fact, if push came to shove, she would have to admit that she hadn't been happy since Pa and her brothers beat the crap out of her boyfriend and made her marry her cousin, Bruce. Bruce was a stupid man, and because of that, and maybe because of a little bit of inbreeding, she gave birth to three children, most of whom were as dumb as posts. Although, like many a mother before her, she became quite enamored of her youngest, Darrell, the blue-eyed baby-wonder. Darrell was a happy baby, a happy child, and a funny and mostly happy young man. And he made Eunice happy. Well, as happy as Eunice could possibly be, considering the fact that she was little more than a slave, sold off to her stupid cousin. At least he'd had the decency to die.

Eunice's marriage to her cousin was just the way things were in the township of Blantonville, in the far northeast corner of Prophesy County, Oklahoma. Her sister was married to their uncle, her cousin Ruth was married to Bruce's brother, who was even stupider than Bruce, and, truth be told, every woman born a Blanton in Blantonville was married to some relative or other. It was their way of keeping only the Blanton name in the town. It had started as a whim with Eunice's great-great-grandfather, and had become an obsession as time wore on. Boys were allowed to go outside of Blantonville to find a wife, as that would not weaken the Blanton name, not to mention the need for a little fresh DNA added to the mix. But girls were forced, most times, to marry within the family. Her own daughter, Marge, was married to a second cousin, and had produced only one living child, Chandra, now seventeen and pregnant. Chandra had not disclosed the name of the person who'd impregnated her, but Eunice figured it wasn't a Blanton, which made Eunice a little jealous. And in Eunice's world, jealousy became hate, which made Eunice even more surly than usual.

PART ONE

A Fine Mess

ONE

I was sound asleep when the call came in at a little after midnight
on a Friday night, or should I say Saturday morning. Personally,
I don't consider it the next day until I have a cup of coffee
and it's light outside. The call was from my second-in-command,
Emmett Hopkins, who was on phone duty tonight/this morning.
Seems Joynell Blanton had called her parents, claiming her husband
Darrell was fixing to shoot her, and they, of course, had called us.
I sighed hard when I heard that, because it meant I'd have to go
to Blantonville. I wasn't the only one in the department who had
qualms about going to Blantonville, a little township on my side
of the county, home to more than a few people who were a few
tacos shy of a combination plate. In fact, I hadn't met a Blanton
yet who appeared to be playing with all their marbles. And in
Blantonville, a Blanton is all you got. They were like British
royalty back in the olden days – way too much inbreeding. And
since my house was closest to Blantonville – and Emmett was a
chicken shit – he thought he should call me to take care of it.

I left a note on my pillow, kissed my still-sleeping wife goodbye,
pulled on my pants and a shirt, grabbed a jacket in case it was
chilly, and headed to my car. Early fall in my part of Oklahoma
is an iffy thing – you never knew if it was gonna be hot or cold,
warm or cool, or blowing rain and hail. Luckily it was a nice night
– excuse me, morning – no moon, but a million stars shining in
the firmament, no breeze to speak of, and just a slight nip in the
air. I pulled on the jacket and fired up my Jeep.

The trip to Blantonville would usually take upwards of half an
hour, but at this time of night – sorry, morning – with no other vehicles
in sight, I was able to make it in little more than fifteen minutes. Of
course, as a peace officer, I should have stopped myself and given
myself a ticket for speeding, but I chose to give myself a break.

The ME's vehicle was sitting at the end of Darrell Blanton's long
driveway, which ran up a hill and out of sight. I pulled up beside

it. I knew there was a double-wide up there beyond the trees. The ME's assistant was standing next to her vehicle, flanked by a man and woman who seemed real distraught. I got out and went to greet them. The man was tall and lean, the woman short and hefty. They appeared to be my age or thereabouts – fifty-something – and the woman looked like she'd been crying. They were, of course, Joynell Blanton's parents.

'Our daughter Joynell called us saying her husband was gonna kill her, but this lady won't let us go up there—'

I nodded. 'She's right. This is a job for police personnel,' I said. If Darrell Blanton was threatening to shoot his wife then he was probably armed, and an armed Blanton was not a good thing. I was the one being paid the big bucks to put my life on the line, not these civilians. So I went to the back of the Jeep, got out the shotgun (I'd left my service revolver back at the house – not my best move, but then again I was sleep deprived), loaded it, put it on the passenger seat of the Jeep then crawled in, cranked it up and headed toward the double-wide.

I don't dwell on things like feelings. It's just not manly. But I've got to admit that I'm pretty much a happy son-of-a-bitch – at least, in the last half of my life. I mean, I was raised OK; my mama and daddy were good people, although they didn't go in for sparing the rod. And I was in high school before my little sister, Jewel, was born, so that didn't impact me too much, except for the embarrassment factor – you know, proof that my mama and daddy still 'did it.' I just got less attention which, when you're a teenager, is always a good thing. I had lots of friends, played a good game of football for my school and had a virgin girlfriend, and after high school and a stint in the air force, I married and deflowered her, which began the not-so-happy part of my life. We both wanted kids, but it didn't happen for us, which put a damper on the marriage. After twenty-something years, she left me. It took me a while to notice that she was gone. But a couple of years after that, I met Jean McDonnell.

A beautiful woman, a psychiatrist and victim of childhood polio, she's the love of my life. It didn't take the people of Longbranch much time to get over the fact that the hospital's new chief shrink walked with braced legs and crutches. We hadn't known each other long before we discovered she was pregnant. So we got married and had our son, John McDonnell Kovak. She calls him John; I call him Johnny Mac. Now that he's eleven it doesn't seem to confuse him so much.

All this is to say that I'm happy. But I don't think I could ever be as happy as Darrell Blanton was when I found him sitting on the aluminum steps of his double-wide, shotgun over his knees, dead wife at his feet and sporting a big old grin. Like I said, the Blanton elevator doesn't go to the top floor.

'Well, hey, Sheriff!' he greeted me, the grin getting bigger. 'I done kilt Joynell! And boy was she asking for it! Know what she did?'

'Why don't you tell me after you put that shotgun down on the ground, Darrell?' I said, holding my own shotgun barrel down so as not to be too aggressive. Blantons don't deal well with aggression. Or much of anything else.

'Oh, hell, Sheriff, I ain't gonna shoot you! You didn't sneak off and do the horizontal mambo with somebody else, now, did you?' Darrell said, and laughed.

'Put the shotgun down, Darrell. I don't wanna have to hurt you,' I said.

The smile left his face and he sighed. 'Well, OK then,' he said. 'Although I don't know what all the fuss is about. She up and messed around on me, Sheriff! Ain't there a law?' Darrell dropped the shotgun on the ground, barely missing his wife's body.

I walked up and kicked the gun away with my foot, then asked Darrell to stand up. He did, the grin thankfully gone, and I cuffed him and read him his rights.

'But why do I need a lawyer?' he whined as I led him to my Jeep. 'She's the one done the nasty, not me! I ain't messed with nobody but her since the day of our weddin'!' A wide grin spread across his face. 'Nailed the maid of honor in the baptismal font of the church! What a rush, know what I mean?'

'Darrell,' I said, 'you just need to stop talking.'

When Dr Jean McDonnell awoke that Saturday morning, she saw the note on her husband's pillow. She was quite familiar with this type of communication from him, knowing that a call must have come in during the middle of the night for a county emergency. She'd gotten to the point where she could sleep through the phone ringing in the middle of the night, knowing it was almost never for her. The only time it had been for her was when a severely depressed patient had called to say she had just taken twenty Ativan, washed down with Scotch, and figured she should croak in about thirty minutes or so. Since she was calling from her home number, it didn't take a rocket scientist to figure out where she was and get an ambulance there. That had been more than a year ago and the woman had been stabilized on anti-depressants, but the late-night calls for Milt kept coming in at least once every two weeks or so.

Knowing Milt could be gone for most of the day, Jean called her sister-in-law, Jewel, and asked her if she could drop John off with her for a sleepover later. Jewel, of course, said yes. Since Jewel had a pool, a trampoline and a neighbor boy with whom John liked to play, she knew her son would have no objections to these arrangements.

Because Jean had plans. Big plans. First, her undergraduate roommate and medical school buddy, Paula Carmichael, was flying in today, and she had to pick her up at three o'clock at the Tulsa airport. After that, she and Milt's deputy, Jasmine Bodine Hopkins (wife of Milt's chief deputy and best friend, Emmett Hopkins) were hosting a surprise bachelorette party for Milt's civilian clerk, Holly Humphries, who would be marrying Milt's long-time deputy, Dalton Pettigrew, Saturday after next.

Jean had made reservations at the Longbranch Inn for one of their suites. Since the Longbranch Inn made most of its money off its restaurant, and the rooms upstairs were usually empty, she got a good deal and their biggest suite. Jasmine was in charge of finding a stripper and collecting the booze. Since Prophesy County had recently been voted dry, that meant she had to go halfway to Tulsa to find a liquor store. Where she was going to find a stripper was a mystery to Jean.

Jean had already bought items to decorate the suite – streamers, balloons and flowers, and had had a banner made that said 'Holly and Dalton Forever' that she planned to string up. By noon, with still no word from Milt, Jean took John to the Longbranch Inn, where they had lunch, then went upstairs to check out their suite. John blew up balloons while Jean paid a busboy from the restaurant to hang up the banner over the top of the wet bar. She and John strung the streamers around the room and Jean made two very nice flower arrangements out of the flowers she'd brought. When they were finished they left the suite, turning out the lights and locking the door behind them.

By this time it was close to half past one in the afternoon, and they would have to hurry to make it to the Tulsa airport by three. Jean and John jumped in her car and headed north. They pulled into the turn-around at the Tulsa airport at about five minutes after three p.m., and had to make the circle twice before Jean spotted her old friend standing outside the baggage claim area.

Jean exited her vehicle on her crutches, while her friend Paula pulled her luggage down the curb and they met by the back of Jean's extra-large SUV.

They hugged, then Paula exclaimed: 'Oh my God! You look gorgeous! Marriage becomes you!' She held her friend at arm's length and admired her.

'And you don't look a day older!' Jean lied.

'Ha!' Paula said. 'You must have bad vision, girl. My wrinkles have wrinkles!'

Jean opened the back hatch of the SUV and Paula put her luggage inside. 'Come on,' Jean said. 'I want you to meet my son.'

'Actual proof that the world's oldest living virgin no longer exists, huh?' Paula teased.

Jean elbowed her gently in the ribs. 'Hush!' she said as she led Paula to the door of the back seat of the SUV, where her son was strapped in. She opened the door and said, 'John, I want you to meet my good friend, Doctor Carmichael. Paula, this is my son, John Kovak.'

Paula stuck her hand in and shook John's proffered one. 'Are you sick?' she asked him.

John gave her a confused look, then said tentatively, 'No.'

'Good. Then you don't have to call me "doctor" anything. The name's Paula. If you're not allowed to call me that, try Aunt Paula.' She turned and grinned at Jean. 'Unless you feel that's inappropriate?'

Jean laughed. 'Not in the least. Come on,' she said, opening the passenger-side door for Paula. 'I'm taking John by his "other" aunt's house for a sleepover while we party hearty tonight—'

'Can we go see Dad first?' John asked from the back seat.

Jean looked at Paula, who shrugged. 'You're the boss,' Paula said.

'Sure, why not?' Jean said. 'I want you to meet Milt anyway. Better before the party than after. You'll be more coherent.'

'Hush!' Paula said.

Color me surprised when I heard the side door to the station open and saw my wife and son come sauntering in, followed by a woman I could only assume was Jean's old college roommate, who had flown down to spend some time with us on her way to a job interview in Houston. Jean had described her to me many times – a party girl with a serious IQ, who rarely studied but always aced her classes, had men falling all over her but never took any of them seriously. So I was surprised by the woman I saw. She had short-cut gray hair, a face devoid of make-up, and was heavily wrinkled for her age, which would have to be early fifties, like my wife. She was so skinny you could actually see her bones, and when she spoke she had a smoker's raspy voice. Not at all the woman I'd imagined.

'Well, hey there, y'all!' I said. I stood up and held out my hand for the newcomer. 'Milt Kovak,' I said.

'Hi,' she said. She turned to Jean and said, 'He is *too* good-looking! I don't know *what* you were talking about!'

Jean laughed and, after a minute, so did I. OK, Jean hadn't said I wasn't good-looking. It was a joke, I guess.

Jean took her friend's arm, looked at me and said, 'As I'm sure you've figured out, honey, this is Paula.'

'Nice to meet you,' I said.

Paula shook her head. 'So you're the redneck sheriff Jean refused to leave this burg for, huh?'

I don't like being called a redneck. Maybe because it's too close to the truth, but really, it's just rude.

Jean closed the door behind her. 'Remember tonight's the surprise bachelorette party for Holly.'

'Damn, totally forgot about that. Been a busy morning,' I said.

'What was the emergency?' she asked.

I looked at my son and the stranger – I guess I should say Paula – and said, 'No biggie. I'll tell you about it later.' To Johnny Mac, I said, 'So what are you up to today?'

'I'm going to Aunt Jewel's house,' he said, 'if you're gonna be busy. If you're coming home I'd rather stay with you.'

Johnny Mac's been like that since my heart attack last spring. Since I had the attack in front of him, he's sort of been like my shadow. I'm afraid he thinks I'm going to croak any minute. I keep trying to tell him that the quadruple bypass they gave me means I'm gonna keep going for at least another fifty years. I don't think he believes me.

'Well, I could be here for a while, kiddo,' I said. 'Got me a bad guy in the pokey. And a drunk teenager in the second cell. Kinda standing room only around here today.'

'Two cells?' Paula asked, then laughed. I bristled.

Johnny Mac nodded. He was well versed in the priorities of my profession. 'OK, then. I guess I'll go to Aunt Jewel's,' he said.

I grabbed his head and gave it a smooch. 'Dad!' he said in that way they have of drawing three little letters out to sound like a four-syllable word.

Holly Humphries sat at her station in the bullpen, doing some paperwork – a little overtime would come in handy for the honeymoon, she thought. The front door opened and Ronnie Jacobs came in, carrying a pizza box. Ronnie worked for Bubba's Pizza and Pasta on the town square, close to the Longbranch Inn, and was short and skinny, with a pimply face and crooked teeth, wearing too-big jeans and showing off his Calvin Klein's. He wore a baseball hat backwards.

'Here's your pizza,' Ronnie said.

'I didn't order pizza,' Holly said, although she thought it might not be a bad idea. 'Any name on the order?'

'Yeah. Darrell?'

Holly shook her head and laughed. It wasn't the first time a prisoner had ordered a pizza from an unconfiscated cell phone in the jail. Milt had put Darrell in the cells before Holly had come in, and she'd assumed Milt had checked him for contraband. She walked around the bullpen, the ring of keys for the cells in her hand. 'Come on,' she said. 'I just hope he has money, 'cause I don't think the sheriff will approve this!'

She unlocked the steel door that led into the cells. That door was supposed to stay locked, but half the time the deputies forgot to do it. Milt, at least, *had* locked up after depositing Darrell Blanton in his cell.

There was a knock on the door and Holly Humphries stuck her head in. 'Milt! Come quick, we got a problem!' Seeing Jean and Johnny Mac – and the stranger – she said, 'So sorry, Jean. It's an emergency. Hi, Johnny Mac!' She nodded to the stranger and then her head disappeared.

'Go,' Jean said. 'We're going to Jewel's.' She gave me a quick kiss and I was out the door, following Holly.

Holly was right, as usual. The drunk teenager was convulsing in his cell. 'You call an ambulance?' I asked her.

'Of course,' she said. 'Help me.'

I glanced over at Darrell's cell. 'Pizza?'

Holly shrugged.

Ronnie, the pizza delivery guy, said, 'You want I should leave now, or you need some help?' He was peering curiously into the cell with the convulsing teenager.

'Out!' I said with some enthusiasm.

Holly and I went in the cell and she showed me how to hold his shoulders while she stuck a wooden, doctor-type stick in his mouth, holding his tongue down.

'Jeez, what's with him?' Darrell Blanton asked from the next cell, chomping on a pepperoni and double cheese slice. 'Boy sure can't hold his liquor, huh?'

'Just shut up, Darrell,' I said, trying to hold the convulsing boy's shoulders down.

'Why you telling me to shut up? My mama says telling someone to "shut up" is rude! So you're being rude to me! Why you being rude to me? I ain't done nothing to you!'

The door to the cells burst open and two EMTs entered. I knew them both. Jasper Thorne, a fifty-something black guy with a big mustache and a bigger attitude, and Drew Gleeson, who had moved from Tulsa to Longbranch when he was offered the lead position at the fire station for the EMTs less than six months ago, which might have been one of the reasons ol' Jasper had a big attitude.

'What's up, Sheriff?' Drew asked as they maneuvered the gurney into the cell.

'He came in last night drunk and disorderly. Now he seems to be having a seizure,' I said.

Drew cocked his head at Darrell Blanton as he and Jasper checked the kid's vitals.

'Killed his wife,' I said.

Drew looked shocked.

Jasper said, 'Man, those Blantons. Ain't nobody safe around them inbred crackers.'

'Hey! I heard that!' Darrell said from the next cell.

'Let's roll him,' Drew said, and he and Jasper got the boy onto the gurney. 'What's his name?' he asked me.

'Larry. He's seventeen. That's all we got out of him,' I told him.

'Let's go!' Drew said, heading out the door.

Holly and I followed them out. Once in the foyer, Drew said, 'Shit. I left the bag. I'll be right back.' He headed back to the cells while I helped Jasper take the gurney out to the ambulance. Before we even got there, Drew was back, emergency bag in his hand, and they got poor Larry in the back of the ambulance, Drew riding with him, while Jasper got in the cab, hit the sirens, and they were out of there.

It was after four o'clock in the afternoon when Jean dropped Johnny Mac off at his aunt Jewel's house. Paula came in with her and Jean introduced her to Milt's sister.

They shook hands and Paula looked around the opulent foyer, letting out a low whistle. 'So this is Oklahoma chic, huh?' she said.

Jewel laughed self-consciously and looked at Jean. Jean just shrugged her shoulders and proceeded to go over phone numbers and all the other stuff moms did when leaving their children in someone else's care. Then, after giving her son a big kiss, she and Paula got back in the car and headed off, and Johnny Mac stood staring at his aunt Jewel.

'Well,' Aunt Jewel said, staring out the window at the retreating SUV. 'She's interesting.'

'She wants me to call her Aunt Paula,' Johnny Mac said.

'Are you going to?' Jewel asked him.

He shrugged his shoulders. 'I don't know. Maybe.' He shrugged again. 'Maybe not. Can I go over to Matt's?' he finally asked, mentioning the boy his age who lived next door.

'Why don't we call him and see if he can come over here?'
Aunt Jewel responded.

Johnny Mac shrugged. He was always uncomfortable in Aunt
Jewel's house, and knew Matt was too. There were too many things
that could break if you breathed hard on them. Aunt Jewel's house
was just too fancy, and what he'd heard his mom call 'fussy'. That
made sense to him. He thought of the mosaic tile floor in the foyer
with a ginormous chandelier hanging down from the second-floor
ceiling, and the fancy double staircase with the shiny wood railing
you shouldn't touch because it would leave a mark. But there was
always outside, and it was nice out today, so he and Matt could
play out there on the trampoline, maybe, or even in the pool. He
wouldn't get cold, no matter how much Aunt Jewel might fuss
about it. All three of her kids were off now, one in college and
the older two out in the world. Johnny Mac guessed maybe she
just needed somebody to fuss over, and he was her only
candidate.

Jean and Paula headed back to Jean's house on Mountain Falls
Road, and Jean had to endure her friend's strident remarks all the
way there. 'So you got cows here, huh?' she said upon seeing
barbed-wire fences, beyond which were many heads of cattle.
'Moo.' And she laughed. Then, as they turned on to Mountain
Falls Road, Paula snorted and said, 'They call *this* a mountain?'

Jean, who loved her home at the top of Mountain Falls Road,
couldn't help herself. 'Better than the *mountains* there are in
Illinois.'

'Ooo! She's sensitive about her hillbilly home!' Paula said and
laughed.

'That's redneck. Not hillbilly. Try to keep your vernacular
straight!' Jean said.

'Well, my goodness! Look who finally grew a backbone!' Paula
returned.

Jean was oh-so-grateful to finally pull into her long driveway.
'This,' she said, pointing to the house, 'is my home.'

Paula was silent for a moment, then finally said, 'Very nice.'

Reaching behind her for her crutches, Jean responded, 'Yes, it is.'

Once inside with Paula's luggage, Jean continued, 'The guest
room is upstairs. There are two bedrooms up there – one is John's

and the other, closest to the stairs, is the guest room. The guest bath is right across the hall. John was supposed to clean it for you. Let me know if it's not satisfactory. There's a large open area at the head of the stairs that's mostly John's play space. He was supposed to clean that up, too, but again, let me know if it's a mess.'

'I take it you don't get up there often,' Paula said, picking up her bags.

'I can do it. I'd just rather not,' Jean responded.

Paula smiled – a genuine smile this time. 'I know you can do it. You could always do whatever you set your mind to.'

As Paula headed up the stairs, Jean removed herself to the first-floor master suite she shared with Milt. Jean was not a clothes horse – far from it. She liked to wear pants to cover the brace that she still wore on her left leg, and had a uniform of dark pants and lighter, button-down shirts that she wore to work – brown pants with a tan-striped button-down, black pants with a white button-down (and in the winter she had a nice black blazer she wore with it), and navy blue pants with a light blue button-down. She had ten long-sleeved button-downs for winter and twelve short-sleeved button-downs for summer. Around the house she usually just wore blue jeans and a T-shirt – often ones formerly worn by Milt.

But tonight was a special occasion. Tonight she wanted to please the guest of honor, Holly Humphries, soon to be Holly Pettigrew – if she made up her mind to take Dalton's name when they got married in two weeks. As far as Jean knew, that decision hadn't been made yet. But because this party was for Holly, Jean had decided to get a little reckless with her wardrobe. She'd actually gone to Tulsa two weeks prior and invested in tonight's garments.

Holly was an adventurous sort – although she'd stopped cold turkey wearing the Goth-white makeup and had let two of the five holes in her ears heal-up, she still preferred fishnets, tutus and Grateful Dead T-shirts, and dyed her hair many varied colors. For that reason, Jean had decided to branch out – in honor of Holly. She'd bought a multicolored peasant skirt and a hot-pink lacy peasant blouse. She could do nothing about her footwear – stuck as she was with the orthopedic shoes that could strip even Marilyn

Monroe of her sex appeal. But she was ready to strut her stuff tonight – and she might even get a little bit high. She could always sleep in the hotel room if she wasn't able to drive home.

She put on more make-up than she generally wore, added earrings and bracelets, and headed into the foyer as Paula was just coming down the stairs – in the same baggy cargo shorts, Birkenstocks and camp shirt she'd worn on the plane. Jean decided to ignore it. Why get things started up again? She wanted to get to know her old friend again, not just trade snipes with her. But, she thought, Paula was going to have to stop with the Oklahoma bashing for that to happen.

Holly Humphries was from Oklahoma City and had been raised in various foster homes. She had no relatives and most of her former friends were still on the streets of that city. So the bachelorette party invitees were almost exclusively from the sheriff's department – Jean, wife of the sheriff, Jasmine, the sheriff's deputy, Nita Skitteridge, also a deputy, and Maryanne Dobbins, wife of a deputy. Paula Carmichael, Jean's friend, Loretta Hawkins, waitress at the Longbranch Inn, and June Pettigrew, Dalton's cousin and the only one in Dalton's extended family that Jean and Jasmine felt was young enough to enjoy such an event, were the only real civilians. With Holly, that totaled eight females and what turned out to be a great deal of booze that Jasmine had procured from the liquor store on the highway to Tulsa: four bottles of wine – two white, two red – a case of Bud Lite, a quart of vodka, a fifth of tequila and an assortment of mixers and fruit. Loretta had arranged for appetizers to be delivered from downstairs every hour on the hour, and Jean had brought bowls to fill with nuts and chocolate to put around the room. It was going to be a grand affair.

Dalton's cousin, June, was escorting Holly to the event, telling her they had to go by the Longbranch Inn to check on her mama, who had just had surgery and was staying there to recuperate. June watched a lot of *Law & Order* reruns and had seen an episode where a rich lady had stayed in a fancy hotel after having a facelift. June thought that was very high class, even if the lady did end up dead. June and Holly were supposed to be on their way to the movies, which translated to Holly as 'dress so you can be seen in the dark.' Her hair had a new bright yellow rinse, and she wore a tie-dye T-shirt of yellow, pink and green that fell almost to her knees, and hot pink leggings, both of which stopped at her red high-top sneakers. It took June, in her sensible stretch pants and polyester top, more than a minute to talk Holly into going upstairs with her, as Holly felt it would be best for her to wait in the car. She wasn't all that crazy about June's mother, who'd been Dalton's daddy's baby sister and had treated Dalton's mother poorly. But with a sigh, the good-natured Holly left the car and took the elevator up to the rooms of the Longbranch Inn.

Having been signaled by June, the rest of the women were hiding behind furniture when the door opened and Holly and June walked in. All jumped up and yelled 'Surprise!' at the top of their lungs. Holly burst into tears.

We were having a quiet afternoon, finally. The drunk teenager, Larry, had gone and was all but forgotten, and Darrell Blanton was being uncharacteristically quiet. I was thinking of heading home in a while to bask in the quiet of my empty house, leaving Anthony Dobbins, the first African-American deputy in the history of the Prophesy County sheriff's department, in charge of the prisoner. I'd watch a Cowboys game I had on tape and drink a few beers. My idea of fun.

I'm not sure what time it was when Anthony came into my office and said, 'Sheriff, we got a problem.'

'What's that?' I asked him.

'Looks like Darrell Blanton is dead,' he said.

It took a while to calm Holly down. She kept saying, 'I've never, ever had a party before! I can't believe . . .' sob, sob, 'y'all did this for me!'

Jean sat beside her on the sofa in the living room of the suite and patted her on the shoulder. She knew Holly's history, the fact that she'd been raised in foster homes since the age of three, had run away from the last one when she was sixteen and lived on the street for two years. But she'd pulled herself up, gotten her GED, taken some courses at a local community college and learned how to do make-up for films, which is what led to her meeting Dalton in the first place. But that was an entirely different story.

As far as Jean was concerned, Holly was one of the most

well-adjusted women she'd ever met, not just one of the most well-adjusted former foster kids. She appeared to know who she was and what she wanted, while at the same time possessing a great big heart that tended to accommodate most people who crossed her path. Add all that to the fact that she was as smart as a whip and you had a great foil for Dalton Pettigrew – a big puppy dog of a guy with lots of love but not a lot of smarts. While not one to bet on other people's happiness, in Jean's professional opinion theirs would be a good marriage.

'What's with the waterworks?' Paula demanded. 'This is a goddamn party, right?'

Jean said, 'Paula . . .'

'Holly, you need a drink!' Jasmine said. 'What'll it be? Beer, wine or a mixed drink? Loretta used to be the bartender at the Longbranch Inn before the county went dry – she can fix most anything, right, Loretta?'

'You bet,' Loretta said. 'What's your poison, Holly?'

Holly gulped in some air, wiped her eyes with a tissue and said, 'Can I have a tequila sunrise, please?'

Loretta grinned. 'One tequila sunrise coming right up!' and headed to the wet bar where everything had been set up. 'You want some of these stuffed mushrooms to go with it, or how about a jalapeño popper? That should go well with tequila!'

Holly nodded. 'Yes, please. One of the poppers. Hey, everybody,' she said to the other women there, 'y'all get started on the booze and the food! I don't want to be the only one here drunk and fat!'

'You don't have to tell me twice,' Paula mumbled and was the first in line at the drink station.

The other women laughed, got up from their seats and headed to the wet bar. Loretta brought Holly her drink, two poppers and a mushroom. 'Thank you,' Holly said, and took a big sip. She sighed. 'OK, I'm feeling better.'

Jean laughed and hugged her. 'And this is just the beginning.'

As Paula came back with a bottle of red wine and a glass, Holly asked her, 'So how long have you and Jean known each other?'

'Ha!' Paula said, sitting down on the other side of Jean. 'I'm not about to give out how many years; suffice it to say, we met on our first day in college. We were assigned the same room.'

'Yes,' Jean said, a smile on her face. 'You should have seen me. Too tall and too awkward, embarrassed about my braces and crutches, trying to slink into the room without anybody actually seeing me. And then there *she* is—' Jean said, pointing at Paula. 'This beautiful blonde girl with big boobs wearing the shortest skirt I'd ever seen, and legs that went on forever—'

'Stop!' Paula said, taking a deep drink of the wine. 'Now they're just going to compare that description to the husk they see before them!'

'What husk?' Holly said. 'You look wonderful.'

Paula snorted. 'I've heard about southern hospitality, but this is ridiculous!'

Jean patted Paula's hand. 'You look fine,' she said, noticing that the bottle of wine Paula had brought back from the wet bar only a short while ago was already half gone.

Jean couldn't help remembering how Paula liked to drink in their undergraduate days. She would stay out all night with one boy or another, then go to class still drunk but managed to make an 'A' anyway. In medical school, though, things had gotten a little tougher for her. There was that time at the end of their first year when Paula had got drunk and totally missed the final testing. She'd lost her first year and had to start over again. Jean couldn't help but wonder if her drinking was still a problem.

'What do you mean, dead?' I demanded of Anthony.

'Well, what we normally mean when we say dead, Sheriff. As in not breathing, bit the big one, kicked the bucket, gone to the big double-wide in the sky—'

'Stop!' I said, and got up and followed him back to the cells.

And there he was – Darrell Blanton – lying on the cot we called a bed, looking like a little boy asleep. Except he wasn't. There's a stillness in death that doesn't mimic sleep. Even in sleep there is animation – not so in death. In death, there's only the shell left – everything else, even with a Blanton, is long gone.

'Jesus H. Christ!' I muttered under my breath. 'What happened?'

Anthony shook his head. 'No idea. Can't find a mark on him.'

'Call the ME,' I said as I walked into the cell to check out the body.

Chandra Blanton put her hands under her swelling belly and lifted the baby to get a little relief for her bladder. She could barely count the number of times she'd been to the bathroom that day for nothing more than a false alarm. And Chandra, unlike many Blantons, could actually count. She wasn't sure if it had been a good idea to tell her mee-maw about the sheriff's wife's party going on upstairs at the Longbranch Inn, but somehow it had seemed to please Mee-maw, and anything that pleased Mee-maw was a relief to Chandra and her mama. A happy Mee-maw was a calm Mee-maw, and everybody wanted a calm Mee-maw.

Chandra had gotten the job at the Longbranch Inn right after she found out she was pregnant. She hadn't told her soon-to-be employers about the pregnancy, though, because she'd been pretty sure she wouldn't have gotten the job. Once on the job, however, she knew they couldn't fire her because of her pregnancy. When the time came, she planned on saying the baby was a preemie, no matter how big he was. And yes, wonder of wonders, she was having a boy. The last ten pregnancies in Blantonville had produced girls, which didn't bode well for weddings in fifteen or sixteen years. But her son would have his pick of anybody he wanted to marry. And because his own daddy wasn't a Blanton, Chandra was pretty sure he'd be one up on most of his cousins.

Chandra's job at the Longbranch Inn was to answer the phone, file paperwork and jot down money in and out in a ledger that went to the accountant every two weeks. She was good at her job and the powers that be were happy with her work. So it was with some misgivings that she looked up and saw her mee-maw, Eunice Blanton, her mama, Marge Blanton, and her uncle, Earl Blanton, all coming in the front door of the Longbranch Inn. Uncle Earl was walking like he had a corn cob up his butt, Chandra thought. She came around the desk and tried to stop them before they got far enough into the inn to be seen by her boss.

'What're y'all doing?' Chandra asked, with just a touch of panic in her voice.

'Where's that sheriff's wife having her party?' Eunice demanded.

'Ah, Mee-maw, I can't give out that information! It's against the rules!' Chandra tried, knowing it was to no avail.

'Piss on your sorry rules! I'm gonna teach that sheriff a lesson, jailing my boy! I mean, he didn't mean Joynell no harm! That was an accident, clear as day!'

'What happened?' Chandra asked.

'Nothing!' Eunice said. 'Darrell was cleaning his gun and it musta accidentally gone off and killed Joynell. And now that damn sheriff's locked up my boy! I ain't having it! So tell me where that party thing is happening!'

'Mee-maw, I can't!' Chandra wailed.

'You want that baby born out in the streets, girl? Or you wanna come home to your mama and me and have that baby in a bed?' Mee-maw demanded.

Chandra had no alternative. She knew her mee-maw wasn't kidding around. She'd throw her out on the street in a New York minute. Chandra sighed. 'Suite 214, second floor.' Mee-maw grabbed Chandra's arm. 'Lead the way, girl!'

'Gonna have to take the body back to the morgue and do an autopsy. First blush, can't see a thing wrong with the boy,' the county coroner said.

'Could it be a heart attack?' I asked him.

'Could be,' he said. 'Or just about anything. Except a gunshot or stabbing. Oh, or strangulation. Or suffocation—'

'Got it,' I said, and walked out of the cell.

The coroner's staff bundled up Darrell, put him on a stretcher and carted him off. It was the second time that day we'd had an ambulance at the front door.

I wandered into the bullpen and saw Anthony shutting down. We closed the office at around six on a Saturday, with an on-call person answering phone calls or emergencies – except when we had guests. Anthony had been on babysitting duty tonight, with Dalton on-call, as both their women were busy elsewhere. It was after seven in the evening now, and with our two guests gone Anthony was no longer on babysitting duty. I walked up to him and asked, 'Hey, since our wives are both at that shindig at the Longbranch Inn, you wanna go grab a bite to eat?'

'Ah, wow, Sheriff, yeah that would be great, but I just called Nita's husband and made some plans. There's a *Doctor Who* festival on TV tonight and we're gonna barbeque. You wanna join us?' Anthony asked as an afterthought, I'm sure. Nita Skitteridge, another deputy, was Anthony's cousin and the first African-American woman deputy in the history of Prophesy County, Oklahoma. I'd hired 'em both, me being the forward thinker that I am.

'No, that's OK. I'm not a big *Doctor Who* fan. Got a ball game on tape at home. Think I'll pick up some fried chicken and head that way.'

'You sure? I make some mean pork ribs! And Will said Nita made a mess of beans before she left.'

I sighed. 'Sounds good, but I best head home. Y'all have a good time,' I said and headed back to my office. Should I go pick up my son? With Darrell dead, I could put Joynell Blanton's murder down as done. I put my feet up on my desk and watched as the lights down the hall blinked off.

TWO

Aunt Jewel called Matt's mom and asked if Matt could come over, and his mom said of course, so Johnny Mac went to the front porch to watch for him. He saw Matt come out of his front door just as a boy was coming up the street on a bicycle. He waved frantically to Matt, who went to meet the boy on the sidewalk. Matt waved Johnny Mac over and Johnny Mac met the two boys at the base of Aunt Jewel's driveway.

'Hey, Johnny Mac, this is Cody.' To Cody, he said, 'Johnny Mac lives out in the country but his aunt lives right here.' Cody stuck out his hand and Johnny Mac shook it like his dad had taught him.

'Hey,' he said.

'Hey,' Cody said.

Cody was short and stocky, with dark hair, blue eyes and pale skin. He was in Matt's sixth-grade class, so Johnny Mac figured they were all around his age – eleven or twelve.

'Matt, listen,' Cody said. 'I saw this guy dragging a dog into the woods over there,' he said, pointing toward the forest of trees behind the last house on the cul-de-sac. 'I think he's gonna kill it. I'm gonna go try to stop him. Y'all wanna come?'

Matt and Johnny Mac looked at each other, and Johnny Mac looked back at his Aunt Jewel's house. 'What do I tell her?' Johnny Mac asked Matt.

'She doesn't have a PlayStation, does she?' Matt asked.

'Uh uh,' Johnny Mac answered.

'Then tell her I got a new game for my PlayStation and we're gonna play it at my house.'

'Cool,' Johnny Mac said, and went in his aunt's house to spread the lie.

There was a knock on the hotel suite's door and Jasmine whispered to Jean, 'That's got to be Rex the stripper!'

'Oh, God, no,' Paula said, shaking her head. 'This has got to be the redneck version of hell.'

Jasmine refused to look at Jean's friend or in any way acknowledge her comment, and headed to the door while the other women in the room stuffed their faces with appetizers and booze.

When Jasmine opened the door she saw Rex, the college kid she'd hired to strip, standing there, but he appeared to be asleep. He then fell on top of her, knocking her to the floor. Three people barged in behind him. Even from her position on the floor, Jasmine's cop training came in useful. She memorized their descriptions for later: an old woman came in first, in her late sixties/early seventies, with white hair and blue eyes covered in cat's-eye-framed glasses. She had a high forehead and several missing teeth. Immediately behind her was another woman, possibly in her mid- to late-thirties and about fifty pounds overweight, with impossibly red hair in the old Farrah Fawcett cut from the seventies. She had the same blue eyes as the older woman, with nearly identical glasses. The man who came in behind her was short, blond and chubby, and was trying desperately to pull something out of his pants. It only took a moment for Jasmine to realize it was a shotgun. Unfortunately, as he tugged the shotgun out, his pants fell down, exposing dirty whitey-tighties and hairless thighs.

'For God's sake, Earl!' the old woman said between clinched teeth. 'Pull up those pants and make yourself decent!'

The last one in the door, Jasmine noticed, was a seriously pregnant young woman, probably still in her teens, who clung to the walls and appeared as scared as the bachelorette party members.

'OK, listen up, you bitches!' Eunice Blanton shouted, silencing the noise from the women, some of whom were still screaming due to the intrusion, while others were still laughing at Earl's whitey-tighties. 'Which one of you is the sheriff's wife?'

Jean used one of her crutches to rise up from the sofa where she sat between Holly and Paula. Both grabbed her arm, trying to get her to sit back down, but Jean shook them off.

'I'm Jean McDonnell. The sheriff is my husband. Who are you and what are you doing here?'

'Shut up!' Eunice said. Turning to Jasmine, she pointed her gun and said, 'You! You're a deputy, right? I saw you when you served papers on my cousin Wilmer. Marge, check her for a weapon.' Turning to the rest of the women, she said, 'OK, how many more of you whores are deputies?'

Nita raised her hand. The woman said, 'Earl, check her for a weapon. Anybody else carrying? 'Cause if I find a gun in somebody's purse, everybody's gonna get hurt, understand me?' To her granddaughter, she said, 'Chandra, go check the purses—'

'Mee-maw, I can't get involved in this! I'll lose my job!'

'Shut up and do as I say!' Eunice shrieked.

'I never carry where there's alcohol,' Jasmine said.

'Me neither,' Nita said.

'OK,' Eunice said. 'But don't mind me if I check anyway, as you bitches are probably lying! Chandra, go check them purses! Now, you, Deputy,' she said, pointing the gun at Jasmine, who was still stood near the unconscious body of the stripper, 'go sit with these other bitches.'

Jasmine did as she was told. Jean was still standing, and addressed Eunice. 'Please tell us what's going on,' she said.

'Oh, now it's "please," is it?' Eunice said, smirking. 'Didn't hear no "please" earlier, now, did I, Mrs Sheriff?'

'We can't help you if we don't know what you want,' Jean said, her tone moderate.

'Well, aren't you the fancy one,' Eunice said. 'Being all helpful and all butter wouldn't melt in your mouth! What makes me think you'd knife me in the back given half the chance?'

'I mean you no harm,' Jean said. 'I'd just like this over with as quickly and harmlessly as possible.'

'Well, I'm with you on the quick, but not so much on the harmless,' Eunice said. She walked further into the suite and picked up the room phone that sat on a table next to the sofa. 'Now, Mrs Sheriff, you sit down here 'fore you fall down – didn't know you was a gimp – and call your hubby. You tell him to let my son go in the next hour or I start shooting a hostage every ten minutes after that, okie doke?'

I had my hand on the side door to the parking lot when my cell phone rang. I checked the screen and saw it was my wife. Grinning, I picked it up and said, 'How drunk are you?'

'Milt, there's a situation,' Jean said, and she didn't sound drunk or even happy.

'What's up, babe?' I asked, heading back into my office to sit down.

'There's a woman here who says you've arrested her son.' There was a short silence and then she said, 'Darrell Blanton. She says to release him in the next half hour or she'll start shooting hostages.'

'How many people she got?' I asked, my stomach sinking to my knees.

'Two others and—' Jean started, then I heard a new voice.

'Listen to me, Mr Thinks-he's-all-that! I'm not kidding around! I want my boy back. You know it was an accident him killing Joynell! That boy never meant nobody no harm! So you let him out or your missus and her friends here are gonna be hurting real bad!'

'Mrs Blanton, listen to me—' I started, but she interrupted.

'I ain't listening to a thing you say, Mr Sheriff! I've said my piece! Let my boy go and I'll let your women go, got that?'

Then she hung up in my ear.

We have this doohickey installed on Holly's phone where, with just a punch of three code numbers, you could contact all the deputies' cell phones at one time and talk to them on speaker. I ran out to the bullpen and hit the code.

Chandra didn't know what to do. She didn't find any guns in the purses, like the lady deputies had said, but each had a cell phone. She picked one out of a purse and stuck it in her pocket. She wasn't sure what she was going to do. All she knew was she didn't want to be part of this, didn't want to be involved in hurting anybody, and she sure as hell didn't want to have her baby in prison! She'd heard they took your baby away when you had it in prison and, since her whole family was here in this room, if she went to prison they'd all be going to prison too, and her baby would go into the system as there'd be no immediate family to care for him. Maybe she should use the phone in her pocket to call Mike, the baby's father. She'd been attracted to him in the first place because he was smart. She didn't know a lot of smart people, living in Blantonville and being home-schooled, so to speak. At least, that's what the Blanton mamas told the truant officers when they came snooping around. Chandra was lucky that she liked to read – as opposed to most Blantons – and had basically schooled herself. She thought maybe Mike could take the baby, or, even better, figure a way out for Chandra. She *really* didn't want to go to prison.

'Mee-maw,' Chandra said, 'I gotta go make.'

'Baby dancing on your bladder?' Mee-maw said with a frown. 'They do that.' To the sheriff's wife, she asked, 'Where's the bathroom?'

The sheriff's wife pointed and Chandra hauled ass into the bathroom. It hadn't been a lie. She did have to make, but she also intended to call Mike. She turned on the water faucet in the sink to cover the sound of her conversation, turned on the deputy's cell phone, and dialed.

It took less than fifteen minutes for my staff to show up. Emmett Hopkins, whose wife, Jasmine, was at the scene; Dalton Pettigrew, whose betrothed, Holly, was there; Anthony Dobbins, whose wife, Maryanne, was there; and Nita Skitteridge's husband, Will. Will's not on my staff but his wife was also at the scene.

After I'd placed the call to my staff, I'd placed another one to Charlie Smith, police chief of Longbranch. After all, the deed was being done within the city limits. After I explained what was going on, Charlie said, 'What do you need?'

'Wondered if I could borrow some guys in case we need to take down the inn,' I said.

'You got 'em for whatever reason. And me too. You got a plan?' he asked.

'Not yet,' I admitted. 'But I got my guys coming in. Hopefully we can think of something.'

'I'm on my way to your place.'

'Thanks, Charlie.'

Jean wasn't particularly surprised that the only women visibly upset by this turn of events were the civilians – Anthony's wife, Maryanne, and Dalton's cousin, June. Loretta, the longtime Longbranch Inn waitress, had basically seen it all and didn't seem the least bit fazed, although she might just have a tough exterior, Jean thought. The remaining civilian, her old friend Paula, seemed more pissed off by the whole thing than scared. The rest of them – two deputies and Holly, the civilian clerk, were outwardly calm, but Jean could see the wheels moving behind the eyes of both Jasmine and Nita. She hoped they wouldn't do anything rash, but knew someone had to do something. She also knew her husband.

He wouldn't let a prisoner out of jail because his mother was holding them hostage. And it sounded like this woman's son had killed his wife, so there was no way Milt was letting a murderer go. But there were three Blantons with guns. The good guys had none.

Mike Reynolds was a very sad young man. The girl he loved was having their baby but refused to marry him. He'd been warned by everybody he knew not to mess with a Blanton girl, but love wants what love wants, and Chandra Blanton was his woman now and forever more. Lately, though, she wouldn't even see him, not even when he came into the Longbranch Inn for lunch. When his cell phone rang, he didn't recognize the number, and was happily surprised when he heard Chandra's voice on the other end of the line.

'Mike, listen—' she started.

'Hey, baby,' he said. 'I'm so glad you cal—'

'Shut up, Mike! I'm in trouble—'

'The baby?' he said, panicked.

'No, hush. It's my mee-maw! She's holding the sheriff's wife and a bunch of deputies hostage until the sheriff lets my uncle Darrell out of jail. And she's pulled me into this and I don't know what to do!' And then she started to bawl.

'Oh, Jesus!' Mike said, taking a deep breath. 'Y'all at the Longbranch?'

'Yes, in suite 214, on the second floor! But they've got guns! Mee-maw and Mama and Uncle Earl!'

Mike took a deep breath. 'OK, baby, listen up. Any way you can get out of the room?'

'I doubt Mee-maw would let me.'

'Try, but if you can't, stay as far away from them as you can.'

'Oh, God, you're not going to kill them, are you?'

'No! Of course not!' he said, thinking, last resort, maybe. 'Just do as I say. Can I call you back?'

'Probably not a good idea. This is one of the deputies' phones, and if Mee-maw caught me with it there'd be hell to pay.'

'OK, I'll try to get word to you. I don't know how now, but I'll try. I love you,' he said.

Chandra sighed on the other end of the line. 'I know. I guess I love you, too. And I think maybe marrying you might be a pretty good idea, seeing as most of my relatives are gonna be either dead or in jail.'

'Sounds like a plan,' Mike said, unable to keep the smile from spreading across his face.

After he hung up, Mike Reynolds left his desk and headed for his boss's office, but was surprised when Charlie Smith, police chief of Longbranch, Oklahoma, met him halfway.

'Reynolds, grab some guys and meet the sheriff at the Longbranch Inn. We got some shit going down there—'

'Ah, Chief,' Mike said. 'About that . . .'

We sorta took over the restaurant at the Longbranch Inn. We had the owner close the place down and send all his staff home. But before they left, I did find out one good thing: Loretta, my favorite waitress and one of the party members, had made a standing order for appetizers to be delivered every hour. They were working their way through the menu: stuffed mushrooms and jalapeño poppers had already been delivered; next up was fried cheese sticks, then Buffalo wings and potato skin boats, with an assortment of desserts to be delivered right before ten, when the restaurant closed.

The owner remarked that he hadn't been able to find his desk clerk when he was getting his people out.

Charlie nodded at me. 'That's OK,' I told him. 'We know where she is.'

Personally, I planned on buying Chandra Blanton a great big oversized teddy bear for that baby of hers. She'd done the bravest thing I've ever heard a Blanton doing – namely calling the cops on her own kin. And the cop she called, Mike Reynolds, was sitting at the table now with me and Charlie Smith. I stood up and thanked the Longbranch Inn's owner for his cooperation, adding: 'But I think it's best you take off home now. We don't know what's gonna happen and we need to keep civilian exposure down to a minimum.'

He stood up too and shook my hand. 'Y'all try not to burn the place down, now, ya hear? This is a landmark building, remember?'

'We'll keep that in mind,' I said as I nodded to Anthony Dobbins, who came and escorted the owner out of his own building.

After Anthony closed and locked the front door of the Longbranch

Inn I heaved a great big sigh, as I was about to reveal the seriously screwed-up mess in which we now found ourselves. 'OK, here's the deal,' I told Charlie and his men, since mine already knew. 'Eunice Blanton is holding my wife, Emmett's wife, Anthony's wife, Dalton's fiancée and Will's wife – oh, and Dalton's cousin, and Loretta, of course, and oh, shit, and what's her name, a friend of my wife's, whatever . . . Anyway, she's holding all these women hostage upstairs. With her are – Mike?' I said, turning that part over to him.

'According to Chandra, besides her mee-maw, Eunice, there's her mother, Marge, and her uncle Earl. Chandra says Eunice and both her mama and uncle are armed,' Mike recounted, a little breathless, but he was more or less in the same position as me and all my guys – that is, loving somebody who was up in that godforsaken room.

'Well,' I said, clearing my throat again. 'As y'all know, Darrell shot his wife and I arrested and jailed him. What y'all don't know is—' I hesitated, cleared my throat again and said, 'Old Darrell kicked the bucket in the pokey. We don't know why. Not a mark on him. They're doing an autopsy right now. Unfortunately, we got thirty minutes – well, now, make that fifteen – to produce the boy before Eunice Blanton starts shooting hostages.' I looked around at the assemblage. 'Any bright ideas?'

Matt and Johnny Mac snuck into Matt's parents' garage, where they found two bikes. Matt grabbed his own personal bike and pointed at a girl's bike for Johnny Mac. 'That's my little sister's. You can use it,' he told Johnny Mac.

Johnny Mac just looked at it. 'It's a girl's bike,' he said.

'Well, duh. My sister's a girl, stupid!' Matt said.

'You want me to ride around on a *girl's* bike?'

'Or you can walk, but we'll be long gone. It's up to you,' Matt said.

Johnny Mac sighed. He saw little alternative and time was wasting. That dog could be dead by now. 'OK,' he said, lifted the kick-stand of the girl's bike and walked it out of the garage.

Cody was waiting at the end of the driveway. Matt and Johnny Mac mounted their bikes and followed Cody toward the end of the cul-de-sac. Johnny Mac was grateful that the new boy didn't seem to take notice of the girl's bike he was riding.

They skirted around the house at the end of the cul-de-sac, finding an asphalt path that led to the hike-and-bike trail that encircled the subdivision. Once on the trail, they cycled over it to the beginning of the woods, and were soon following a path deeper into the small forest. They hadn't gone far when Johnny Mac looked behind him and could no longer see the subdivision Aunt Jewel lived in. All he saw were more trees. And he noticed it had gotten darker. Glancing up, he could barely see the sun, which he knew would be going down soon. The trees above him formed an almost umbrella-like canopy that shielded them from the sun's rays. He lost his balance, and he and his girl's bike fell over in the underbrush.

'Your old man is cuttin' it real close, Mrs Sheriff,' Eunice Blanton said. 'You think he's gonna call me and let me know what's happening?'

Jean thought the question wasn't rhetorical. Eunice really wanted to know. 'I'm sure he will,' Jean said, keeping her voice calm and steady.

'Ah, hell, what do you know?' Eunice said, contempt in her voice. 'I think you'll be the first one I shoot! What do you think, ladies? You think it's only right that the sheriff should lose his wife first?'

The woman sitting next to the sheriff's wife stood up. 'Look, lady,' she said, 'I have nothing to do with any of this. I stopped to visit a friend on my way to Houston for a job interview. I think you should just let me go—'

Eunice turned to her son, Earl, and used her head to point at the woman standing. 'Make her shut up,' she told her son.

Earl walked up to Paula and pushed her down to the sofa. 'Hey!' Paula shouted.

'Shut up!' Earl said, and turned back around to his mother. 'That good, Mama?'

'If it ain't I'll let you kill her,' Eunice said. 'Now, as I was saying 'fore I was so rudely interrupted, the sheriff's the one who arrested my boy and that boy never did a bad thing in his life!' Eunice looked around at her other two children. 'Ain't that right?'

'Sure,' Earl said, remembering the time Darrell tricked him into putting his hand in that vice then turned it until he broke five bones in Earl's hand.

But Marge didn't say anything, knowing her mama didn't really care for her opinion one way or the other. She had a lot she could say about her youngest brother, but she knew the little bastard would eventually get his comeuppance – if not on earth, then in hell.

Dalton Pettigrew stood very quietly by the elevator of the Longbranch Inn. Dalton had learned to be quiet over the years, opting not to say too much least he get the usual reactions: from Milt, a rubbing of the forehead and a squinting of the eyes; from Emmett, a clearing of the throat with a glance anywhere but at Dalton; from Jasmine, just a rolling of the eyes. Nita Skitteridge would look at him bug-eyed and say, 'What did you say?' loud enough for everyone to hear. Her cousin, Anthony, was Dalton's only friend (other than Milt, of course), and even he sometimes looked confused or befuddled by what came out of Dalton's mouth. Holly was the only one who understood him and would gently correct any misconception on Dalton's part. She loved him just as much as if he were smart.

But fear of condemnation was not what made Dalton quiet this day. It was fear, all right, mixed with an anger he had never felt in his life. An anger so outrageous he would gladly strangle the woman who kept his Holly hostage. He wasn't sure if he could wait for Milt and them to come up with a plan; his Holly was in danger right now, and something needed to be done.

He turned and looked at the elevator behind him. Just step in, push the button for the second floor, go to suite 214 and bust the door down. But he didn't know where everybody was in the room; it would take a minute to place everyone and figure out who was bad and who was good. In that minute, Dalton figured, they'd riddle him with bullets. He didn't mind taking a bullet for Holly, but he really wanted to marry her and have a life. He wanted that more than he had ever wanted anything.

It had taken a while, but even his mama had gotten used to Holly's look – the tattoos and piercings, the tutus and fishnets, the hair that was sometimes black, sometimes blue, and occasionally pink-striped. It had taken him but a minute. Almost immediately he could see her heart, and that's all he really wanted to see. Well, that and a killer body, he had to admit. His mama had always said about loose women, 'Why buy the cow when you can get the milk for free?' Meaning, he was pretty sure, why marry a girl who'd let you do the deed before the wedding? Well, his mama was wrong about that, but Dalton wasn't going to tell her. Making love to Holly had been the most wonderful moment of his life, and he wanted moments like that to continue for eons to come. Yeah, his mama had been dead wrong about that.

The assembled peace officers came up with a first move. They needed to know where everybody was, and the only way to find that out was to get into the suite. Since Loretta had a standing order for appetizers to be sent up every hour, and since the next appetizer in line – the fried mozzarella sticks – was already assembled and ready to go, they decided to send a 'waiter' up with the food. Mike Reynolds volunteered to be that waiter. He'd told Chandra he'd try to find a way to let her know what was going on. He wouldn't be able to talk to her, he was pretty sure about that, but maybe just his presence would be some reassurance for her.

The powers that be also decided to send two more guys up with Mike – Anthony Dobbins and Dalton Pettigrew. Anthony had the keys to the rooms on either side of suite 214, and he and Dalton would split up and try to listen in to the goings-on where their women were being held hostage.

Mike changed from his police uniform into a waiter's uniform he found hanging in the staff lounge, found a tray, put the two large plates of fried cheese sticks on it, along with several napkins, and headed for the elevator.

Dalton Pettigrew hit the elevator button for him, squeezed his arm so tight Mike was afraid he'd drop the tray, then held the door open so Mike and Anthony could enter. Mike gave them both a nod and a weak smile. Anthony's wife and Dalton's fiancée were up there, just like his was. He felt like they were passengers on the *Titanic*, only the tables were turned and the men were safe while the women were about to go down with the ship. But, he thought to himself, not on my watch!

Suite 214 was in the middle of the long hallway, about five

doors away from the elevator, on the side facing the town square. Dalton and Anthony moved to their allotted rooms and shut themselves in, while Mike walked up to the door of suite 214 and rapped loudly.

'Who the hell is that?' Eunice Blanton screeched, whirling around to point her gun at the door.

'It's just a waiter!' Jasmine said. 'We're supposed to get appetizers sent up every hour, and it's just about time.'

'Earl! Move that boy's body,' she said, indicating Rex the stripper. She waved her gun at Jasmine. 'You, get up and answer door. Don't let him in.'

Earl dragged Rex's unconscious body behind the sofa, hiding it from view of the doorway.

Jasmine went to the door and opened it. She recognized Mike Reynolds from the Longbranch police department. She nodded ever so slightly to show her recognition and he nodded back.

'Ma'am, I've got the mozzarella sticks here,' he said in a loud voice.

'Just give me the tray, please,' Jasmine said.

'Oh, no, ma'am,' Mike said, pushing past Jasmine. 'It'd be too heavy for you.'

Walking into the suite, he smiled brightly and said, 'Hey, ladies! Y'all having fun?'

'Put them cheese sticks on the coffee table, boy, and haul your ass out of here. We're having a party, don't ya see?' Eunice Blanton said.

'Yes, ma'am,' Mike said, smiling brightly at his future grandmother-in-law, in awe of how un-scary she looked. From Chandra's reactions to her 'mee-maw,' he always figured her to have horns growing out of her head, or at least a crooked witch's nose. But she was just a fairly wrinkled old lady with tightly permed, mostly white hair, wearing a house dress the likes of which he hadn't seen since his own grandmother's passing some ten years back. Since Chandra had never allowed him to pick her up anywhere near Blantonville, he'd never seen any of her kin and they'd never seen him. Which had worked out well under the circumstances.

He snuck a peak at Chandra, sitting in a straight-back chair toward the back of the room away from the rest, just like he'd asked her to. She was holding her belly, and the look on her face was full of hope. But he knew that look would vanish because he had to leave.

He saw Jasmine sit down on the couch and made note in his mind of where everybody was. Then, with the silly smile still plastered on his face, he left the suite. Unlike a real waiter, Mike didn't notice that he hadn't been tipped.

'Hey, guys, wait up!' Johnny Mac called as the other boys rode out of sight. He got up and dusted himself off, then picked up the girl's bike. Jumping back on it, he rode like the wind to try to catch up with the other boys. But after a hard five minutes, they were still nowhere to be found. Johnny Mac started to get scared. He stopped the bike, his feet on the hard-packed ground of the small forest. The woods were dark and unearthly still, not a leaf moving on any of the trees. He looked up. The sky – what little he could see through the trees – was getting darker by the minute, and it shouldn't be.

It was still daylight savings time, which meant it didn't get dark until eight or nine. But the thing that worried him was that he heard no birds. You always hear birds in the woods, he thought. But where the heck were they? And where the heck were the other boys? He thought about turning around and going back to his aunt Jewel's house, but then Matt and his friend would think he was a chicken shit. And he wasn't. They were assholes, as far as Johnny Mac was concerned. Surely at least Matt had noticed that Johnny Mac was no longer behind them. Or were they playing some kind of joke on him?

He felt the wind pick up and grow stronger. Looking up, he saw the tops of the trees almost bent over from the wind. Then he heard a noise every Oklahoman recognizes from birth: the unmistakable sound of a freight train bearing down on him.

THREE

Anthony Dobbins hadn't told anyone yet, but Maryanne was eight weeks pregnant. They wanted to wait until she was further along before they told anybody, even their own parents. They'd lost two pregnancies around week eight, and this was a nervous time for them normally, but, Anthony thought, with this going on and Maryanne being held captive by that lunatic old bitch, he couldn't help but think that the stress alone could end the pregnancy.

Anthony and Maryanne had been married for nine years and together for fifteen. They'd been high-school sweethearts at Longbranch High, Anthony a linebacker on the football team and Maryanne a band majorette. They had also gone to the same church for most of their lives and, as he finally told Maryanne on their wedding night, he'd fallen in love with her the first time she did a solo in the children's choir when they'd been little more than ten years old. Basically, Maryanne was Anthony's whole life. If something happened to her up in suite 214 he didn't know if he would be able to keep on living. Somehow, he doubted if he could.

When Mike Reynolds came out of the suite, Anthony peeked out of his door and saw Dalton follow Mike to the elevator. Anthony wasn't far behind the two.

Once downstairs, they headed straight to the table where Milt, Emmett and Charlie Smith sat.

'Well?' Milt said, standing up. The other men at the table also stood. Milt looked at Anthony and Dalton. 'Why are y'all back down here? I wanted you to stay up there! Keep an ear out!'

'Oh,' Dalton said.

'Just let us hear what Mike has to say,' Anthony pleaded.

Milt nodded and Mike said, 'Chandra was right. There's three of them: Eunice, Marge and Earl. They're close to the door. The couch is in the center of the room, sideways to the fireplace, facing the front door, and Mrs Kovak and some gray-haired woman—'

'That'd be her college friend, Paula,' Milt said.

Mike nodded. 'They're both on the couch, along with Holly and Jasmine. There's a big redheaded lady—'

'My cousin, June,' Dalton said.

Mike nodded at him. 'She's in a chair just to the right of the sofa as you walk in, and Loretta is in a chair to the left. Nita and Mrs Dobbins are in the love seat opposite the sofa. The whole seating arrangement is like a square. Nita and Mrs Dobbins have their backs to the Blantons.'

Anthony asked, 'Could you see my wife's face? Did she look all right?'

'Yeah,' Mike said. 'I saw her fine when I put the cheese sticks on the coffee table. I mean, she looked scared, but they all did. At least, the civilians did.'

Milt touched Anthony on the shoulder. 'We're all worried about our wives—' he started, but Anthony interrupted.

'Maryanne's pregnant. About eight weeks.' He sighed and said, 'We lost her last two pregnancies at about eight weeks.'

Milt's hand on Anthony's shoulder tightened. 'We'll get her out,' Milt said. 'We'll get 'em all out.'

Jewel heard the tornado warning sirens only seconds before she heard the sound of the freight train. She ran out of the front door and looked at the sky. She only saw blue sky, until she turned to the west, where it was pitch black, except for a gray funnel shape. It was the largest tornado she'd ever seen, and having been raised in Oklahoma she'd seen her share. Her husband was at work but Johnny Mac was next door. She ran to her neighbors and flung open the door, only to almost hit Laurie Potter, Matt's mom, in the face. 'Where are the boys?' they asked simultaneously.

Then, stunned, they both just looked at each other. 'They're at your house,' Laurie almost whispered.

'No, they're at yours,' Jewel said, a catch in her voice. She stepped back on the sidewalk and looked to the west. 'No time!' she said, grabbing Laurie's arm. 'Shelter, now!'

They ran into Jewel's backyard, beyond the pool on the other side of the trampoline, just to the right of the shed that housed the garden equipment and pool supplies, and flung open the door to the storm shelter, scurrying down into its darkened depths.

I'm not sure I can explain how I felt that day sitting in the restaurant of the Longbranch Inn, surrounded by both town and county law enforcement personnel, half of whom were in the same boat as me – the love of their life threatened by a crazy old lady who'd only let them go when she saw her son. Unfortunately, but fortunately unbeknownst to that crazy old bat, said son was as dead as a doornail, and I had no idea why. This would be the new ME's first autopsy, and I wasn't expecting a speedy answer on that – if I got one at all. I figured that by tomorrow I'd have to send the body off to the state guys to get any real answers. But by tomorrow, all the women upstairs could be dead. *Would* be dead. If we didn't do something, and do it damn quick.

I picked up my cell phone and called the phone number for suite 214. Eunice Blanton picked up on the first ring. 'What the hell's taking so long?' she demanded.

'We have a slight hitch at our end, Mrs Blanton—'

'Don't you try to trick me, you devil!' Eunice spat into the phone. 'I know what you cops like to do – twist things around, make it like up is down and down is up! Well, I ain't having none of that shit, I can tell you right now!' I heard a commotion on the other end of the line. Then the old woman came back on. 'Say goodbye to wifey!' she said.

Then I heard Jean's voice. 'Milt, I'm sorry,' my wife said.

'Baby, hold on! We're coming—'

'Well, you'll be too late,' Eunice Blanton said.

'Wait! Eunice, listen! Please!' I begged, trying to come up with a convincing lie. 'The state bureau guys came down on this and they're not letting him go yet. I'm trying everything I can, and I've got a plan! I'll get your boy to you as soon as I can! You just gotta be patient, and please don't shoot my wife. We've got a little boy—'

'Yeah? Me, too! And you done locked him up for no good reason!'

'I'm getting him out, Eunice, I promise you that. Just give me another hour,' I begged.

The old bitty sighed, then said, 'One hour. Then I'm gonna start killin' 'em two at a time!' And the line went dead in my ear.

I'd no sooner hung up the phone when it started beeping. I hit the screen and found a flashing icon – the weather icon. I punched it and the screen lit up, showing a tornado touching down in the Bishop area. I exited that and dialed my sister's home number: no answer, so I tried her cell, but still no answer. I hoped that meant she and Johnny Mac were in the shelter and either she'd forgotten her phone or her cell service wasn't working because of the storm.

Turning to the assembled lawmen, I said, 'We got a tornado in Bishop. Any volunteers to go there and assist?'

Neither Emmett nor I raised our hands, and I wasn't about to call upstairs to see if Dalton or Anthony wanted to volunteer. It would be a waste of breath. Charlie Smith said, 'You guys stay here. I'll get some off-duty guys to go up there, and you,' he said, pointing to two of his men, 'go to the fire station, get the rescue van and call the volunteer firefighters, if they haven't already been called, and call our off-duty guys, and y'all head up to Bishop.'

'Yes, sir,' both men said in unison and were out the door.

'When it rains, it pours,' I heard someone say under their breath. Couldn't figure out who it was, but, truth be known, I didn't really care.

Johnny Mac left the girl's bike where it was and found a depression at the base of a tree trunk. He hunkered down in that, his hands finding a sturdy tree root and grabbing on to it. He closed his eyes and prayed.

Jean could feel herself beginning to lose it. Normally a woman in control of her emotions, she'd never been held captive before and was beginning to think that maybe this was her breaking point. She hoped, if she did break, she could come back from it. She'd seen too many patients who never did – whatever their trauma. She reached for Holly's hand and was amazed when Holly patted hers with her free hand and whispered, 'It's gonna be OK, Jean. Trust me.'

Jean had mixed feelings about this – respect and awe for Holly's ability to handle this situation, like so many other things in her short life, and a little anger at Holly's ability to handle this situation, like so many other things in her short life. Was this young woman for real? Where was the panic? Where was the angst? Where was the screaming and crying that Jean wanted to indulge in?

From the other side of her, Paula whispered, 'What the hell have you gotten me into, Jean? I can't believe we're even at this stupid party with all these hicks—'

Jean sighed. 'Paula, just shut the hell up. Really.'

Paula opened her mouth to speak but Jean just glared at her, so she shut it again.

Jean tried some meditative breathing to calm herself, but it didn't work. To give herself a break, she had to admit that she was the only one of the women who'd been personally threatened not once but twice. That pissed her off – which in the circumstances was a good thing. She had a good life; she'd been happy up until about an hour ago. She loved her husband, her son, her job – everything. Who in the hell did this woman think she was, trying to take all that away from her?

She squeezed Holly's hand and whispered, 'We need to get this bitch!'

The two Longbranch police officers headed straight to the firehouse, where they found several volunteer firefighters already readying the rescue van. The officers grabbed what they needed – ropes, shovels, drills, saws – piled them in the trunk of their squad car and, with sirens blazing and flashers brightening the evening as it grew dark, followed the rescue van headed north toward the township of Bishop, the richest part of Prophesy County, infested with doctors, lawyers and bankers.

They were halfway there when the officer riding shotgun shouted, 'Shit! Look!' He was pointing out of the driver's-side window. The driver glanced that way and almost lost control of the squad car. He figured the sirens had kept them from hearing the sound of the freight train. The tornado, which the driver calculated to be about a mile across at the bottom, maybe a category four if not a five, was headed straight at them. He saw the rescue van in front of them veer off the highway, heading for a ditch. The driver followed suit, breaking, and he and his partner clambered out of the squad car and hit the ditch with the volunteers, all lying flat on their stomachs. The driver couldn't help glancing up as he heard the might of the tornado bearing down on them. He was just in time to see his squad car get picked up in the twister, twirled around and thrown. He covered his head, hoping the car would miss them as it came crashing down.

Johnny Mac heard the sound of the horrible freight train crashing through the tiny forest, could see trees being ripped up from their roots. 'Not my tree, God,' he prayed. 'Please, not my tree!' He held onto the root with all his strength, one arm having worked through the dirt to the other side of it, so that now his arm was around it, securing him more tightly – he hoped.

Johnny Mac didn't cry. He wasn't a baby. He admitted he was scared shitless, something he wouldn't mention to his mother – if he made it out of this alive – because she didn't like him using cuss words. But, he figured, scared shitless was the only way to describe the feeling he had right now. He hoped Matt and the other boy were OK, and that Aunt Jewel had made it to her shelter and wasn't out looking for him in this. God, if something happened to Aunt Jewel because he'd lied to her, he would never forgive himself – and he knew his dad never would either. The guilt almost brought tears to his eyes, but he choked them down, deciding that living through this was his best course.

Johnny Mac felt his legs being lifted and he wrapped his arms even tighter around the tree root, squeezing his eyes shut to protect them from the debris flying around. The noise was so profound he couldn't hear his own thoughts – although he wasn't sure at that moment if he had any. It seemed to last forever. At one point he felt he was vertical, his feet up in the air and his head down toward the tree root. He screamed once or twice, but got grit in his mouth and shut it. He wasn't sure how long he could hold on. His arms were on fire; he felt his shoes being torn from his feet. It was hard to breathe and his chest felt tight.

And then it passed. His body fell back to earth, knocking the breath out of him. Debris fell to the ground around him, and the horrible noise subsided as the funnel cloud moved on. But it was so dark in what was left of the forest that he could barely see his hands in front of his face. He stuck his hand in his pocket and was glad to feel the small flashlight his dad insisted he carry at all times. Not that he did – carry it all the time, that is. Half the time he forgot it, along with his lucky rabbit's foot and his lucky dollar bill on his bedside table. But today he had them all, although the flashlight was going to be handier than either the rabbit's foot or his lucky dollar bill. Then he smiled, thinking that both of those charms, along with his prayer to God, had already paid off. He wasn't dead.

Jasper Thorne and Drew Gleeson, Longbranch EMTs, were heading to Bishop when they saw the Longbranch police department squad car flipped over in the middle of the highway. Jasper, who was driving, slammed on the break and swerved to miss it, and the ambulance came to rest across the two lanes.

'Jesus H. Christ on a bicycle!' Jasper muttered.

Drew was out of his side of the ambulance, heading for the squad car, when he heard a shout from the other side of the road. Looking that way, he saw several bedraggled people pulling themselves out of a ditch. Drew headed in their direction, followed by Jasper.

'You guys all right?' he called out.

There was some nodding of heads and a couple of shakes, but everybody looked in one piece. The lone woman in the group had blood on her face and Drew went to her first.

'Jasper, you got the bag?' he asked his partner.

'On my way,' he said, heading back to the ambulance for it.

Drew sat the woman down and said, 'Who are you guys?'

'We're volunteer firefighters,' she said. 'Except for the two cops, of course.'

'I expect we were headed the same place as y'all – Bishop?' one of the officers said.

'Yeah,' Drew said, taking the bag that Jasper had brought to him and opening it. He took out some alcohol wipes and set to work on the blood on the woman's face. 'Y'all get a look at the twister?' Drew asked.

'Yeah, I did,' the driver said. 'I'd say it was a mile across at the bottom, at least a C-4 if not a C-5. We were lucky, it just clipped us. Got our squad car, which was right behind the rescue van, but didn't touch the van.'

'Anybody else hurt?' Jasper asked the men standing around.

One guy, who was holding his arm, said, 'I think I may have broken my arm.'

Jasper took him to the open back doors of the ambulance and sat him down while he checked his arm.

Meanwhile, Drew found the cut on the woman's head. It was small but deep and was still bleeding. He also took her to the ambulance, sitting her down next to the guy with the broken arm, then found some butterfly bandages to close the wound and stop the bleeding.

Looking at both the injured, Drew said, 'We need to keep going to Bishop. We can leave y'all here with the squad car, after we move it off the highway, or y'all can come with us and we'll stash you somewhere in Bishop.'

The woman stood up. 'Hey, it's a scratch. They're going to need all the bodies they can get up there.'

'I'm fine, too,' said the guy with the broken arm. 'We all got jobs to do.'

Drew looked at Jasper. 'Is it broken?' he asked.

'Like a two-dollar watch,' Jasper said.

Drew looked at the guy. 'Well, we can't let you be part of the rescue party 'cause of that arm,' he said. 'We'll take you with us, but the best I can do is to let you take notes – if you can write with your left hand,' he said, noting that it was his right arm that was broken.

'No problem,' the volunteer firefighter said. 'I'm a southpaw.'

'Good,' Drew said, slapping him on his good arm. 'Both of y'all hop in the back here while we move the squad car.'

The five remaining volunteer firefighters, the two police officers and the two EMTs managed to rock and slide the upside-down car to the side of the road and remove it from the highway. Then the firefighters and the cops got in the rescue van, while the EMTs got back in the ambulance with the two injured firefighters, and they headed toward Bishop, sirens blasting away again.

We had an hour. To do what I didn't know. The fact that Darrell Blanton was dead was pretty much putting a wrench in the works, I can tell you that. I saw this movie once, called, I think, *Weekend at Bernie's,* where these guys used all kinds of contraptions to make it look like this guy Bernie was still alive when he wasn't. I supposed I could stand Darrell's corpse up under the window of suite 214 and get him to wave at his mama. I decided not to share this idea with the rest of the guys. The problem of who killed ol' Darrell wasn't bothering me too much at the moment. I really didn't care. All I cared about were the hostages, and I'd care about them the most even if my wife wasn't one of 'em. Adding her to the mix just plain threw the thought of Darrell's killer right out of my mind.

We were a little ahead now. We knew where our people were and where the bad guys were. We could go in guns blazing, but five'd get you ten, and one of our women would get hit by somebody – either them or us. And just because everybody up there was in those positions when Mike was there didn't mean they were going to stay in those positions. Maybe what I should do – what I should have done at the very beginning – is call in the state guys with their hostage negotiators and SWAT teams and let them do their thing.

Except these guys, these pros, always had an acceptable hostage body count – some formula that figured a certain percentage of loss was to be expected. Well, I didn't expect it. Not any loss, not on my watch. I was getting my wife back, as were Emmett and Anthony and Will. And Dalton and Mike Reynolds were getting their fiancées back. And we were getting Loretta and June and even Paula out of there as well. Nobody was going to die. Maybe Eunice Blanton, but that was it.

I used my cell phone to call Anthony's cell. He answered on the first ring. I'd instructed both him and Dalton to turn their ringers off and keep their phones on vibrate. I called Anthony instead of Dalton because with Dalton's less-than-extensive knowledge of all things electronic he could have just as easily turned his volume up. It wouldn't be cool for Eunice Blanton to hear a phone ringing in another room.

'Hello?' Anthony whispered.

'Can you hear anything from next door?' I asked him.

'A little bit,' he said. 'I got one of the glasses out of the bathroom and held it against the wall and I can hear the occasional word, but nobody's talking much in there. Not even the old bat. I heard her on the phone with you, I'm thinking?'

'Yeah, I called up there.'

'Yeah, I figured. We got another hour, huh?'

'Yeah,' I said.

'I'll keep listening and call you if I hear anything pertinent,' Anthony said.

'Roger and out,' I said.

'Mama, I feel sick,' Earl Blanton said, using the hand that wasn't holding the shotgun to rub his stomach.

Eunice turned to her son then glanced at the former bowls of chocolate Jean had placed around the room. She slapped Earl in the face. 'You think now's the time to eat your weight in candy, you idiot!'

'But, Mama, it was just sittin' there—' Earl started.

Eunice slapped him again. Earl said, 'Ow, Mama!' and moved his tummy hand to his face. 'You don't gotta do that!'

'Well, if not me, then who? Somebody's gotta set your stupid Blanton ass straight!' Eunice turned back to the assembled. 'See what I gotta put up with?' she said to no one in particular. To her son, she said, 'Don't you even think about getting started on them nuts, you hear me?'

'But, Mama, they got nigger-toes!' Earl said, only to see all the hostages look up at him – the white women with shock on their faces while the two black women in the group just glared at him.

'They got another name?' he asked in all innocence.

'Brazil nuts!' the black deputy said, her teeth clinched.

'Huh,' he said. 'I didn't know that. Thanks, ma'am.'

Nita just shook her head and turned back around.

There came a groaning from behind the couch and Eunice Blanton swung around, her gun pointed at the noise. It was the boy who'd been about to knock on the door when they burst in. She had no idea why a boy would be coming to an all-girl party, but it had worked out OK.

'You, deputy,' Eunice said, brandishing her weapon at Jasmine. 'See to him.'

Rex Kitchens had a bitch of a headache. Worse than a hangover, he thought. He knew he had a gig to do, the money from which kept him in beer and Buffalo wings, but, feeling around, he noticed he was still wearing his break-away firefighter costume.

He opened one eye and saw that lady, the deputy, who had hired him. 'Did I fall down?' he asked her.

'More or less,' Jasmine said, helping him to sit up and propping him against the side of the chair in which Dalton's cousin June sat.

Rex looked up and saw the three Blantons with their guns pointed directly at him.

He grabbed Jasmine's arm and pulled her down to where she could hear him whisper, 'They got guns!'

'Yeah, Rex, they sure do. We're all being held hostage,' she said.

'Me, too?' he asked.

Jasmine looked at Eunice and Eunice nodded her head. Looking back at Rex, Jasmine said, 'Yeah, you, too.'

'Am I still gonna get paid?' he asked.

Even though the twister had passed, Johnny Mac was still scared shitless. Trees were down all around him. He didn't know which way would lead back to Aunt Jewel's house, and he sure as heck didn't know where Matt and the other boy were. What if they'd been hurt? Maybe he should go looking for them. But he didn't see how he could get that girl's bike through all the rubble. Then he looked at the spot where he thought he'd dropped the bike. No bike there. He stood up and walked gingerly toward the spot. His shoes were gone, and they were good ones, too. His first pair of Nikes, with a glow-in-the-dark Nike swirl. His mom had paid a lot of money for them. His mom. He wished she were here now. Actually, no, not really. She'd have a hard time walking. He guessed what he wished was that he was with her. At that party, watching the ladies get drunk and sitting in a corner eating all those appetizers his mom had told him had been ordered. He liked chicken wings and jalapeño poppers. He was like his dad – he liked the hot stuff. Although Dad couldn't eat that stuff anymore. Mama said bland food was all he could have. Doctor's orders. He wasn't sure if that was his dad's doctor's orders, or his mom the doctor's orders.

But none of that musing was getting him out of this mess. He took a few more steps, wincing as he stepped on something sharp. He looked at his foot, still covered in his new Fruit of the Loom socks. The shoes and the socks had been some of the new purchases for going back to school. He doubted if the socks were going to make it. But there was no tear in the sock this time, and no blood coming from a cut on his foot. He'd just have to walk more carefully. Looking steadily at the ground, Johnny Mac took several more steps until he was at the rubble where he thought he'd left the bike. He lifted some branches and saw a strange metal thing he thought might have come from a car – he didn't want to think about *that* flying through the air so close to him – but didn't see the bike. Beyond the rubble, and past a few downed trees, he saw what looked like the trail. Gingerly, he headed that way.

*   *   *

Jewel tried to open the door to the shelter but it was stuck. She asked Laurie to help, and between the two of them they managed to dislodge whatever had been pinning down the double doors of the shelter. When they got out, they saw what it was: Jewel's refrigerator door – with jelly, mustard, mayo and ketchup still in their allotted spaces. Jewel looked up and saw that her house was mostly gone.

Although a shock to her system, she figured it wasn't all that bad. The house had been her husband's first wife's home and she was more than happy to see it gone. But then she sobered: Johnny Mac. Where was he?

'Where are the boys?' Laurie Potter asked, anguish in her voice. 'Matthew said he was going to your house! He wouldn't lie!'

Jewel just looked at her next-door neighbor. How naive was this woman? Having raised three children – two of them boys – Jewel knew one thing for sure: they lied. Boys lied about anything, while girls lied mostly about boys.

Laurie's house was more intact than Jewel's so they went that way, hoping to find a working phone or a cell phone. Jewel had no idea where hers was. But then again, she rarely did, which was a bone of contention between her and Harmon, her husband.

The bedroom wing was missing from Laurie's house but the living room looked unscathed. Books still sat on the shelves, magazines were still laid on the coffee table and there were toys in a box by the fireplace. They heard a screech of tires and both ran out to the driveway. Bobby Potter came out of his car fast, running up to his wife and grabbing her.

'Are you OK?' he asked.

'Where's Miranda?' Laurie asked, looking for her youngest, Matt's little sister, owner of the now missing girl's bike.

Miranda came out of the back seat of the car. 'Mommy, what's wrong with our house?'

'Where's Matt?' Bobby asked his wife.

Laurie put her hands to her face and began to cry. Jewel said, 'My nephew was here – he told me he was going to Matt's. Matt told Laurie they were coming to my house.'

Bobby nodded. 'So where are they?'

'I have no idea,' Jewel said, feeling the tears begin to sting her eyes.

Bobby Potter was a big man, about six foot three or four, with massive shoulders. A former college-level wrestler, he'd almost made it to the Olympic tryouts but was benched due to a severe inner-ear infection. He hadn't been on good terms with his ears since.

Bobby patted Jewel on the arm. 'Don't worry,' he said, 'we'll find the little shits. They think they've been in a tornado now, huh? Wait until you two get hold of 'em, huh?' he said and laughed.

Neither woman laughed back.

Ronnie Jacobs, the pizza delivery guy from Bubba's Pizza and Pasta, had been on his way to Bishop to deliver a pepperoni and bell pepper extra large. He was playing an old Randy Travis CD of his mom's, not listening to the radio. If he had had the radio on, he might have realized what he was driving into. As it was, the extreme southeast edge of the twister grabbed his Toyota Celica and flipped it over four times, turning it in circles like a whirling dervish until it came to rest on its roof. Ronnie hung upside down in the driver's seat, only his safety belt keeping him in place. His hat had fallen off and his hair, which needed to be cut, was hanging straight down. Ronnie didn't notice. He was out like a light.

FOUR

Marge Blanton had been a sad little girl, a sad teenager, and had grown into a sad woman. She'd married her second cousin, Kenny Blanton, when she was sixteen, at her parents' insistence. She didn't love Kenny and he really didn't love her. He just liked her big boobs, and his idea of romance was jumping on her at unexpected times. She lost her first baby when she was four months pregnant; her second was stillborn. Her third pregnancy ended just weeks after it had begun. But the fourth, which had resulted in her beautiful daughter Chandra, had been a success. And only Marge and one other person knew why.

His name was Gary Roberts, and he'd mistakenly come to Blantonville to try to sell vacuum cleaners. Luckily he'd come to Marge's trailer first and she'd set him straight. Nobody in Blantonville liked door-to-door salesmen. In fact, there was a rumor that a Fuller Brush man had come to town once back in her mama's day and had never been seen again.

Kenny, Marge's husband, was at work in the body shop he and some of his cousins owned right outside of Blantonville, so Marge had been alone in the house with Gary Roberts, the vacuum cleaner salesman. It was the first time – maybe ever – that Marge had talked to a man outside of the Blanton clan. And she'd found him fascinating. He'd shown up at ten in the morning; by three that afternoon, after a lovely lunch (Elvis sandwiches – peanut butter and banana – with a Marge flare of added bacon and Lays potato chips), they'd ended up on the built-in sofa of Marge's single-wide.

When she'd found out she was pregnant, she hadn't immediately thought it could be Gary's. She'd just assumed it was Kenny's, as he had pounced on her many times between her tryst with Gary the vacuum cleaner salesman and her finding out that she was pregnant. As the pregnancy wore on, she'd tried not to get her hopes up – they had been dashed so many times before. But when the baby had been born alive and began to thrive, she'd had to wonder. Was it the fresh genes? How come every pregnancy with her second cousin had failed but one dalliance with an outsider and she bore the perfect child? By the time Chandra was six months old, Marge could see a definite resemblance between her beautiful baby girl and the vacuum cleaner salesman.

Gary had left her his business card, so she had an address. She wrote him the following letter:

> *Dear Gary,*
> *This may come as a shock to you, but you have given me the greatest joy in my life – our beautiful daughter, Chandra. She's six months old and looks just like you! I don't want to put any pressure on you, but if you are so inclined, please come by and get me and the baby and take us away from here. If I don't hear from you, I guess that means no.*
> *Sincerely,*
> *Marge Blanton*

Needless to say, Marge never heard from the man. Chandra was now seventeen and Marge had never told anyone about Gary the vacuum cleaner salesman. But now her little girl was pregnant and, as far as Marge knew, Chandra had never even glanced at any of the Blanton boys. She could only hope that the daddy of her grand-baby, like the daddy of her own baby, was from outside the invisible walls of Blantonville.

Marge knew it was the vacuum cleaner salesman in Chandra that made her stand up, just a little bit, to Mee-maw. It was the vacuum cleaner salesman in Chandra that had her sitting away from the rest of them, refusing to be a part of this madness of Mee-maw's. If Marge had just a little bit of that defiance, she could turn the gun in her hand on her mama – maybe not kill her, but at least slow her down. Enough, anyway, to get Marge and Chandra out of this mess. Oh, and maybe save a hostage or two.

Drew Gleeson, the EMT, was almost glad about the tornado, except for the people who were injured or even dead. He was sorry about that. But at least the activity was keeping his mind off Joynell Blanton.

Drew had never in his life messed with a married woman, but

Joynell was different. She wasn't like most women. She was smart and tough while at the same time gentle and feminine. And she was beautiful. Beautiful in a way most women weren't, in Drew's opinion. She had an inner beauty – and it shone through her like a light inside a Halloween pumpkin. She was the love of his life. And that goddam husband of hers had gone and killed her. It was bad enough that the way Drew had met her was when the asshole had knocked her down the aluminum stairs of their double-wide and broken her ankle. The asshole hadn't even been there when Drew had shown up in the ambulance. He'd been on his own that day, Jasper having taken the day off for his father-in-law's funeral. And there she'd been, sitting on the steps to the trailer, cradling her swollen ankle. Maybe it wasn't love at first sight, but it was definitely lust at first sight. Then he'd seen the ring on her left hand and got himself in check. But on the ride to the hospital, with her lying on the gurney right behind him as he drove, they got to talking and, although she'd never said anything directly against her husband, he'd got the vibe that she hadn't accidentally fallen down the steps. He'd hated Darrell Blanton ever since, and now . . . and now . . .

Drew was driving the ambulance, and tried to push that thought out of his mind as he felt the tears starting. Not only was it not manly – in Drew's opinion – for a man to cry, it could cause an accident, and he already had injured people in the back of the ambulance. But still and all, he wasn't paying that much attention and almost ran into the back of the rescue van. Slamming on his brakes, he could see beyond the van and ascertain the problem. Two firefighters were heading toward a Toyota Celica resting upside down in their lane of the highway.

Drew reached behind him for their emergency bag and jumped out of the ambulance, Jasper two feet ahead of him.

There was a young man in the driver's seat of the Toyota, hanging upside down and not moving. Drew felt for a pulse and found one beating strong.

'He's alive,' he told the firefighters. 'We need to cut the seatbelt. First, though, Jasper, bring the backboard.'

Grumbling under his breath, Jasper headed for the ambulance while one of the firefighters went to the rescue van for clippers to cut the belt. When they both got back to the Toyota, Jasper laid the backboard down as close to the kid as they could get, while the firefighter clipped the seatbelt.

Drew and Jasper both had hold of the boy's head and shoulders, and were able to gently release him onto the backboard.

'Now what?' Jasper asked Drew. 'We go back with what we got or keep going?'

That, as far as Drew was concerned, was the $64,000 question. With this guy in the back the ambulance would be pretty much full. Did he take this kid back to Longbranch to the hospital, or hope that the clinic in Bishop was still there and could take care of him? In the end he decided that they needed to get the unconscious young man and the firefighter with the broken arm to the Longbranch hospital. Checking out the head injury of the female firefighter, he discovered that the cut had stopped bleeding and the woman insisted she had no headache or any other residual effects. Her eyes looked clear, which suggested no concussion.

'OK,' Drew said, removing the pencil flashlight from her pupils, 'I guess you're good to go.' He looked at one of the firefighters standing by. 'OK with y'all if she goes with you?'

'Ah, hell, man, she's senior,' the firefighter said. 'I got no say in that A-tall.'

The woman stood up. 'So I'm outta here,' she said.

'I reckon so,' Drew said and smiled at her. She gave him a mock salute and led the other two firefighters back to the rescue van.

'Ideas!' I said to the men standing around with their thumbs up their butts. 'Come on, y'all. Ideas!'

'We could sneak up there, then bust the door down and take the Blantons down,' Emmett Hopkins suggested, his forehead sweaty, although the air conditioning in the Longbranch Inn kept the restaurant permanently chilly.

'I considered that,' I said, 'but I'm afraid Eunice would shoot one of the hostages.'

'Not if we shoot her first!' Emmett said, his face turning red with the tension and stress of the occasion. Emmett Hopkins, former police chief of Longbranch, Oklahoma, current head deputy of the Prophesy County, Oklahoma sheriff's department and one of the most level-headed men I've ever known, was about to lose it, and I was afraid that if Emmett lost it I wouldn't be far behind.

'Well, that has some merit,' I thought. OK, I sorta wanted to shoot the old lady, but I knew that wasn't what I *should* be thinking.

'Too iffy,' Charlie Smith said. 'She could have one of the hostages with her, or be standing close to them. Just because they were where Mike said they were when he was up there doesn't mean they're still in those positions.'

That pissed me off. I'd already considered that and I wasn't too happy with Charlie thinking I hadn't. But this wasn't the time for a pissing contest. I had bigger fish to fry.

'Maybe we should call in the state boys,' Emmett suggested.

'You wanna wait for them to get here? Usually takes 'em a couple of hours to get all the paperwork done and their asses in gear. I'm not sure about yours, but my wife will be dead by then,' I said.

Emmett nodded his head. 'You're right. The time for calling in the state has long gone.' And the look he gave me then made me question my motives. But what was done was done, and now it was time for ideas and action.

'What if we send somebody else up there?' Charlie suggested. 'The staff's supposed to bring up desserts at closing, which is usually ten o'clock, but we could send someone up with the desserts and say we're closing early because of the storm—'

'Shit!' I said, jumping up. 'The storm!' I turned to Mike. 'Did they have the TV on or a radio in the room?'

'No, sir,' Mike said.

I grinned real big. 'Then we gotta evacuate 'cause that tornado could be heading to Longbranch, donja think?'

Johnny Mac used his flashlight to illuminate the way through what was left of the forest, calling out Matt's name as he went. No one answered him, but he kept walking. He wasn't sure which way he was going – he'd gotten all turned around in his head – but he hoped he was heading in the direction they'd taken rather than back to his aunt's subdivision. As careful as he was, watching where he stepped, he tripped over something right in front of him and fell on his face. The flashlight flew out of his hand.

He pulled himself up and looked for the flashlight, scared that he'd lost it. But he saw the light shining on some rubble, and was thankful the bulb hadn't broken when it went flying out of his hand. It was as he was trying to stand up that he noticed what he had tripped over. A bike. A boy's bike.

'Matt!' he yelled at the top of his lungs. 'Cody!'

He heard something. Just a slight something. He twirled around, not sure which direction it had come from. 'Louder!' he said.

'Here!' came a small voice.

'Keep talking!' Johnny Mac shouted. 'So I can find you!'

'I'm over here. Is that you, Matt's friend?' came the voice.

Johnny Mac felt his heart sink. It wasn't Matt calling out to him. He was glad that he'd found Cody but he really wanted to find his friend.

'Is Matt with you?' Johnny Mac called as he headed in the direction of the voice.

'I dunno where he is,' the voice said. 'And I'm stuck. I think a tree landed on me or something!'

Using his flashlight, Johnny Mac saw a depression in the ground with fingers wiggling out of it. He grabbed the fingers. 'You OK?' he asked Cody.

'I can't move my legs,' Cody said.

'I'm gonna try to move some of this stuff!' Johnny Mac said.

'Just be careful! Don't make it worse, OK?'

'I'll try not to,' Johnny Mac said, thinking, *Duh, like that would be my goal?*

He was just lifting a large branch when something hit him from behind, bowling him over.

The room was quiet. The old woman, Eunice, was looking out the window at the town square and her daughter was leaning against the door while her son stood in front of the women, glaring at them, the shotgun resting by his side.

Paula stood up. 'This sucks!' she said, and headed for the wet bar.

Earl's right arm suddenly seemed to have a mind of its own. It lifted the shotgun up and then he pulled the trigger. Paula went down.

The decision had been made for Mike Reynolds to reprise his role as waiter and go to suite 214 with the message about the storm. He had just stepped out of the elevator when he heard the gunshot. He froze, only for a moment, then, dropping the tray of desserts, pulled out his gun and ran to the door of suite 214. Both Dalton and Anthony had left their rooms and were close behind Mike. Mike hit the door with the heel of his boot and charged inside.

Marge Blanton was standing, leaning against the wall right next to the door to suite 214. When it crashed open and she saw the waiter with his gun drawn Marge screamed, then used the pistol in her hand to knock him out.

Johnny Mac didn't know what had hit him. All he knew was that he'd lost his flashlight again. He tried to sit up, but all he got for his efforts was a wet face. He reached out and touched fur.

'Stop!' he said between licks. 'Enough!'

The dog said, 'Woof!'

Johnny Mac stood up, again saw his flashlight shining against a tree trunk and went to pick it up.

'What's goin' on?' Cody's voice asked.

'I think that dog we were looking for found us,' Johnny Mac said. 'Looks like a cross between a golden retriever and a Shetland pony?'

'Yeah, that's him,' Cody confirmed.

The dog headed in the direction of Cody's voice and began licking the fingers sticking out from the debris. 'Hey, boy,' Cody said. 'Good boy!'

Johnny Mac pulled the dog away from the debris. 'If you wanna help,' he told the animal, 'get some of this stuff off him.'

The dog cocked his head, as if listening but not fully comprehending. Johnny Mac began pulling smaller tree limbs and assorted stuff off Cody. All this dog needed was a little show and tell. He reached down with his mouth and pulled up a bigger branch, moving it away from the trapped boy.

'Good dog!' Johnny Mac said, rubbing the dog's fur. 'You're one smart cookie!'

Grinning at the compliment, the dog grabbed another branch while Johnny Mac continued his work. Finally they got to the real problem: a tree limb about a foot in diameter and about two Johnny Macs long was across Cody's legs.

'Can you wiggle your toes?' Johnny Mac asked Cody, remembering his mother the doctor asking him the same thing when he fell out of that tree one time.

Cody said, 'Did they move?'

Johnny Mac didn't have the heart to tell him that his toes hadn't moved one bit. 'We're gonna get this off you now,' he told Cody. Turning to the dog, he said, 'You take this side and I'll take the other. Let's roll it off of him.'

The golden retriever/Shetland seemed to understand and began using his snout to roll the large branch off, with Johnny Mac rolling the other end. The fact that Cody didn't scream from pain kinda worried Johnny Mac. They got it off and Johnny Mac almost cried out at the sight of Cody's legs, but caught himself in time. One was really smashed and all bloody, with a bone sticking out. The other was bloody too, but maybe just from scrapes? Johnny Mac hoped so. But how was he gonna get this kid outta here? He couldn't lift him. Cody was short, but stocky. First things first, Johnny Mac thought. He took off his shirt and began to wrap it round the broken leg.

FIVE

A nthony, still unseen by anyone in the hostage suite, grabbed Dalton before he could rush in. Both the old lady and her daughter had guns trained on the hostages. Anthony figured that if he and Dalton went rushing in there with their guns drawn there would more than likely be a blood bath. He put his hand over Dalton's mouth and dragged him back to suite 212 where Anthony had been stationed. He shoved Dalton as best he could – Dalton being as big as he was and all – into the suite and shut the door behind the two of them.

'What'd you do that for?' Dalton demanded.

'Shhh!' Anthony said, pointing at the thin wall separating them from the hostages. 'If we'd gone rushing in there they woulda shot somebody – either us, or where the guns were pointed: at the women!'

Dalton dropped to the bed, his head in his hands. 'I can't stand much more of this, Anthony.'

Anthony sat down next to him and patted him on the shoulder. 'I know, big guy. Me neither. Honest to God.'

Holly and Jean both jumped up as Eunice Blanton whirled around from the window and Marge Blanton, still leaning against the door, simply said, 'Oh, shit.' The remaining civilians screamed and the deputies half stood up before Eunice turned the gun on them.

'Sit down now!' she yelled, waving the gun. Holly and Jean were both by Paula now, Holly kneeling while Jean leaned on her crutches, trying to see the damage. 'She dead?' Eunice asked.

Chandra, who had been sitting as far away from the rest as possible, as instructed, jumped up when she saw Mike fall from her own mama's attack, and ran to him.

With tears in her eyes, Holly looked up at Jean and nodded. 'I'm so sorry, Jean.'

'Goddammit, Earl!' Eunice said, turning on her son. 'Why'd you go and do that for?'

'I dunno, Mama! She just got up and I didn't know what she was doing and I just sorta . . . you know . . . kinda shot her. It was an accident really.' He looked at his mother sheepishly, then brightened and said, 'Just like Darrell shooting Joynell! An accident!'

Eunice backhanded her son with her gun hand, busting his lip and starting the blackening process of his left eye. 'Don't you never compare yourself to Darrell! You ain't a wart on that boy's ass!'

'Mama!' Earl wailed, swiping at the blood coming from his busted lip. 'Why you gotta say such mean things?'

Eunice sighed. 'You just bring out the ornery in me, Earl.' Turning away from him, she said mostly to herself, 'You remind me too much of your stupid father.' To her daughter, she said, 'Good going, Marge, girl. At least you got some sense. Is that that damn waiter fella? Why's he got a gun?'

Marge shrugged. 'I dunno, Mama,' she said. To her own daughter, Chandra, who was cradling the waiter's head in what was left of her lap, Marge said, 'Girl, get away from him! He'll get you all bloody!'

Chandra gently laid Mike's head on the floor and stood up, walking as close to her mama as she could get. She whispered, 'Mama, he's my baby's daddy.'

Turning her mouth away from her own mama, Marge asked, 'You diddled the waiter?'

'Mama, he's a cop. He came up here undercover,' Chandra said.

'Shit!' Marge said, a little louder than she meant to. 'Girl,' she said, her voice now a whisper, 'don't tell your mee-maw or the boy's dead for sure.'

Tears welled up in Chandra's eyes. 'Mama, we gotta do something! This has gotten way out of hand!'

Meanwhile, Jean turned on Eunice. 'Look what you've done!' she said, her voice loud, her body shaking with anger. 'You need to call this off immediately before anyone else gets hurt! That man killed my friend! It was no accident and you know it—'

'Shut the hell up,' Eunice said in a tired voice. 'I'm gonna kill you next myself. So go sit down. And you, bride-to-be, you go with her.' She looked at Holly long and hard. 'You love this man you're marrying?' she asked.

'Yes, ma'am, with all my heart,' Holly answered.

'Lucky girl,' Eunice said, turning back to the window. 'I loved me a man once.'

Earl and Marge exchanged looks. She wasn't talking about Daddy, Marge thought. There was never any love lost between those two. So, Marge set to thinking, Mama had her a man before Daddy. As the oldest of Eunice's children, Marge couldn't help but hope that maybe her real daddy hadn't been a Blanton either. Maybe if she was only half-Blanton she'd have the guts – like her own daughter – to do something about this situation. She didn't necessarily want her mama to meet a bloody end but, well, truth be known, it wouldn't hurt much if she wasn't around.

'Ah, ma'am?' Rex Kitchens said from the floor. 'You think it'd be OK for me to get going now? I have another gig after this one.'

Eunice turned to him. 'Gig? What's a gig?'

'Another performance. I'm a performer,' Rex said proudly.

'Well, you ain't been performing none here.' She turned to the other women. 'Y'all wanna see this boy's show?'

No one said anything. They looked at Eunice, horrified.

'Marge, you and Earl wanna see his show?'

'Sure, Mama,' Earl said quickly. Feeling only half-Blanton, Marge just shrugged and looked away, then smiled to herself. Oh, yeah, she thought, I'm sure as hell not a full-blooded Blanton!

Eunice turned to the boy. 'OK, whatja got?'

Rex stood up, a little uncertain. 'Well, ma'am, let me get my boom box from over there.'

Eunice nodded her head and Rex went to a table near the front door where someone had placed the boom box. He brought it to the coffee table and turned on the music. 'Baby Got Back' came out loud and strong and Rex began to gyrate. Eunice frowned, wondering what kind of performance this was. When Rex pulled away his fireman's suit, showing nothing but a G-string underneath, Eunice picked up a chair from the small table by the window and body-slammed the stripper. He went down in a heap as she began beating the boom box into submission.

Drew Gleeson and Jasper Thorne drew up to the Longbranch Memorial Hospital's ambulance bay. Jumping out, they both opened the doors and helped the firefighter with the broken arm down, then let him walk in on his own, while the two EMTs dragged out the gurney holding the injured and unconscious pizza guy, pulled out its legs and rolled him into the hospital. They deposited the injured, Drew filled out and signed a couple of forms then, sirens blazing, Drew put the pedal to the metal and hauled ass toward Bishop. There hadn't been any communication from anyone in Bishop yet, to his knowledge. Not even the firefighters and the two cops had radioed any information. But then he supposed he probably wouldn't hear it – they'd be radioing their own people. It would have been polite to keep him in the loop, though, he thought.

Getting pissed about that helped to take his mind off Joynell, so he thought he'd get more pissed. Just get good and mad, he told himself. Maybe knock a few heads together. That would take care of some of the crap building up in his heart and his head.

He'd been just about ready to ask Joynell to leave Darrell. It hadn't taken long, just these past two to three months for him to know that she was the one – the love of his life. He'd have given up his new job in a heartbeat if she'd said yes. Go back to Tulsa and get his old job back. It paid pretty well – not as good as his new job but well enough. Blantons didn't venture far from home, so there'd be no fear of Darrell coming after them if they were in Tulsa. And if Joynell could have gotten a job they'd have done pretty well financially. She'd been a cafeteria lady at the elementary school not far from Blantonville when she'd met Darrell. She could probably have got another job like that, he thought. But that was not to be – not now that asshole Darrell Blanton had gone and killed her. Drew could hardly keep his anger in check, and it had little to do with the police and firefighters not keeping him in the loop. It was Blanton. That black-hearted SOB! He'd torn Drew's own heart out with his selfish and cowardly act. At least he couldn't hurt anyone anymore . . .

Get your mind off it! he yelled at himself. Stop thinking about her! It's over. She's gone. And then he found himself bawling and had to pull the ambulance over because he couldn't see.

Johnny Mac studied the situation as the dog studied him. Cody, still lying in the slight depression in the forest floor, closed his eyes and hoped he wasn't going to die.

Finally, Johnny Mac saw what he needed. About fifty yards from him was a tree limb that hadn't been chopped up or defoliated from the storm. It was one of the rare elms in this part of Oklahoma (Johnny Mac, of course, being eleven years old, was not aware of this), and had large leaves and strong, smaller limbs. He could use it as a litter – get Cody on it somehow and pull him out of this mess!

He went over to Cody, whose eyes were still closed and said, 'Cody? You dead?'

Cody opened his eyes. 'Sure hope not,' he said.

Johnny Mac breathed a sigh of relief. 'You're alive. Look, I found a bushy tree limb I think we can use as a litter—'

'What's a litter?' Cody asked, his voice weak.

'It's something you can use to lay a person on and drag them out. Don't you watch westerns?'

'No, my dad likes Steven Seagal movies. I don't think he makes westerns,' Cody said. 'But that litter thing – that sounds good.'

'Yeah, I know,' Johnny Mac said. 'But I've got to get you on it. What can you move?'

Cody lifted his left arm, then his right. 'My arms,' he said. He lifted his head. 'My head,' he said. He tried again to move his legs but nothing was happening until the left foot stretched out like Cody was trying to be a ballerina. 'Hey! My foot!' Cody smiled up at Johnny Mac and Johnny Mac smiled back.

'Now we're making progress!' Johnny Mac said.

'Woof!' The golden retriever/Shetland barked in agreement.

Anthony and Dalton were both at the wall connecting their suite with the suite next door, both holding glasses to the wall and listening. They heard Jean berating the old bitch for killing her friend.

'We need to call this in to Milt,' Anthony whispered as he put down his glass and moved to the other side of the suite where the bathroom was. He went inside and shut the door, pulled out his cell phone and rang Milt.

'Hey, what's up?' Milt asked.

'They got Mike,' Anthony said. 'Hit him over the head. We all heard a gunshot. Mike got there first and rushed in and that's when they got him—'

'Who'd they shoot?' Milt asked, his voice low but steely.

Anthony gulped in air and said, 'We listened through the wall and heard your wife yelling at the old bitch about shooting her friend. I'm real sorry, Milt.'

'My wife's alive?'

'Yes, sir. They shot her friend, and I think maybe she's dead,' Anthony said.

'OK,' Milt said. There was silence for a long moment.

'Milt,' Anthony said, 'I think there may be a problem with Dalton. He's losing it. I had to pull him away from the door before those people saw us. And I had to practically gag him and drag him into my suite.'

'He's in there with you now?' Milt asked.

'Yes, sir, but I'm in the bathroom with the door closed, so he can't hear me,' Anthony said.

'You OK staying up there for a while?' Milt asked.

'Sure, yes, sir.'

'Then send Dalton back down. And watch him to make sure he gets in the elevator.'

'Yes, sir,' Anthony said, and hung up.

Jean had gone to Catholic schools from kindergarten through to her senior year of high school. Her co-ed grammar school had given way to an all-girl high school. Her mother wanted her to go on to a convent after graduation and become a nun, but one of her teachers, Sister Mary Celeste, had told her, when Jean mentioned her mother's wish, that it probably wasn't a good idea.

'You're a cripple, Margaret Jean. We need girls of sound mind *and* body. Tell your mother it's not going to happen,' the nun had said.

Jean never told her mother this – it would have only hurt her to think that the church she loved so much wouldn't accept her daughter as she was. Rose McDonnell had been steadfast in her belief that Margaret Jean could do anything she put her mind to – crutches or no crutches.

The all-girl high school had an associated all-boy high school, and the two would occasionally get together for parties and dances. Jean went because her mother insisted, but she was the very definition of a wallflower. She'd find a place to sit, lean her crutches against the nearest wall, and endure. During her freshman year she got asked to dance at least once at every get-together, but then the boy would notice the crutches; sometimes he would blush, sometimes he would just swagger away, but always he would leave. By her sophomore year, even the new boys had been told that Margaret Jean, sitting over there by herself, was a gimp. Stay away. By the time Jean graduated from high school, she hadn't even talked to a boy – at least, not one related to her in some way – in two years.

So the day she'd walked onto the campus of Northwestern University had been an eye-opener. There'd been boys everywhere. Thin ones, fat ones, cute ones and not-so-cute ones. Everywhere. Then she'd walked into her dorm room, her mother and father carrying her belongings in behind her, and seen Paula for the first time. Four years of a private girls' school and never a crush – until that moment. Beautiful, blonde, blue-eyed, voluptuous Paula, sitting on her single bed barefooted and her legs crossed, wearing short-shorts and a halter top. On seeing her, Jean's father had turned immediately and left the room. John McDonnell (for whom Jean's son would be named) didn't believe in facing temptation. Better, he always said, to run from it like your feet were on fire.

Jean had lived a very sheltered life and, at seventeen, knew nothing about homosexuality. She just knew that her new room-mate was one of the most fascinating girls she'd ever seen, and that she immediately liked her a lot. It would be a long time and many psychology classes later before Jean would be able to recognize what had been going on in her heart those first few months, maybe years, of her relationship with Paula. She had always been grateful that Paula had never noticed, or, more likely, since Paula had been quite worldly, had decided not to acknowledge it.

But now Jean couldn't take her eyes off the body of her friend. The small carcass left on the floor didn't look like it could possibly be that of the Paula of old. Jean could feel the tears burning the backs of her eyes. She couldn't let them out – not here, not now. Not in front of this horrible old woman and her crazy-stupid son!

Next to her, Holly stood up. 'Ma'am?' she said, talking to the old woman.

Eunice sighed. 'What now?'

'Can we get something to cover up the body?' Holly asked.

'Like a blanket from one of the bedrooms? And maybe something for the waiter and that stripper boy. You know, like a cold compress or something?'

Eunice glanced down at the unconscious again stripper boy. 'You order such a thing for your stupid party?'

'No, ma'am,' Holly answered. 'It was a surprise party. I didn't know anything about it.'

'Humph,' the old woman said. 'Well, I just don't truck with such things. A woman should only see the privates of her husband, not every Tom, Dick and Harry who wants to walk around dangling their dick! It's just not proper!' She sighed again and said, 'Well, go ahead and get a blanket for the body.' To her daughter, she said, 'Marge, you go with her. I don't know that there ain't another door in the bedroom and she's just sneaky enough to try to leave.'

'Oh, no, ma'am!' Holly said. 'I'd never leave my friends—'

'Just go!' Eunice said.

So Marge led Holly out the living room and into the bedroom of the suite. Jean watched them go. Covering Paula wasn't going to change anything. She'd still be there – stiff and lifeless under a blanket, instead of in plain view. Holly was right, of course, Jean thought. It was the respectful thing to do, not only for Paula but for the other women in the room. The civilians surely didn't need to have that constantly in sight.

The good memories kept flooding in – Paula insisting that Jean go with her to a bar on Jean's twenty-first birthday and paying to get her good and drunk. Jean had gotten her first kiss that night – from a boy who was almost as drunk as she was. And she'd liked it a lot. She never saw him again – but, since she couldn't remember exactly what he looked like, she may have seen him and just not known it. Paula had said, 'You can kiss a lot of boys and it's OK. You just can't sleep with all of them because then they'll call you names.'

Jean would never forget the look in Paula's eyes when she'd said this, or the sound of her voice. It had been a sad sound, her eyes guarded and dark. But it wasn't until medical school that another girl from their undergraduate days had managed to put Paula's words in perspective. She'd walked up to Jean in the cafeteria – shortly after Paula had vacated the table – and asked, 'Are you still hanging with that skank?'

'What?' Jean hadn't been sure who she was talking about.

'Paula the punching bag!' Seeing the confused look on Jean's face, the woman had sat down with her tray. 'Oh, come on, McDonnell! Don't tell me you don't know about pushover Paula? She's worked her way steadily through every fraternity house on campus – even the service fraternities!' the girl had said with a laugh.

'Paula's my friend—' Jean had started.

'Some friend! Did she at least give you her leftovers?' the girl had teased.

Jean had stood up, balancing her crutches and her tray. 'Maybe you should mind your own business!' she had said with some heat, feeling her face burning and hoping she wasn't blushing. She'd wanted to slap the woman but hadn't had a hand free.

Holly and Marge came back with a blanket and covered Paula's body. Jean watched, wondering now, for the first time, what had gone on in Paula's life prior to their first meeting that would cause such behavior. From her studies and her patients, she now knew that kind of acting out from a young woman was usually caused by some sort of sexual abuse. She wished she had talked to her friend about it way before her visit and tried to help her instead of pushing it out of her mind and never mentioning it.

Jean could feel the tears starting to fall. In her husband's vernacular, Jean admitted to herself that Paula now looked like she'd been 'rode hard and put up wet.' Not only that, she obviously had a serious drinking problem. Jean had failed her friend. There was no two ways about that.

'What are we gonna do about Mike?' I asked the room in general.

There were some shrugs and a couple of 'I don't knows', but that was about it.

'Charlie?' I asked.

Charlie looked forlorn. 'I don't know what we *can* do,' he said. 'Any more than what we can do for the rest of them up there. Any word from Anthony? Are they talking?'

I picked up the phone and dialed.

Jasmine had managed to inform Nita Skitteridge that the 'waiter' on the floor was actually a city cop and the two stared at each other, wishing they could confer. Finally, Nita whispered to her cousin's wife, 'Maryanne, go trade places with Jasmine. Say it makes you nervous to sit with your back to them.'

'No!' Maryanne hissed back. 'I'm not drawing any attention to myself. You know that the pregnant black chick is always the first to go in these kinds of things!'

'You're pregnant?' Nita said, clasping Maryanne's hand. 'Wonderful! And an even better excuse to sit facing them. Tell 'em it makes you nauseous to have your back to them!'

'No!' Maryanne said, removing her hand from Nita's.

'Do you wanna get out of here? Then do it!' Nita said.

Maryanne sighed. She stood shakily to her feet. 'Miz Blanton, ma'am,' she said.

Eunice whirled around. 'Sit down! How many times I gotta tell you bitches!'

'Ma'am, I'm early pregnant, and sitting with my back to y'all is making me kinda queasy. OK if I trade places with someone on the sofa?'

Jasmine jumped up before the always helpful Holly could. 'I've got no problem sitting with my back to y'all,' Jasmine said.

Eunice shook her head. 'You bitches are more trouble than you're worth!' She sighed. 'This sure ain't getting my boy back! Go ahead. Switch places.'

She turned away, not noticing that she had just allowed the two deputies to sit side by side. Eunice may not have noticed, but her daughter Marge did. And didn't say a thing.

Bobby Potter, Johnny Mac's friend Matt's father, looked from his wife and Jewel to what was left of the woods at the end of the cul-de-sac. 'You don't think . . .' he started, but couldn't complete his thought out loud.

Laurie, Matt's mother, said, 'No! He knows he's not allowed in those woods! He wouldn't do that!'

Jewel and Bobby looked at each other. 'Oh, yeah he would,' Bobby said.

'I'm afraid he's right,' Jewel said, tears stinging her eyes. 'I'm going in—'

Her thought was interrupted by the sound of screeching tires. Jewel turned to look behind her, toward her own home, and saw her husband, Harmon Monk, jump out of his car, screaming, 'Jewel Anne!' at the top of his lungs.

Jewel ran toward him. 'Harmon! I'm here! I'm OK!'

Harmon turned at the sound of her voice and ran to her, lifting her in his arms and squeezing her tight. 'Oh, Jesus! I saw the house – I thought – oh, Jesus!'

Jewel squirmed out of his arms. 'Honey, Johnny Mac was here. He left the house a little before the storm broke and we can't find him. He said he was going to Matt's house, and Matt said they were coming to our house—'

Harmon shook his head, and he too looked toward what was left of the small forest at the end of the cul-de-sac. 'You don't think . . .' he started.

Jewel nodded her head. 'Yeah, Bobby and I both think that. Laurie – well, Laurie lives in her own little Never Land.'

They walked back to where Bobby, Laurie and their daughter Miranda were standing in their driveway. Bobby and Harmon shook hands. Harmon was about the same height as Bobby, but slender. If he'd been one to play sports in high school he'd have done long-distance running – but he hadn't been a social type back then, and college had never been in his future. Bobby said, 'You wanna go with me in there?' He nodded toward the woods.

'Nothin' to it but to do it,' Harmon said.

'But, Daddy,' Miranda, Matt's sister said, 'remember when we left earlier we saw Cody riding toward our house? Maybe Matt and Johnny Mac are with him?'

Laurie jumped on that. 'I'm sure that's it! They went back to Cody's house with him! Bobby, go check!'

'Cody who?' Harmon asked.

'McIntosh,' Bobby said. 'Terry and Carolyn's boy.'

'The guy with the Porsche?' Harmon asked.

'Yeah, she's a real beaut, huh?'

'Bobby, try to stay focused!' Laurie said.

'Well, OK,' Harmon said. 'Let's drive over to the McIntoshes house and find the boys.'

SIX

J ean heard moaning behind her and turned to see the pregnant girl
bent over, clutching her stomach. The girl's mother, Marge, also
heard. Marge rushed to her daughter's aid and Jean stood up,
leaning heavily on her crutches. 'Mrs Blanton,' she said to the old
lady, 'I'm an MD. May I go to your granddaughter's assistance?'

Eunice, who was staring out the window, glanced only briefly
at her granddaughter. 'Whatever,' she said and turned back to the
window.

Jean moved to the girl, Chandra Blanton, and asked, 'Contractions?'

'Yes, ma'am, I think so,' the girl said between deep breaths.

'How far apart are they?' Jean asked, pulling up a chair and
feeling Chandra's extended belly.

'I dunno. Maybe like fifteen minutes?' Chandra said.

Jean looked up at the old lady. 'Mrs Blanton, I need to examine
your granddaughter. May I please take her into one of the
bedrooms? She needs a little privacy.'

Without turning away from the window, the old lady shrugged.
'Whatever.'

With Marge's help, Chandra stood up and the three moved into
the bedroom. Once inside, Chandra said, 'Please shut the door.'
Jean did so, at which point the hunched-over girl straightened and
said, 'Sorry, but that was for Mee-maw's benefit. I'm fine. But the
daddy of my baby isn't. He's lying on the floor out there and for
all I know he's brain-dead!'

Marge sighed. 'I can't believe you messed with a cop!'

'Mama, just give it a rest. He's a good man. Better than any
Blanton I've ever met!'

Marge grunted. 'Honey, that ain't saying much. You just be sure
Mama don't find out!'

'She won't if you keep your mouth shut!' Chandra said.

'Young lady, that's no way to talk to your mama!' Marge said.

'Well, Mama, I gotta tell you, this whole thing is getting on
my nerves! I never should have been brought into this, and you

never should have gotten involved either!' Chandra said, staring daggers at Marge.

'Hell, girl, I didn't know what she was doing! She handed me a gun and said "come on," and I just came on,' Marge said.

Chandra shook her head and settled down on the edge of the bed. 'See, Mama, that's the problem! All you ever do is say "how high?" whenever Mee-maw says "jump,"' Chandra said with disgust in her voice.

'I hate to break into this meaningful mother-daughter exchange, but my friend has just been killed and your mother keeps threatening to take my life,' Jean said, frowning at Marge. 'So I'm not in a particularly good mood at the moment. If either of you know a way out of this, let's just get it done!'

Chandra brightened and turned to Jean. 'That's just it! I've got an idea! If I go into labor, Mee-maw's gonna have to call for an ambulance, right?'

Marge shook her head. 'Not hardly,' she said. 'Your mee-maw delivered you and half the babies in Blantonville. She's not about to call an ambulance.'

'What if there was something wrong?' Jean asked. 'Like the baby was breech. Or the cord was around its—'

'His,' Chandra corrected.

'OK,' Jean said, '*his* neck. Surely she'd see the need for an ambulance then?'

Marge was still shaking her head. 'You done told her you're a doctor. Between the two of y'all she'll figure it'll be taken care of.'

'Mama, you don't know that!' Chandra said.

'OK, just say I'm right and you two go through with this and pretend the baby's coming right now and there's something wrong going on in there. But Mama decides that this doctor here and herself can deliver him. And then nothing happens. No baby yet. What do you think she's gonna do?'

Chandra's shoulders fell and Jean sank down on the bed next to her.

'Well, now what?' Chandra said. 'She thinks you're in here examining me because I'm in labor. What do we do now?'

Jean stood and balanced herself on her crutches. 'Braxton-Hicks,' she said, and headed out the door.

*   *   *

The phone on the table rang and I jumped to answer. 'Hello?' I said, sorta breathless, although the only thing I'd moved was my arm.

'So where's my boy?' Eunice Blanton demanded.

I moved my arm again to look at my watch. Fifteen minutes left of the new deadline. 'I'm still working on it, ma'am,' I said.

'I'm getting well and damned tired of sitting up here while you're sitting down there with your thumb up your behind! I want my boy and I want him now!'

There was a commotion on the line and then I heard Holly's voice. 'Milt?'

'Holly, you OK?' I asked, realizing I shouldn't have said her name out loud because Dalton grabbed the phone out of my hand.

'Holly, baby, you OK?' he demanded.

I didn't hear her reply, but told Dalton, 'Ask her about Mike!'

He asked, then turned to me and said, 'Still unconscious.'

'Shit,' I said, while there were other expletives expressed throughout the room.

Dalton handed the phone back to me. 'It's that old bat,' he said.

'Miz Blanton—' I started.

'Old bat? Is that what your boy called me? Maybe I should start with his pretty little girl first, huh, Sheriff? What you think? I can always shoot your wife second!' And she hung up.

So we all sat there for a full minute before anybody spoke. Since it was my mess, I thought I'd do the honors. 'OK, so sending Mike up there didn't work. Now the old bitch just has another hostage. Anybody got any more bright ideas?'

The silence that followed that question was so loud it coulda busted an eardrum.

Johnny Mac found a ball of string in Cody's pocket. There were also three Skittles, thirty-four cents in various coins, a pocket knife and another flashlight. Johnny Mac figured he could use both flashlights now that it was getting dark. He took one of the Skittles – cherry, his favorite – and gave the other two to Cody. He figured he needed nourishment due to his injury.

He lashed the branch with all the leaves to a medium-sized limb that he could use to pull the litter, then used more string to tie the flattest limb he could find to Cody's injured leg. Once that was done, he got his hands in Cody's armpits and began to pull. When Cody let out a bloodcurdling scream, Johnny Mac figured the Skittles had done their job – Cody was no longer in what Johnny Mac's mother the doctor called shock. That was good for Cody, Johnny Mac supposed, but he was gonna have to listen to it the whole way out of here. One good thing, though, was that maybe the screaming would help Matt find them.

Johnny Mac continued to pull Cody to the litter. The dog disagreed with this move and nipped at Johnny Mac's leg. Johnny Mac shook him off, so the oversized golden retriever/Shetland simply knocked Johnny Mac over. Luckily, he didn't land on Cody.

'What are you doing?' Johnny Mac demanded of the dog.

'Woof!' the dog said, then ran away further into what was left of the woods, barking away.

Johnny Mac looked down at Cody, whose eyes were bloodshot and leaking tears. 'You OK?' he asked.

'No! It didn't hurt so much before!' Cody whined. 'Why's it hurting now?'

'I think you were in shock. Then I gave you those Skittles and it brought you out of it,' Johnny Mac explained, to the best of his knowledge.

Cody sat up as best he could and stuck his finger down his throat.

Johnny Mac shoved his hand away. 'What're you doing?' he demanded.

'Getting rid of those Skittles! I liked it better when I didn't hurt!' Cody shouted.

Johnny Mac, still sitting on his butt on the debris left by the tornado, said, 'I don't think it works that way.' He got up and moved to Cody's upper body, leaning down to grab his armpits once again.

'It's gonna hurt!' Cody said.

'Yeah, you bet it is,' Johnny Mac said, and began to haul the boy onto the litter.

Ronnie Jacobs, the pizza guy, was dreaming. He dreamed about Lucinda, the girl he loved. He dreamed they were in his car, driving away from Prophesy County, heading for the west coast. Maybe LA, maybe 'Frisco. That would be cool. California was the coolest.

He could learn to surf. Lucinda could become an actress-slash-model, like she wanted to. They'd make a bucketful of money and buy a house on the beach, and he could go surfing every day until he became a professional surfer, and then Lucinda would retire at the top of her actress-slash-model career and they'd move to Hawaii, where he'd make a ton of money winning every surfing competition there was.

It was the same dream Ronnie had been having, asleep or awake, since he had first met Lucinda eight and a half months earlier. It had been love at first sight for him; it had taken Lucinda a little longer. But the powers that be were against their relationship, and his dream began to turn dark, evil lurking around them.

Ronnie awoke with a start but smiled when he saw his Lucinda sitting beside his hospital bed.

Harmon Monk, Johnny Mac's uncle, and Bobby Potter, Matt's dad, jumped in Bobby's car, which was still idling in the driveway, and headed down the hill. Both men's homes sat atop a hill that looked down on the rest of the subdivision, with its $500,000-plus homes, swimming pools and recreation centers, incredible landscaping, and artfully spaced copse of trees. Little of that was present at the moment – an occasional house spared, a group of trees missed.

'Where do these people live?' Harmon asked, speaking of Cody's parents, Terry and Carolyn McIntosh.

'On High Grove, down the hill,' Bobby responded, keeping his eye on the road to avoid the debris left by the tornado's path. Big as the tornado had been, it had still jumped around a lot. There would be a group of two or three houses ripped down to their foundations, then one or two left totally alone. Bobby turned left on High Grove and slammed his foot on the brake.

There were overturned cars in the middle of the street, and not one house was standing.

'Shit,' Bobby said under his breath.

Both men stared at the destruction in front of them. 'Ah, God,' Harmon said, 'the boys. You think they're in there?'

Bobby shook his head. 'No,' he said emphatically. 'The boys are in the woods, just like we thought at first. They're not in this . . . hell.'

'But what about the McIntoshes?'

'Terry was probably at work,' Bobby said. 'But Carolyn – she's a stay-at-home mom.'

'Which house is theirs?' Harmon asked.

Bobby pointed in the general direction of the destruction on the left side of the street. 'Third house in – I think. If you can figure out which is the third.'

Harmon opened the shotgun-side door. 'I guess we're gonna find out,' he said as he bailed from the car and headed in the general direction of the third house on the left.

Bobby bailed out after him.

Jean noticed that the last exchange Eunice Blanton had had with Milt had been far less heated than her previous exchanges. Now the old woman was back at her new post, staring out the window at the county courthouse on the town square. As a professional, Jean was privy to certain conditions, and was ready to diagnose Eunice Blanton with situational depression. Seriously depressed people – either chronic or situational – were prone to go in one of two directions: self-injury or lashing out violence. In this instance, Jean was betting that Eunice had past the lashing out stage and was well on her way to self-injury. If she could just get Eunice's son out of the picture she could come up with something, but she just didn't know how to get rid of him. He had proved himself to be the wild card here – he'd already shot and killed Paula just for standing up. Everyone's nerves were on edge – why wouldn't they be? – but Earl could be a real problem: stupid and dangerous is not a good combination, Jean thought.

The two police officers from Longbranch arrived with the volunteer firefighters at what was left of the town square of Bishop. They saw a man with a clipboard ordering other people around and figured he might be in charge.

Getting out of the crowded rescue van, they headed toward the man with the clipboard.

'Longbranch police department,' the tall one said, sticking out his hand. 'We're here to help in whatever way we can.'

The man with the clipboard shook the police officer's outstretched hand. 'Harley Minton,' he said. 'Mayor of Bishop. Thanks for coming. We were expecting an ambulance. They with y'all?'

'No, sir,' the police officer said. 'We had some problems getting here. Lost our vehicle to the twister, a firefighter broke his arm, and then we found a guy upside down in his car, unconscious. The EMTs had to take them back to the hospital, not knowing if your clinic here was in any shape—'

'Not hardly! Our only ambulance had to cart Doctor Crane, two nurses and four patients back to Longbranch Memorial. The clinic itself is long gone – and all the supplies with it. The ambulance is not back yet, and we're finding injured people all over the damn place.' The mayor sighed. 'But that's what I need you and the fire boys to do. Just drive into a bad area and do a walk-through, see if you can find any more injured. As for the dead, we'll deal with them later.' He handed the policeman three walkie-talkies. 'Use these to call in any injured. We're staging here, so I can send an ambulance to your location – if we ever get any fucking ambulances back!'

'Yes, sir,' the police officer said, just as three ambulances pulled in – one with the Tulsa fire department logo and two with the Oklahoma City fire department logo. The officer gave a thumbs-up sign to his honor, the mayor, and headed back to his partner and the Longbranch firefighters to tell them their instructions.

He said, 'We've got three walkie-talkies. I think we should pair up, head to a hard-hit area and do a walk-through. Ma'am,' he said to the senior female firefighter, 'why don't you take one of your guys, then the other two can pair up, and me and my partner will pair up. Sound OK to y'all?' he asked the assembled.

There were positive responses all around, so they loaded back into the rescue van and headed toward the many upscale subdivisions that made up the county's richest community.

They had just driven off and were not looking back when Drew Gleeson and Jasper Thorne pulled the Longbranch Memorial Hospital's ambulance up to the town square.

Johnny Mac got Cody settled on the litter, went to the front, grabbed the tied-on branch and began to pull. Almost immediately the branch came loose and he almost fell over as he'd been pulling hard. 'Shit,' he said under his breath, then instinctively looked around to make sure his mother hadn't heard.

'What's the matter?' Cody almost screamed from his position on the litter.

'The thing I made to pull this just came off.' He leaned down and grabbed hold of two branches of the elm, one in each hand, and began to pull again. 'Here we go,' he said, more to himself than Cody. He'd only gone a few yards when he was forced to a complete stop by two things: one, the litter had gotten too heavy to pull, and two, Cody was screaming louder than usual.

He turned to look at Cody and saw that the golden retriever/ Shetland had returned and was bucking for a free ride – right on top of Cody. Johnny Mac hurriedly set down the litter and ran to the back, attempting to pull the dog off Cody. He wouldn't budge. He just seemed to smile big and say, 'Woof!'

'Get him off me!' Cody yelled, pushing at the dog, tears streaming down his face. Johnny Mac grabbed the giant dog by the scruff of his neck and pulled with all his might. The dog rose from his position, and Johnny Mac fell on his butt. The dog came over to him and lolled out an enormous tongue that he used to liberally wash Johnny Mac's face.

'Gawd! Stop!' Johnny Mac told the dog, trying not to laugh, knowing it was likely to encourage him. It was because of the face washing that he hadn't immediately noticed that Cody was no longer screaming. When he got himself up off the ground, he saw why. Cody was – well, dead, maybe?

Johnny Mac scurried over to the litter and grabbed Cody's wrist. Johnny Mac's mom had taught him how to check for a pulse – because of his dad's heart condition, although his dad denied he had one any more – so he checked, and found a beat. It wasn't as strong as his mom's or his dad's, both of whom he'd practiced on, but it was there.

'Look what you did!' he scolded the dog. 'Now he's unconscious.' Thinking about it for a moment, he added, 'Well, at least he's not in pain, huh? And he's not screaming. That was getting on my nerves.'

Johnny Mac grabbed the litter by the two branches and continued to head in the direction he'd been going – having no idea which direction that might be.

Harmon Monk was the first to reach the third house on the left, the home of Terry and Carolyn McIntosh, Cody's parents. All he could hear was a hissing sound, coming not just from the third house on the left but a lot of homes, left and right. He turned back to Bobby, who was following behind him. 'The gas lines are broken. Be careful, don't spark anything or we'll all go up!'

Bobby stopped in his tracks, looking at all the debris around him. A lot of it was metal: bits and pieces of kitchen appliances, bathroom fixtures and small objects of all sorts. Across the street from where they stood they could also see a totally intact, big brass tuba.

Both began to walk gingerly toward the McIntoshes home. Bobby called out, 'Carolyn! Carolyn McIntosh! You here?'

'Hello?' came a small voice from somewhere in the debris.

'That's her!' Bobby said and started to hurry toward the sound.

Harmon grabbed him by the arm. 'Slow down, Bobby! We have to be careful.'

'Shit!' Bobby said, but slowed. He called out again. 'Carolyn! Keep talking so we can find you!'

'I'm in the kitchen!' she called back. 'It's in the back of the house!'

They waded carefully through the debris, heading, hopefully, in the direction of the kitchen.

'There's an awful smell, y'all,' Carolyn called out. 'I think the gas line is busted. Y'all be careful!'

'Yes, ma'am,' Harmon called back, 'we're trying. You just keep talking and we'll find you.'

'Who are y'all anyway?' Carolyn asked.

'It's me, Bobby Potter, Laurie's husband. And I got Jewel Monk's husband, Harmon, with me.'

'Well, I'll be damned!' Carolyn said. 'Thanks, y'all. I really mean it!'

And then they found her. Or part of her – the part that was sticking out from under her Sub-Zero refrigerator. Harmon immediately fell to his knees next to her.

'Hey, Carolyn,' he said, 'how are you feeling?'

'Not bad considering I have a $15,000 refrigerator on top of me. I told Terry we didn't need such an expensive one – I would have been fine with a Kenmore, ya know?'

'Should we try to lift it?' Bobby asked.

Harmon and Bobby looked at each other. 'I dunno,' Harmon said.

'Well, if we don't lift it off her,' Bobby said, 'then we won't get her out of here, and how long before the inevitable fires start?'

Harmon said, 'You're right.'

Bobby, being a wrestler and a body builder, was assigned the task of attempting to lift the $15,000 refrigerator off the prone woman, the idea being that as soon as he had it high enough Harmon would slide Carolyn out and Bobby would lower the refrigerator to the floor – very carefully, of course. It wasn't so much because of the expensive refrigerator itself as it was about the spark that might occur if he dropped it.

And it worked. Bobby lifted the bottom end of the refrigerator that was resting on Carolyn's chest high enough for Harmon to slide her out – and, miracles of miracles, her mom jeans were barely rumpled. Not a broken bone, not a scratch. With Harmon's help, Carolyn McIntosh was standing within a minute of her freedom, her blonde hair covered in dust and soot, her pretty face smeared with dirt, but otherwise fine.

'Let's get out of here,' Harmon suggested.

'Bobby, have you seen Cody? Is he at your house?' Carolyn asked. 'He took off about an hour before the storm, said he was going to play with Matt.'

Bobby shook his head. 'We'd hoped all the boys were with you, 'cause Harmon's nephew and Matt are also missing, and we think they might all be together.'

'Oh my God!' Carolyn said, grabbing Bobby's arm. 'I thought he'd be safe. They could be hurt or—'

Bobby shook his head. 'Don't go there,' he said, leading her back toward the street. 'Let's just get off your street before it blows up. And we'll go after the boys.'

'Where are you gonna go?' Carolyn demanded.

Bobby Potter said, 'The woods behind our cul-de-sac seem like a good place to start.'

There was the time in medical school when Paula had stayed up into the wee hours of the night with Jean, teaching her mnemonics for parts of the human anatomy for Jean's test the next day. Paula never had to study; she had an eidetic memory and only had to read the material once to have it down pat. Jean wasn't so lucky – she had to work for every 'A' she got, and even for the occasional 'B'.

She remembered one night when they were undergrads, when they talked well into the night about anything and everything. That happened a lot, those first four years. It had been Jean's decision to give up on the roommate situation once they both moved on to med school. She needed alone time to really hunker down and get the job done. Ever since that nun had ruined her mother's dreams for Jean's future, Jean had begun to think there might be a possibility for her own dreams to surface. And ever since she got her first play doctor kit, that's what she wanted to be. A real, live doctor. Sometimes she regretted her decision to live alone during med school, like the time Paula had spent the night just to drill her for her anatomy test the next day. When her studying was basically done for the night, she'd sit in her small apartment and wonder if Paula was busy – on a date or, God forbid, studying. But she never called. She didn't want to seem needy, even if – especially if – that was the reason for the call.

She regretted that now as she stared at the blanket-covered form on the floor by the wet bar. Could she have changed Paula's outcome if she hadn't been so selfish? Then she chided herself: suffering from a little delusion of grandeur, don't you think, Doc? As if she really affected Paula's life at all. But thinking about it, remembering the past, she was pretty sure she'd been Paula's only female friend. *Real* friend, that is. And the males in Paula's life rarely seemed to think of themselves as friends – whether she did or not. Did she confide in those boys? Did she tell them the secrets she never told Jean?

Jean had gone back a few years ago to her med school class reunion. There had been nearly one hundred people there, but not Paula. Her name did come up, though. She'd heard it mentioned here and there, usually followed by less than good-natured laughter. Jean had known only that, upon graduation, Paula had left for a prestigious internship at Johns-Hopkins in Baltimore. The night of the reunion she'd heard that Paula had lost that internship due to a tryst with a patient on his hospital bed. The woman who'd told her that said she'd heard that she'd ended up at Bellevue in New York. Someone else said he'd heard she'd done her residency at a small hospital in Wyoming, but had left there when the hospital chief of staff's wife had caught her in a compromising position with her husband. Since the wife was the hospital administrator, Paula was out of there before she could pull her panties up.

If Jean had confronted her back in the day, if she'd understood what Paula was talking about when she'd said, 'You can kiss a lot of boys and it's OK. You just can't sleep with all of them because then they'll call you names,' maybe she could have done something. What, she had no clue – then or now. How naive was I? Jean asked herself. Or did she just not want to acknowledge it? Paula had dates almost every night – very few were repeats with the same guy. She'd come home in the wee hours, often taking her panties out of her purse to put them in the hamper. Even when they walked the paths to and from classes, there would be the occasional hoot or holler from a boy or a group of boys, most of them lewd to Jean's ears.

Jean hoped that there'd been something good in Paula's life. Someone she'd met along the way who'd loved her and cared about her. She hadn't been that someone for her old friend – she knew that. And if Paula had come here to Oklahoma looking for that, Jean had definitely failed her. Before Paula had been shot dead, Jean had actually been thinking about getting her a room here at the Longbranch Inn, rather than risk bringing her back to her house to torment Milt and herself. Some friend she was, Jean thought. 'Some fucking friend I was!' she mumbled under her breath.

Holly squeezed her hand. 'Did you say something?' she asked.

Jean took a deep breath and shook her head. 'No.' She smiled at the bride-to-be. 'Don't let this sour your idea of marriage, Holly,' Jean said. 'Bachelorette parties rarely end up like this.'

'That's the point,' Holly answered. 'Seems like an omen to me.'

SEVEN

'Baby,' Ronnie Jacobs, the pizza guy, said as he grabbed Lucinda's hand. 'What are you doing here? What if somebody sees you?'

'I don't care, honey-bunch!' the girl said, her big blue eyes misty, her slightly bleached blonde hair falling over her shoulders to touch Ronnie's hand. 'I heard you was hurt and I got here just as soon as I could slip away!'

'I love you!' Ronnie said.

'I love you more!' Lucinda said, and brushed his lips with her own.

'Ain't nobody gonna stop us – never!' Ronnie said.

'I'm so proud of you, baby. You're my hero, Ronnie Jacobs!' Lucinda said, her eyes about to spill tears.

Carolyn McIntosh, Cody's mother, thought about leaving a note for her husband but couldn't figure out where to stick it since there was nothing standing upright and she doubted he'd notice if she just left the note in the middle of the debris. 'Anybody got a cell phone that works?' she asked.

'Mine went out before the storm hit,' Bobby said.

Harmon said, 'I tried calling Jewel Anne from the car but mine was out of service, too.'

'Well,' Carolyn said, crawling into the back seat of the Suburban, 'I guess Terry will find us somehow.' Carolyn shook her head. 'The important thing now is to find the boys. Terry's a grown man and we'll find each other eventually.'

'That's the spirit!' Harmon said, turning to smile at Carolyn in the back seat.

They pulled into the cul-de-sac and up to the Potters' driveway. 'The ladies are all inside. Why don't you join them while we search the woods?' Bobby said.

'Hell, no!' Carolyn said. 'I'm not sitting this one out! My boy's out there and I intend to find him. With or without you guys!'

'Definitely with,' Harmon said.

They all piled out of the Suburban and looked toward the woods. 'Like you said, Harmon,' Bobby glanced at him, 'ain't nothing to it but to do it.'

The dog was walking next to Johnny Mac and the two kept up a steady stream of conversation.

Johnny Mac: 'If we make it outta here, I'm gonna get you a big ol' steak.'

Dog: 'Woof.'

Johnny Mac: 'You like steak?'

Dog: 'Woof!'

Johnny Mac: 'I like steak too. A lot. One time my mama tried to trick me and fixed steaks for her and Daddy and fixed me this hamburger thing. I mean, I was only, like, five, but hell, I knew that wasn't any steak! And I said so! I said, "Where's my steak?" and my daddy laughed his butt off.'

Dog: 'Woof!'

Johnny Mac: 'So, you got an owner, or something? Don't see any tags or anything.'

Dog: 'Woof.'

Johnny Mac: 'I bet whoever it is must be missing you.'

Dog: 'Woof.'

Johnny Mac: 'It wasn't that boy that was dragging you in here, was it?'

Dog: 'Woof.'

'Hey, shit for brains!'

Johnny Mac stopped in his tracks, looking around, shining his flashlight hither and yon. Finally he saw his friend Matt limp out from behind some still-standing trees. Johnny Mac dropped the litter, ran to his friend and hugged him.

'All right already!' Matt said, laughing. 'Boys don't hug!'

'Sure they do!' Johnny Mac said, and slapped his hand on Matt's back. 'Like that.'

'Ow!' Matt said.

Johnny Mac backed away. 'Are you hurt?'

Matt shook his head. 'Just scrapes and bruises. Nothing serious. Who's that?' he asked, pointing at the litter. 'Is that Cody?'

'Yeah. He broke his leg and there's a bone sticking out and everything. I wrapped it in my shirt but he passed out from the pain. Well, that and the dog jumping on him.'

'Woof!' said the dog.

'Hey, is that the dog we came in here looking for?'

'Yeah, that's what Cody said.'

Matt leaned in and rubbed the golden retriever/Shetland's head. 'Jeez, he's a big 'un.'

'Yeah, tell me about it. I had to pull him off Cody and believe me, it wasn't easy,' Johnny Mac said. 'You know which way is out?'

Matt shook his head. 'I dunno. I'm so turned around I don't know which way is up.'

Johnny Mac grinned and pointed at what little could be seen of the sky. 'That's the only direction I'm sure of.'

'It's darker than crap in here. If I hadn't seen your flashlight and heard this beast bark,' he said, again rubbing the head of the very satisfied dog, 'we never would have found each other.'

'So, if we can find each other I don't see why we can't find our way out!' Johnny Mac said with determination.

Matt held out his hand and Johnny Mac shook it. 'Let's do it!' Matt said.

The one thing that kept Jean from totally losing it was the knowledge that her son was safe at his aunt's house in Bishop. He knew nothing about Jean's predicament and, if all went well, never would. After being alone for forty-some odd years, finding Milt and getting pregnant had been a godsend. It had taken some adjustment to come to terms with someone in her bed, someone else suckling her breast, and both of them needing her for this or that. John, at first, for everything; Milt for as many reasons as she needed him.

She worried about what would happen to Milt if she were to die up here. She knew he'd finally found true happiness with her and John, and with one of them gone how would he cope? She knew he'd continue to be a good father – that was just in his nature. But would he grieve too much? Maybe she should just say 'fuck you' to the old bitch and pick up the phone and call him. Tell him it's OK to marry again, as long as he's sure that she really loves John. But it's OK for Milt to find happiness. Not just OK – necessary.

She felt Holly's hand squeeze her own, and didn't notice until then the tears streaming down her face. Jean used her other hand to wipe them away and turned her head to smile weakly at Holly. 'I'm OK,' she told the girl.

Holly laughed slightly. 'Yeah, aren't we all?'

I was pacing. Nine minutes until the old biddy started shooting. I just couldn't sit still any longer. Something had to give. We needed a plan but nobody seemed to be coming up with one. Finally I turned to the group of law enforcement personnel standing there with their thumbs up their butts – just like yours truly.

'I'm going upstairs—' I started.

'Come on, Milt,' Emmett said, standing up from the table.

'Jeez, Kovak, what do you think that will accomplish?' Charlie Smith asked, also standing up from the table.

'I'll go with you, Milt!' Dalton said. He was already standing, having not sat down once since the onset of this business. I was a mite worried that if the boy did sit down he might just die of a broken heart.

'No, thank you, Dalton, but I think it's best if only one of us goes. I'm going to trade myself for the hostages. I need some of y'all standing by in the hall to grab the hostages as they slip out, or start shooting if the old bitch starts shooting.' I shrugged. 'It could go either way.'

'It's not just you she's gonna be shooting, Sheriff!' Emmett said. He never called me Sheriff – always Milt. I figured he was pissed. 'Some if not all of the hostages will be dropping like flies!'

'Well, what the fuck do you propose I do, *Deputy*?' I yelled. I emphasized the 'deputy' because I was pissed he'd called me 'Sheriff,' and also because he just shot holes (excuse the pun) in my grand – if somewhat faulty – scheme.

'OK, everybody,' Charlie Smith said, walking toward me and putting his arm around my shoulders. 'Let's all calm down. We don't need to be at each other's throats.'

I pulled away from Charlie's embrace. I didn't need him being all condescending to me. I wanted a plan! Any plan! I looked at my watch. Seven minutes. Seven minutes until the old bitch shot my wife.

The two Longbranch police officers, along with the Longbranch volunteer firefighters, had just pulled the rescue van onto High Grove Lane, where the former home of Cody McIntosh and his family used to be, when the ruptured gas lines finally blew. It only took the first one to set off all the others, and in seconds the whole street was an inferno.

The blasts sent cracks through the windshield of the rescue van, but there were no injuries. The four firefighters jumped out, grabbed the one hose the rescue van carried and affixed it to the fire hydrant stationed at the corner of the street.

One of the police officers got on the walkie-talkie and called in to the mayor. 'We got a major fire on High Grove Lane. The whole street's gone up. I'm guessing ruptured gas lines. Got any fire engines around? Over.'

'We got a couple on the way. I'll send them up there. Just try to keep it from spreading, OK? Over.'

'That's what we're doing,' the police officer said, then followed up with, 'Out,' and stuck the walkie-talkie in his back pocket.

'You think Cody's gonna be all right?' Matt asked as they pulled the litter along the debris-strewn floor of the woods.

Johnny Mac shrugged. 'Hope so. But that bone sticking out – man.' He shook his head. 'That didn't look good at all. And now he's all, you know, out of it. I just hope he's not dead.'

Matt stopped pulling the litter, which made Johnny Mac stop since if he just pulled his side he and his cargo would be going around in circles.

Matt walked back to where Cody lay and shone the flashlight in his face. Nary a muscle moved. 'He's dead,' Matt announced. 'Shit, are we gonna be in trouble, or what?'

Johnny Mac joined him and looked down at Cody's face, still illuminated by the flashlight. He bent down, lifted Cody's wrist and felt for a pulse. 'Naw, he's not dead. But his pulse is weaker than it was a while ago. We really need to get him out of here.'

'Yeah, no kidding. But which way is out?'

Both boys looked around, wishing they had a clue – but one was provided at that very moment.

'Why'd you start bawlin' back there?' Jasper Thorne, EMT, asked his partner, Drew Gleeson.

Drew hedged for a minute, then said, 'The whole situation just got to me, I guess. And,' he said, thinking fast, 'I was in a bad tornado when I was a kid. It killed my grandpa.'

'Ah, hell, man, I didn't know,' Jasper said. He slugged Drew on the arm. 'Ain't no shame in tears, man. Ain't no shame.'

Drew nodded and looked off into space. They were essentially sitting in the Bishop town square, waiting for a call to pick up the injured to transport them back to Longbranch. They'd been there for ten minutes and no calls yet. Surely there were injured people out there? Drew needed there to be injured people. He needed to jump in the ambulance and rush off, administer emergency care and get people the hell back to Longbranch, sirens blazing, going as fast as the old bus would let him.

And he needed all this, of course, so he could stop thinking about Joynell. Shot dead by that no-good asshole husband of hers, the sweetest woman he'd ever known. Kind, caring and tender, and all those good things you want a woman to be. And still as sexy as hell. He'd never felt like that before. Never in his whole life. Joynell was his one true love, and that goddam Blanton asshole had taken her away from him! Just like his love for Joynell was a new experience in his life, the hatred he'd felt for her husband when he'd looked at him in his cell was something he'd never experienced before either.

Drew could feel the tears welling up again and, despite what his partner had just said, he opted not to get caught blubbering yet again. There might not be no shame, Drew thought, but it was as embarrassing as hell.

My cell phone rang and I dug it out of my pocket and said, 'Kovak.'

The new coroner identified himself.

'Hey,' I greeted him. 'You got any results?'

'Nary a one. Figure it must be like poison or something 'cause he didn't have a mark on him anywhere. So I gotta send him to the state lab. They got all the stuff to do a real autopsy, know what I mean?'

'The two former MEs were able to do a "real autopsy,"' I said, putting some emphasis on the 'real autopsy' comment.

'Well, Milt, they were doctors. I'm a mortician. The county knew what they were getting when they voted me in! They wanna pay me less than a real MD, then they're gonna get somebody who ain't a real MD! Know what I mean?'

I sighed. 'Just send the body to the state guys then—'

'Already done. Sent him out half an hour ago. But I gotta tell you, Milt, the lady that answered the phone said they were back-logged and it could be a couple of days,' the new coroner said.

'Wonderful,' I said. 'Just fucking wonderful.' I hung up the phone.

I went out the front door of the Longbranch Inn and glanced at the sky in all directions, thinking, well, if that tornado was heading here, it was taking its own sweet time. There'd been some rain, and a little lightning and thunder that I could see and hear from the restaurant of the Longbranch Inn, but the rain had stopped and the clouds were dispersing. I put my hands in my pockets and started walking around the inn, thinking.

Fact: Darrell Blanton was dead.

Fact: Eunice Blanton held my wife and seven other – make that eight, or would it be nine by now? – people hostage.

Fact: One of those people was an undercover policeman.

Fact: We had no reinforcements coming – because of my own stupidity.

Fact: Dalton Pettigrew was on the verge of a nervous breakdown.

Fact: Emmett Hopkins was probably thinking about running against me come election time.

Fact: I had not one good idea.

Not one. And my wife, the love of my life, was upstairs in that hell hole with so many loves of so many other lives, and I couldn't get her out. I couldn't tell Eunice Blanton the truth about her boy. She'd go ape-shit. Or would she? I thought it would be really nice to talk this over with Jean. Her being a psychiatrist and all, maybe she could get a handle on this. But I really couldn't tell the old bat that her son was dead! Or could I? I looked at my watch. Four minutes.

Bobby Potter, Matt's father, was a civil engineer who had to inspect sites and buildings and what have you. Therefore, the back of his Suburban was loaded with the tools of his trade. There was a box of flashlights in varying sizes – everything from a huge hand-held searchlight to a tiny mag light and everything in between. He handed out the flashlights and then began handing out tools.

'I'll take the sledge hammer, as I'm the biggest,' Bobby said. 'Here, Carolyn, take this pick ax; Harmon, you bring the first aid kit,' he said, hauling out the biggest first aid kit any of them had ever seen.

And they headed to the end of the cul-de-sac, to the path that led around the last house, across the greenbelt and into the woods, their lights shining brightly on the devastation in front of them.

'Oh my God,' Carolyn breathed. 'Our boys are in here somewhere?'

Harmon Monk patted her shoulder. 'They're OK, Carolyn. I can feel it. They're OK.'

'From your mouth to God's ear,' Carolyn said as they trudged deeper into the woods.

They took turns shouting out the names of their missing children, the lights sweeping the trees and debris. It didn't take long before they literally tripped over a bike. Actually, it was Bobby, in the lead, who did the tripping.

'Well mother-fu—' he started. Then said, 'Excuse me, Carolyn.'

'What is it?' she asked, shining her light on the object that had tripped Bobby.

'It's a bike!' Bobby said. 'My daughter's bike.'

'Your daughter?' Harmon said. 'But she wasn't home when this came down. She's at your house now.'

'So what if Matt and Johnny Mac decided to go do something stupid – like come in here,' Bobby said, flashing his light around, 'and they needed bikes. But Johnny Mac doesn't have one at your house, right?'

'Right,' Harmon answered. 'So he'd borrow Miranda's and follow Matt in here.'

'Hey, now!' Bobby said. 'We don't know who followed who!'

'Sorry,' Harmon said. 'They're in here, all three of 'em, and that's a fact. And we found one girl's bike—'

'And a pair of Nikes,' Carolyn said, coming back from a slight detour and carrying the shoes. 'Anybody recognize these?'

Both men shook their heads. 'They could have come from anywhere,' Harmon said, 'and just got dropped in here when the twister came over.'

'Yeah, but hold on to 'em,' Bobby advised. 'We might run into a barefooted boy.'

Carolyn stuck the child-sized shoes in the back pockets of her jeans and followed the men further into the woods.

Eunice Blanton was still staring out the window at the county courthouse across the street. She thought she'd like to sit down, but figured she'd better not. Don't let 'em think they got you down, girl, she told herself. But truth be known, Eunice was tired. She was going to be seventy years old next week – not that her children noticed – and what with the sugar diabetes, things weren't exactly looking up. No matter how many times she poked herself and smeared her blood in that little doohickey the doctor gave her, the numbers still came out real high – like in the two-hundred range. One thing she did know was that it was supposed to be from eighty to one hundred and twenty. So she wasn't doing so hot. But if she went to the doctor about it he'd probably make her take them damn insulin shots. Lord knew, poking her fingers four times a day was bad enough, but shooting herself with a needle? Uh uh. Wasn't gonna happen.

She missed her boy. She missed Darrell. Darrell always made her laugh. Earl just made her want to hit him most times. Marge? Eunice mentally shrugged. Marge wasn't such a much. She shoulda been a boy. Three boys woulda been great. But the first baby, right out of the chute, ended up a girl. Seemed like everybody in Blantonville was whispering about that. Her having a girl. What was she thinking of? Of course, weren't nothing she coulda done about it. It was in God's hands.

Marge moved in with Eunice when Marge's own husband died, saying she wanted to take care of her mama, but Eunice knew it was really because that worthless husband of hers didn't leave her a pot to piss in. And then Eunice ends up practically raising

Chandra all on her lonesome. Marge didn't even work. But with Eunice's social security, and the social security disability Marge got from her dead husband, they did OK. 'Course, half the time Earl stayed with them, whenever he lost a job and missed his rent and got kicked out on his butt, and of course he never offered a dime. Sometimes he'd bring home a rabbit or a squirrel or, on rare occasions, a deer, but other than that he didn't do much for his keep.

But her Darrell! Now there was a real man! He worked hard to bring home the bacon to his family, had his own double-wide on twenty acres of prime real estate his daddy had left him and took good care of his family. Well, except for accidentally shooting his wife, of course. And Eunice knew in her heart that Joynell had somehow been asking for it. She'd never liked Joynell. She thought she was all hot stuff 'cause her family didn't marry their relatives. But she was just a hairnet working at the elementary school outside Blantonville when Darrell found her. Not like she was such a much, either.

Shit, Eunice thought, when it came to daughters and daughters-in-law she wasn't exactly batting a thousand. And then the little missy, her granddaughter Chandra, goes and gets herself pregnant, and dollars to donuts it wasn't a Blanton who'd done the deed. Now she thinks she's all high and mighty carrying a child, who, rightfully, shouldn't have the Blanton name.

Eunice glanced over at Chandra, sitting away from the rest of them, holding her belly like she was the first girl in history to be knocked-up. Then Eunice noticed the girl was looking a little green around the gills. From her spot by the window, Eunice called out, 'Chandra! You sick?'

Chandra looked up at the old lady. 'I don't rightly know, Mee-maw, but I think this baby is fixin' to come.'

Emmett found me standing up against the wall of the Longbranch Inn opposite the county courthouse. I was standing against the wall because I didn't want the old bat to see me if she happened to look out the window. Emmett saddled up to me.

'Got a light?' he said. Since neither of us smoked – any more, that is – I just looked at him.

'A little levity,' Emmett said and sighed. 'Very little, I guess.'

'You got that right,' I said, staring at the courthouse.

'I didn't mean to undermine you in there,' he said.

I glanced at him but he was staring at the courthouse, too. So I went back to staring at it. 'No real harm,' I said.

'What the fuck are we gonna do, Milt?' he said, and I could tell his real emotions were showing. Emmett had had a lot of loss in his life – first his son who had died of leukemia, then his first wife who had blew her brains out with his service revolver – and he didn't need any more. Besides, Petal, his little girl, who was a year younger than my Johnny Mac, needed her daddy – just like Johnny Mac needed his mama. And, hell, Anthony deserved to see his child born, and Dalton deserved to get married and start a family, and everybody up there had people who loved them and wanted them back safe. And I wasn't doing a damn thing to see to that.

'I'm thinking of calling up ol' Eunice and telling her that her boy's dead. What do you think?' I finally caught his eye.

He looked at me a long moment, shrugged, looked back at the courthouse and said, 'It's something to do.'

'My thinking exactly,' I said. I looked at my watch. Two minutes.

'Marge! For gawd's sake, see to your girl!' Eunice bellowed from her stance at the window. 'If it's more of them Braxton-Hicks thingies, she just needs to go lie down in the bedroom and stop with all the drama!'

'Mee-maw!' Chandra cried. 'I'm not doing drama! I'm hurting real bad here!'

'Huh!' Mee-maw responded. 'That baby don't look more'n seven or eight pounds. Your stupid uncle Earl was fourteen pounds. Liked to rip me to shreds!'

'That why you don't like me, Mama?' Earl asked, standing in the middle of the room, shotgun by his side and his head down, a wayward tear dropping from his eye to the carpet.

'I don't like you 'cause you're worthless, Earl! I done forgave you for ripping me up. Had to go to Longbranch and have Darrell at the hospital 'cause I had to have a C-section after you!' She shook her head. 'I coulda forgiven you most anything if you weren't just so damn worthless.'

What with her depression setting in and the drama her

granddaughter was creating, the old woman had totally forgotten her deadline. If she'd looked at her watch she might have realized it was time to start shooting people.

'I ain't worthless, Mama—' Earl started, looking up at his mother, but Chandra interrupted.

'Excuse me!' she all but shouted. 'I'm having a baby here! Would someone do something!'

Marge ran to her daughter's side. 'Are you for real this time?' she whispered in Chandra's ear.

'Yes!' Chandra hissed back.

Marge turned toward Jean, who was watching the scene. She nodded her head and Jean stood up and walked over to Chandra. 'The real thing?' she asked, speaking softly.

'Oh, yeah!' Chandra said and tried to breathe like she'd seen women do on TV.

Jean showed her how to do it correctly, then asked, 'How close are they?'

'Like all the time! It ain't stopping!' Chandra said.

Jean turned to Marge. 'We need to get her in the bed—'

'No!' Marge whispered. 'The only way to get my brother out of here is if he thinks he's gonna witness childbirth. Blanton men don't hold with that. So let's say she's too close and the men oughta leave.'

'No!' Chandra said. 'Not the men! Then he'll have a gun – ooooooooo – ha ha ha – oooooooo – on my baby's daddy and I can't— Oh, shit!'

Marge stood up. 'Earl, unless you wanna see your niece give birth, I think you oughta step outside.'

Earl looked up at his mother, panic on his face.

'Oh, for gawd's sake! You Blanton men and your stomachs.' Eunice shook her head. 'Go on, get out! Not like you're doing any good here anyway!'

Earl ran for the door, making gagging noises as he went. Marge followed discreetly, looking for all the world like she was just making sure the door shut behind him. Then, without her mother seeing her, she locked it and walked casually back to her daughter.

'Jean, you need some help?' Holly asked.

'Yeah, I've delivered a few babies,' Jasmine said.

Marge gave Jean a negative sign, and Jean said, 'No, but thanks, you guys. I think her mother and I have it.'

Marge helped Jean lay Chandra down on the floor. The women sitting on the sofa and the love seat threw pillows in their general direction, which Jean used to cradle not only Chandra's head but her lower anatomy as well.

Quietly to Marge, Jean asked, 'What's your plan?'

'Well, I've still got my gun. I think maybe I'll just have to shoot Mama.'

EIGHT

A loud explosion rocked the boys nearly off their feet. A fireball lit up the sky in the opposite direction from where they were headed.

'That's gotta be houses going up!' Johnny Mac said with alarm.

Matt nodded his head. 'Yeah, but it's not ours. I mean, not my house or your aunt's. It's too far away. Gotta be down the hill somewhere.'

'Then we should go that way!' Johnny Mac said.

'Yeah, I guess. But I coulda sworn it was that way,' Matt said, pointing behind them.

'We gotta do something, or else Cody—' Johnny Mac started.

'Yeah, I know, I know,' Matt interrupted. 'Just don't say it.'

Both boys stared at Cody's unconscious body for a few moments, then at the dog which, when you thought about it, was the reason they were stuck in this mess in the first place.

'If it hadn't been for the damn dog we wouldn't be here,' Matt said.

The dog said, 'Woof!'

'It's not his fault. It's the fault of the guy who was dragging him in here,' Johnny Mac, who had become somewhat enamored of the dog, said.

'Whatever,' Matt said. He turned his head, straining his ears. 'Listen!' he said, grabbing Johnny Mac's arm.

'Hey, you guys!' said a voice.

'Who's that?' Matt shouted.

'Help me!'

'Keep talking, we'll find you!' Johnny Mac shouted, just as the dog said, 'Woof!' and ran off into the trees, woofing away. 'Let's follow the dog!'

'And leave Cody here?' Matt asked.

Johnny Mac stopped in mid-flight. 'Oh. Yeah. You wanna stay and I'll go find out who that is?'

Matt looked at Cody, resting somewhat peacefully on the litter.
'He should be OK, don't you think?'

'Yeah, come on!' Johnny Mac said and went off after the dog,
which was doing some serious barking.

They found the dog halfway up a really big oak tree, and
doing that by only standing up on his hind feet, his front feet
reaching high into the tree. But he was no longer barking – he
was growling. When the dog saw them, he got down from the
tree and grabbed Johnny Mac's hand with a soft mouth. The dog
pulled Johnny Mac to the tree, stood up and began growling
again.

'Up here,' said a disembodied voice.

Both boys looked up. A teenaged boy was splayed over a large
limb of the oak, his head a bloody mess. 'Can y'all get me down?'
he asked.

A fire truck from Tulsa showed up on High Grove Lane and hooked
up their much bigger hoses to the fire hydrant. The puny hose
being used by the volunteer firefighters from Longbranch hadn't
done a lot of good.

One of the two police officers from Longbranch walked up to
the female volunteer firefighter, whom he had, by watching her,
determined was definitely in charge. 'Wanna leave this to the Tulsa
boys and keep going?' he asked.

'Sounds like a plan,' she said and let loose with a two-finger
whistle and a wave of her hand. The rest of the volunteer firefighters
showed up and they all piled into the rescue van.

'Where to?' she asked the cop.

'Up the hill?' he suggested.

She shrugged. 'Works for me.'

Drew Gleeson and Jasper Thorne were headed up the hill in the
same subdivision, gawking at all the damage. 'You'd think somebody up here would be hurt,' Drew said.

'Yeah. Ya'd think,' Jasper agreed.

'Where should we go?'

'I dunno,' Jasper said. Then got all excited. 'Hey! Look at it!
That's the Longbranch rescue van!'

Seeing it, Drew hit his horn then turned on the siren for a quick 'woop-woop.' The rescue van stopped and the cops and the female firefighter got out of the van.

'Hey, guys!' Drew said, getting out of the van and vigorously pumping hands. 'Y'all find any injured?'

The cops shook their heads and the woman firefighter said, 'No. Found a fire, though. Hate to think someone could have been alive in there when it started.' She shook her head. 'It was a real bad explosion and most of the houses – or what was left of them – went up.'

'Ah, shit, man,' Jasper said. 'That's not good.'

Everyone nodded in agreement with his statement.

'Where y'all headed?' Drew asked.

'Up the hill,' one of the cops said. 'No particular reason, but we thought we'd start there and work our way down.'

Drew looked at Jasper, who nodded. 'We'll follow you up there,' Drew said. 'In case you find survivors.'

Again, they all nodded and got back into their respective vehicles.

'You that guy who was dragging this dog into the woods?' Johnny Mac demanded of the kid in the tree.

'No,' he said.

The dog growled, still standing tall into the tree.

'Dog says you're lying,' Johnny Mac said.

'That dog didn't say shit!' the boy in the tree shouted. 'He's just a stupid, dumb dog!'

Johnny Mac looked at Matt. 'Should we just leave him up there?' he asked his friend.

Matt appeared to think it over. 'Would serve him right,' he finally said. 'I don't like dog killers.'

'Me neither,' Johnny Mac said.

'Hey! I didn't kill that dog! Look! He's right there!' the kid in the tree said, pointing down at the still-growling dog.

'Maybe you just admitted what you were gonna do!' Matt said.

'I'm not saying shit!' the boy said. 'Y'all just be on your way. I'm fine up here. Just fine and dandy.'

'How bad you hurt?' Johnny Mac asked him.

'Not so much,' the boy's voice got softer. 'Just a head injury. You know they bleed a lot.'

Johnny Mac could see that by the pool of blood on the ground that he almost stepped in. He and Matt conferred.

'You think we should try to get him down?' Johnny Mac asked.

'I'm afraid if we do the dog'll tear him to shreds,' Matt whispered.

They both looked at the dog, still holding up the tree and growling.

'Hey, dog,' Johnny Mac said.

The dog jumped down and turned to Johnny Mac, the growl gone and his tail wagging. There was a big old smile on his face.

'Promise you won't hurt this guy if we let him down?' Johnny Mac asked.

The dog cocked his head, as if trying to figure out his instructions. Then he grabbed Johnny Mac's arm again with his soft mouth and pulled him to the tree. He sat down on his hindquarters, looked up into the tree and said, 'Woof!'

Mike Reynolds woke up, his head throbbing. He reached to touch the sore spot and brought back a bloodied hand. 'What the fuck?' he said, staring at his hand, then looked up. He was in the suite again. Oh, right! He remembered. There'd been gun fire and he'd run in and . . . that's all he could remember. All the women in the room were turned with their backs to him, staring at something behind the long sofa. Chandra's mee-maw was just standing by the window, staring out. Where was Chandra, though? He couldn't see her. She wasn't in her chair at the back of the room. Then, just as his vision had slowly cleared, the ringing in his ears abated and he began to hear voices.

'Push! Come on, you can do it, baby girl! Push!'

Mike pulled himself up and hobbled toward the sound. But Chandra's mee-maw must have heard him and turned away from the window, her gun pointing at his heart.

'Where in the hell do you think you're going?' she demanded.

Mike pointed to the back of the sofa, where he could now see his beloved's feet sticking out. 'She's having my baby,' he told the old woman.

Eunice Blanton shook her head and sighed. 'Oh, for God's sake! Go on.' And she turned back to stare out the window again.

*   *   *

'I can't stand much more of this!' Carolyn McIntosh, Cody's mom, said. 'Cody!' she yelled at the top of her lungs.

Both men followed suit, screaming their own boys' names as loud as they could.

'Hey!' came a faint sound from far away.

'Hey!' Harmon bellowed back. 'Who is it?'

'John McDonnell Kovak, sir!' came the faint but shouted answer.

The three adults began to run as fast as they could through the wreckage and debris of the woods.

'Y'all hear that?' Drew Gleeson asked those assembled outside their vehicles on the cul-de-sac at the top of the hill.

There was a chorus of 'yeahs!' in response.

Jasper Thorne pointed toward the woods. 'It came from there!'

'Grab the stretcher and I'll grab the bag,' Drew said and they all – two EMTs, two police officers and five volunteer firefighters – headed down the path to the greenbelt and into the woods.

'I'm here, baby, I'm here,' Mike Reynolds said, holding his beloved's hand and stroking the damp hair away from her forehead.

'Just let her squeeze your hand,' Marge said. 'Come on, sweet girl, breathe, breathe!'

Chandra tried her new breathing techniques but it didn't seem to help the pain even a tiny bit. 'Oh my God!' she screamed. 'Get this damn thing out!'

Jean, who, with some help, had managed to get on the floor between Chandra's raised legs, looked at Marge. 'The cord's around his neck,' she whispered to Marge.

'Ah, shit,' Marge breathed.

'What? What is it?' Mike asked, panicked.

'Oh, God, oh God, my baby!' Chandra screamed, and began to cry as Mike tried without success to calm her.

'We need to get her to the hospital,' Jean said.

'That ain't happening,' said Eunice Blanton from her stance at the window.

Johnny Mac, Matt and the dog ran back to where Cody was lying, still unconscious, on the litter.

'Here we are!' Johnny Mac screamed. 'Can you hear us?'

'Keep yelling!' a grown-up voice said.

So both boys began to yell and both burst into tears – which they would later deny – when they saw Johnny Mac's uncle, Matt's dad and Cody's mom come running to where they were.

The room phone rang. It took two rings before Eunice Blanton turned to acknowledge it. She moved away from the window and picked the phone up off the table.

'What now?' she said into it dejectedly.

'Ma'am,' said the voice of the sheriff, 'I got some real bad news for you.'

'That's been about all you've been giving me, asshole,' Eunice said, trying to get some spunk into her voice.

'Ma'am, Darrell is dead. I'm real sorry, Miz Blanton—'

Eunice dropped the phone and fell on the sofa where Jean had been sitting. Marge saw this, stood up and walked to her mother. The gun in Eunice's hand was pointed at the floor. Marge took it out of her mother's hand with surprising ease, let out a deep breath and picked up the phone's receiver. 'Sheriff, that you?' she asked.

'Yeah, who's this?'

Ignoring his question she said, 'Y'all can come on up now, Mama's disarmed. And we need an ambulance. My baby girl's having a baby and the cord's around its neck.'

'We're on our way,' the sheriff said.

'But be careful. My brother's outside the door and he's armed. He's already shot one lady up here.'

Downstairs, Milt nodded his head, hung up the phone and readied his men to go.

PART TWO

SIMULTANEOUS INVESTIGATIONS

NINE

'There's a boy in a tree back there,' Johnny Mac told his uncle after all the hugging had abated. 'We think he tried to kill this dog here.'

'That's a dog?' Uncle Harmon asked. 'I thought it was a bear.'

The dog, sitting back on his haunches, smiled and wagged his tail without saying a word.

It was at about this juncture in the discussion when all the Longbranch rescue people showed up.

Carolyn McIntosh was down on her hands and knees next to her son. When she saw the EMTs with their medical bag and stretcher she said, 'Over here, y'all! My boy! He's hurt bad.'

Turning to the EMTs, Johnny Mac said, 'I tried to help him.' Tears formed behind his eyes, threatening to spill over. 'I tied my shirt around his leg so that bone wouldn't—'

At that point Cody's mom unwrapped Johnny Mac's shirt, saw the bone sticking out of her son's leg and passed out.

Anthony got a call from Milt. 'We're going in,' Milt said. 'Except the son, Earl Blanton, is outside in the hall and he's armed. Can you check that out and get back to me? See how we should approach this dude.'

'Got it, Milt,' Anthony said and hung up his cell phone. He went to the door, opened it just a crack and peered out toward the door of suite 214.

Earl Blanton was standing in the hallway, all right, his ear to the door of suite 214, his shotgun propped against the opposite wall and his face pointed in the other direction.

Anthony took off his shoes, readied his weapon and walked silently up to Eunice Blanton's only surviving son.

'Hands up. You're under arrest. You have the right to—'

*   *   *

Back inside suite 214, Marge Blanton handed her weapon to Jasmine Hopkins. 'Here ya go,' Marge said. 'I was coerced into this. Wasn't none of my doing.'

She looked at her mother, who was bent over, sobbing fit to beat the band. 'Mama just has this thing for Darrell, is all.' Marge shook her head. 'It's always been like that. Darrell just hung the moon as far as Mama's concerned.'

Eunice stood up and slapped Marge's face. 'Don't you talk about my boy like that! He's dead!' And she fell back down, sobbing.

'Sorry about that, Mama,' Marge said. 'But you got two other children and you done ruined our lives because of him. I hope you're happy!' Marge swung around and went to her own daughter who was lying on the floor, panting and alternately screaming.

The door burst open and Anthony came in, pushing a frazzled Earl in front of him. 'Mama!' Earl cried. 'This black guy is arresting me!'

Eunice paid no attention, but Maryanne Dobbins jumped up from the sofa where she'd been sitting next to the old bat and ran toward her husband. Seeing that, Jasmine turned, pocketed the gun Marge had given her and advanced on Earl. 'I'll take him,' she said to Anthony. She grinned. 'You take your wife.'

And he did – hugging her so tight that Maryanne felt she might break, but she didn't really care.

We weren't far behind Anthony, me and everybody else from downstairs, with Dalton pushing through to the front. Holly was on him in a New York minute, arms and legs entwined around him. Emmett helped his wife with her prisoner and Will and Nita Skitteridge found each other.

I didn't see Jean. I screamed her name at the top of my lungs, my eyes not leaving the corpse covered by a sheet over by the wet bar.

Marge stood up from behind the sofa. 'Sheriff, she's back here with my daughter. We need an ambulance bad.'

I rushed around to where Mike Reynolds and Jean were bent over the pregnant girl. 'There are no ambulances,' I told Jean. 'There was a real bad tornado in Bishop and everybody in the county's up there. We'll have to drive her in a squad car.'

Jean grabbed my arm. 'John?' she whispered.

I shook my head. 'I don't know. I haven't been able to get hold of Jewel. You and me will drop Mike and the girl off at the hospital and head to Bishop.'

Jean nodded.

Marge said, 'I'm going with my daughter!'

'No, ma'am!' I said, ready to cold-cock this woman if she said another word. 'As I understand it, you assaulted a police officer—'

'Ah, Sheriff,' Mike Reynolds said, standing up. 'This lady's gonna be my mother-in-law so let's just put all that down to a domestic squabble, OK?'

I looked from him to Marge to the pregnant girl on the floor. 'Ah, hell, whatever. Y'all get downstairs. We gotta go. Guys! Y'all pick this girl up!'

So Dalton got her head, Anthony got her feet, Mike took her heavy middle and we all headed out, leaving Charlie Smith to clean the place up – after all, it was his jurisdiction.

It took but a minute or two to get the teenaged boy down from the tree. The rescue squad figured this was an easy one.

Both boys pointed at the teenager and started talking on top of each other.

Johnny Mac: 'He's why we were in here—'

Matt: 'He was trying to kill the dog—'

Teenager: 'No, I wasn't.'

'OK, guys,' Bobby Potter, Matt's dad, said, ruffling his son's hair. 'We'll sort all this out once we get this kid to the hospital.'

'But, Dad—' Matt started.

'Let's get you home. Your mama's pretty upset,' Bobby said.

Matt looked sheepish. 'Bet she's more than upset,' he said.

'She's about a minute away from qualifying for a straitjacket, but she'll be OK once she sees you.'

Carolyn McIntosh was roused by Drew Gleeson and smelling salts. Drew and Jasper already had Cody on a stretcher, an oxygen mask on his face.

'My boy—' Carolyn started.

'He's OK,' Drew told her. 'Can you stand up?'

Carolyn nodded and Drew helped her to a standing position.

'I take it you wanna ride in the ambulance with him?' he asked
her.

Carolyn just gave him a look, since the word 'duh' was now
out of favor.

Mike Reynolds rode up front with me, while Jean and the mama
rode in the back with the pregnant girl stretched out over them,
her head in her mama's lap and her pelvic area in Jean's, while
Jean tried to stop the baby from pushing out.

We were about ten minutes away from the hospital, but when
we got there we saw two ambulances in the bay and no one came
running out to help.

'Mike, run in and get a gurney! Quick!' I said.

Which he did, coming out followed by a five-foot-nothing,
eighty-five-pound nurse who was yelling at him and who looked
like she could take him out no problem at that moment. I was at
the back door of the squad car, but left it to stop the nurse.

'Sheriff Kovak,' I told her. 'We got a pregnant girl with the
cord around the baby's neck.'

She moved into action, telling me and Mike how to get Chandra
on the gurney and making us push it in past the other gurneys
lined up like cords of wood in the hallways of the ER. Some held
bleeding patients who bitched and moaned, while some held people
who were out cold and not bitching at all. But mostly it was pure
mayhem, plain and simple.

An orderly grabbed my side of the gurney and I stopped, letting
Mike and Marge continue on. I turned and headed for the front
door, where my wife waited in the car. Now we were off to find
our son.

Johnny Mac feared for his ribs as his aunt Jewel tried to squeeze
the life out of him. He knew it was just an exuberant hug, but still
and all, it kinda hurt – especially after the day he'd had.

'If you ever try that again, young man—' she started once she'd
stopped hugging him.

But Uncle Harmon intervened. 'Not now, Jewel Anne. Let's just
be grateful he's OK.'

Aunt Jewel nodded her head. 'Oh, I am,' she said, 'I am,' and
squeezed him again.

'We got any phones working yet?' Uncle Harmon asked the room. Negative responses were all he got. Turning to Jewel and pulling her away from Johnny Mac, he whispered, 'We gotta let Milt and Jean know he's OK.'

'I know. Should we use your car and take him home or what?' Jewel asked. 'We can't use mine. It's under the rubble that used to be our garage.'

'Just don't think about it,' Harmon said, holding her close. 'We're gonna take this one hour at a time. As for taking Johnny Mac to Milt and Jean, I think it's best if we stay put. They'll come to us.'

Jewel went back to holding her nephew, while Johnny Mac and Matt – who was in a similar situation with his mother – just looked at each other and rolled their eyes.

I've witnessed a few tornadoes, growing up in Oklahoma and all, but the devastation from this one wasn't like anything I'd ever seen before. As I used the sirens and lights on Mike's city squad car the roadsides were lit up as we sped past and I saw tossed farm equipment – a ten-ton tractor sitting on its butt like a dog begging for a bone – cars tossed hither and yon and dead cattle here and there. As we neared Bishop I turned on the searchlight and turned off the siren and strobe lights, moving the searchlight this way and that to see what was there.

It wasn't pretty, and my stomach was heaving at the thought that my son could be somewhere in all this wreckage. It looked like a nuclear bomb had gone off – rubble everywhere. What used to be a Chevy dealership on the south end of town was now gone, and if you didn't know it had been there you certainly wouldn't know now. A tire store on the other side of the road had a broken glass picture window and a Toyota Celica sitting upside down on its roof. Billboards – on the outskirts of Bishop only, they weren't allowed inside the city limits – were long gone, not even their posts stuck up now. As we moved into town, I could see that the north side of the town square – that used to house a fancy boutique, an organic produce store, a jewelry store so expensive I'd have to take out a government loan to buy my wife the cheapest thing in there, and a men's haberdashery – was nothing but a memory. The east side had lost at least half its shops, with only the post office

and half a dry cleaning establishment still standing. The west side
had a twenty-four-foot inboard motorboat sticking out of the front
of what used to be a real estate office, and the State Farm office
next to it had no front at all. The south side, however, was totally
untouched. Tornadoes are curious things.

The middle of the square used to house a gazebo, picnic tables
and benches and tall, old trees, flowerbeds and such, but now there
were only people milling about, a fire truck, an ambulance and a
man with a clipboard. I drove up to him in the squad car and stuck
my badge out the window.

'Sheriff Kovak,' I said. 'Me and my deputy here are headed up
to Lazy Hill Lane. Any problems up there?'

'Yeah, the Longbranch ambulance just took a kid off to the
hospital from there.'

'A kid?' I said, my stomach heaving even more.

'Yeah, him and his mom, and somebody needs to give that lady
a sedative, know what I mean?'

My stomach settled, but I felt for the mama. I nodded my head.
'Yeah, I know what you mean. OK if we head up that way?' I
asked him.

'Just be careful. It's a mess up there. Pretty hard hit,' he said.

My stomach did its thing again and Jean – my deputy – and I
headed up the hill. We passed a street with two fire trucks fighting
a pretty bad blaze and kept going higher up. There was rubble
and debris everywhere, with only an occasional standing house.
In this neighborhood the bill was gonna run into the hundreds of
millions.

Jean was holding my hand so tight I thought she'd break a finger,
but I didn't complain. I was too damned scared to say a word. All
I could think was my boy, my boy . . . My mind wouldn't allow
me to go any further than that.

Then we were on Lazy Hill Lane, the cul-de-sac where my
sister and her husband lived. Except there was no house there.
Just rubble and a swimming pool empty of water but full of debris,
including my sister's fancy black-and-gold toilet from the master
bath.

Jean and I jumped out of the squad car and screamed Johnny
Mac's name and my sister's name at the tops of our lungs, holding
on to each other like we'd fly away if we weren't grounded by

each other's need. Tears were streaming down my wife's face, and I knew I wasn't far behind in the tear stakes, when the door to the house next door burst open and our son came running out.

Lucinda stood outside pizza guy Ronnie Jacobs' hospital room, talking to the doctor about her beloved's condition. 'But is he gonna be OK, Doctor?' she asked.

'He should be fine, young lady,' the doctor answered. 'But he has a concussion and a possible head injury, and he's lost a lot of blood from the head wound so we need to keep him here for a while.'

'How long?' Lucinda whined.

'Maybe a week,' the doctor answered. 'We're at a crucial point right now – he could still slip into a coma so he needs around-the-clock attention. That's why he's still in ICU.'

'But they won't let me stay with him!' Lucinda cried, a tear slowly leaking from her baby blue eyes and traveling down her peaches-and-cream cheek.

The doctor patted her on the arm, not at all immune to her charms – or the thirty-six Ds peeking out of her low-cut blouse. 'I'll see what I can do. Are you two legally married?' he asked.

Lucinda shook her head as another tear threatened to stain her lovely face. 'Not yet. We're fixin' to, though.'

The doctor sighed. 'Well, I'll do my best.' He squeezed her arm then walked off, and Lucinda went back into Ronnie Jacobs' room.

She leaned down and kissed him on the lips. 'Honey bear, I'm not sure they're gonna let me stay,' she said, more tears blotting her cheeks. 'They're gonna keep you in this eye-see-you place 'cause you're so sick.'

Ronnie tried to sit up. 'I'm sick?' he said. 'What's wrong with me?'

'Your head, honey-bunch. Remember?'

'What happened to my head?' Ronnie asked, touching the top of his head with his hand and feeling only bandages. 'Is there something wrong with my head?'

Lucinda said, 'Uh oh,' and began to cry in earnest.

TEN

Three days later, things had begun to calm down. We had Johnny Mac home with us where he belonged, and my sister and her husband were in the guest room upstairs. Their house was totally demolished and they had to wait for the insurance inspector and all the crap that comes with a major tornado. The town of Bishop had been declared a disaster area by the governor, and although I hadn't voted for him, I had to agree with him on this. The whole place *was* pretty much a disaster.

My sister's kids – Leonard, Marlene and Carl – had all been calling non-stop, checking on their mama and Harmon and us, too. Leonard was married and living in Houston where he was apprenticing with Jewel's old neighbor, Chuck Lancaster, at his insurance office. Since Chuck's mother (who played the part of Chuck's secretary/receptionist) had passed on, I don't think Leonard was much more than that, but Chuck kept promising Leonard that he'd let him take over the agency when it was time for Chuck to retire.

Marlene was living in Dallas where she was some high-up muckity-muck with Southwest Airlines. She was married and had a baby girl. Her husband, I think his name is Jordan or George, I'm never sure, also works at the airlines, and before the baby came along they spent as much time as possible anywhere but in Dallas, which is easy to do, I hear, if you work for an airline.

Carl was in his last year at OU in Norman, studying accounting, hoping to become a CPA like his dead daddy. He was the closest of the three to Prophesy County, and the one who wanted to come home the most, but since his mom and stepdad were bunking with us Jewel kept telling him there wasn't room and he needed to stay where he was, but that she and Harmon would come up over the weekend to see him. Jewel was worried she'd hurt his feelings, but as Harmon told me, when Jewel was out of hearing range, 'That boy's too sensitive. He needs to grow a pair.'

I couldn't say I disagreed.

All in all, the body count wasn't as bad as it could have been.

Since the tornado hit on a Saturday, most kids were at home and not in the schools, one of which had been demolished. Most people got to their shelters and took in folks who didn't have one. There were plenty of injured – most treated and released – some serious. So far, on this third day, we had six dead and two hundred and thirty-three injured. The other boy who had been with Johnny Mac on their misadventure – Cody, the one whose leg got broken so bad – was still in the hospital, but the broken leg was his only real injury (if you ignored the bruises and abrasions that all three boys had), and the doctors operated and put in pins and other stuff and said he'd be walking with a cast and crutches at least until Christmas, if not longer.

The teenaged boy Johnny Mac and his friend Matt had found was still in the hospital, having slipped into a coma from his head injury, and his mama told me when I asked that it didn't look good.

Somehow, and I'm not sure exactly how, the giant dog that had helped or hindered – depending on who you talked to – the boys was lying in front of the cold fireplace in my living room, waiting, I suppose, for someone to build a fire. I told Johnny Mac that we needed to put a notice in the paper that we'd found him, but that if nobody called in a month we'd have to make other arrangements. Johnny Mac is pretty set on those other arrangements being us keeping him. I'm not sure – considering what he's consumed so far – that we could afford to keep him. Johnny Mac named him, of course. I kept telling him not to, that there might be an owner out there somewhere, but Johnny Mac ignored me and started calling him Tornado – or Nado, for short. Evinrude, my tabby cat I've had since before Johnny Mac was born, is not so sure about Tornado. The first day the dog came to our house, Evinrude took one look and bolted. The only way I know he's been around is that his bowl is empty, but even though we moved it to a high counter, I think that dog could be the one emptying it out. I did see a glimpse of the cat yesterday, peeking around the edge of the garage. When he saw me he hissed and ran off. I think, as far as Evinrude is concerned, I'm in the doghouse. Excuse the pun.

Jean had been charged with doing the very hardest thing I ever have to do in my job – mainly notifying the next of kin for her friend Paula Carmichael. I told her I'd do it, but she said she had to. I'm not sure why, but I left her to it. It was obviously something she felt she needed to do, and I made sure she was alone in our bedroom so she could make the call.

Eunice and Earl Blanton were partaking of our guest quarters in the county jail, although, as I'd told Mike Reynolds, I hadn't arrested Marge Blanton. When it came right down to it she was the one that got the whole thing stopped in the first place, so I figured – even though I still considered her almost as guilty as the others – I should let her go. She was pretty busy – as were Mike and Chandra – with the bouncing eight pound and four ounce baby boy that Chandra had delivered just minutes after Jean and I had hightailed it out the hospital.

Now I had one little old thing left on my plate: namely figuring out who the hell had killed Darrell Blanton. The state lab boys had to run extra blood tests, but finally found a poison akin to digitalis, which is a type of drug used for congestive heart failure. As far as his mama knew, Darrell Blanton didn't have a heart condition of any kind.

The guy at the state lab said, 'Brand names include Digoxin, Lantoxin, Crystodigin, Purodigin, and you can get it in either tablet or liquid form. There are also poisons from other natural sources such as the oleander which provide a similar effect and are easy to find. And Sheriff, if it relieves your mind, there was nothing much y'all coulda done to help this poor slob. The reaction time is immediate.'

I took notes, thanked him and hung up.

I sat at my desk at the station, which, like any other Tuesday, was filled with my deputies and Holly at the command center minding the phones, and all was right with my world. Except we had two dead bodies: Darrell Blanton and Paula Carmichael. Of course, we knew who killed Paula, so that was no biggie. Every woman in suite 214 that fateful night saw Earl Blanton shoot her, and Earl was more than happy to admit it – he kept saying it was an accident, like Darrell shooting Joynell. So the county prosecutor was as happy as a clam to take his statement – and those of all the women present – and offered him twenty-five years to life.

As for Darrell, well, not so much. I thought back to that day. Me and Holly and Anthony in the shop, Darrell and the drunk teenager in the cells. Darrell eating pizza and the teenager convulsing. Holly had called 9-1-1 and the EMTs had showed up. An hour later Anthony had found Darrell dead in his cell.

So what the hell happened? Then a thought came to me. One of the EMTs – Drew Gleeson, the new guy from Tulsa – had said he'd left his bag in the cells and went back for it. An EMT, a bag full of medicine and Darrell – was that a sum that equaled guilt? After all, Drew and Jasper were the only ones present that night who'd have had access to those kind of drugs, and Drew was the one who retrieved his bag, which meant he'd have been alone with Darrell. But why would he want to kill him? It didn't make any sense, but it at least meant a good talking to with Mr Gleeson. I sighed. Shit, I thought. I had me a suspect.

Jean found an ID card in Paula's wallet with the name and phone number of her next of kin: her mother, Vivian Carmichael, with an area code for Kansas City, Kansas. She dialed the number and it was answered after two rings.

'Mrs Carmichael?' Jean asked.

'No. May I tell her who's calling?' the female voice asked.

'Jean McDonnell. In regards to Paula,' she told her.

'One moment, please,' the woman said and put down the phone.

It was more like two minutes before Jean heard the voice of an elderly woman say, 'Doctor McDonnell? This is Vivian Carmichael. What's my daughter done now?'

'Mrs Carmichael, I'm so sorry to do this by telephone, but I thought you should have this information immediately—' Jean started, but Vivian Carmichael interrupted.

'Whatever it is I'm not throwing any more money at it! The girl is fifty-five years old, for crying out loud! She needs to face the music for once!'

'Ma'am, Paula didn't do anything. She . . . ma'am, she's dead. She was killed here—'

Jean stopped talking. She didn't know where to go from there. All her training had flown out the window. This was too personal. This was Paula.

Finally the older woman said, 'How was she killed?'

'We were in a hostage situation—'

'Excuse me?' Vivian Carmichael demanded.

'We were at a—' Jean couldn't bring herself to say bachelorette
party, as that would somehow – in Paula's mother's mind – make
it appear as if Paula was somehow to blame, so she said instead,
'Wedding shower. And there was a home invasion. Paula was shot.'

Again, silence from the other end of the line. Finally Jean could
hear a shuffle, then Vivian Carmichael said, 'Oh my God. You're
serious.'

'Yes, ma'am. I'm so sorry.'

'Did she suffer?'

'No,' Jean said. 'It was instantaneous.'

'Where is she – I mean, her body – where is it now?' Paula's
mother asked.

'It's still at the morgue—'

With a stronger voice, Mrs Carmichael said, 'Well, I want her
home. Right away.'

'Yes, ma'am.'

'And Doctor McDonnell, I know you were my daughter's only
real friend all these years. Would you do me – and Paula – the
honor of accompanying her home?'

Jean was silent for a moment, surprised by the request. Finally
she said, 'Of course. I'll make arrangements right away.'

'I'll send you a check—' Mrs Carmichael started, but Jean
interrupted.

'Please, don't. I'd like to take care of it, if you don't mind.'

'Yes, of course. Please call me with the details.'

'As soon as—' Jean stopped when she realized she was talking
to dead air.

The really unfortunate thing about my sister and her husband
bunking with us was that, because I had to be at the sheriff's
department, Harmon had to be at his used-car part stores (one of
which was hurt pretty bad by the tornado), and Jean had to be at
the hospital, Jewel felt righteous about volunteering to cook dinner
every night.

Let me tell you, there's nothing righteous about my sister's
cooking. Unless you like your pasta mushy and your potatoes al
dente, your chicken rare and your beef well done (otherwise
known as burnt to shit). My sister never saw a vegetable that
couldn't be boiled within an inch of its life, or a fruit that wouldn't

be better coming from a can. How Harmon could stand it I'll never know.

Wait, that's a lie. I do know.

Jewel and Harmon met while she was still in high school. He was a dropout that hung around the burger joint where Jewel went to meet her friends. The two fell madly in love and my daddy took umbrage to that. Jewel was fifteen and Harmon Monk – the son of a drunken pig farmer – was twenty-two. So my daddy, with me by his side, went up to Harmon's daddy's pig farm and explained to Harmon that, what with me being a deputy and all, I was gonna throw him under the jail for statutory rape. He protested that he'd never touched my sister and I believed him, but we nevertheless put the fear of God into the boy. And with his father's encouragement – at the end of a spiked belt – Harmon up and joined the army.

Jewel went to college, got knocked up by Henry Hotchkiss, and with Daddy barely in his grave it was my duty to force my sister into marrying the boy. Fifteen years later he was killed, so my sister and her kids came to live with me, and Harmon Monk – married with two daughters – came a-courting.

He'd loved my sister all those years, and now with six used-car part stores all across our end of Oklahoma and a big ol' house in Bishop, he decided I might think he was now good enough for her.

There was the small matter of his marriage, but I guess you could say that Harmon's wife left graciously enough, after she cleared all their accounts and got a lawyer to get her a God-awful amount in child support. Jewel and Harmon were married shortly after that. The kids loved him. Harmon's two girls, who he only saw one weekend a month, tolerated Jewel and her kids, and all was well in their world. Except that my sister couldn't cook worth a damn. But Harmon was a tall, skinny drink of water, and I doubted if food was very much a priority in his life.

Unfortunately, food *is* a priority in mine. After my heart attack this past summer, I've been on a strict diet – even though I had a quadruple bypass and should be good to go for another twenty years or so. Jean insists on it, and she and Loretta, our favorite waitress at the Longbranch Inn and one of the ladies held hostage with Jean, had conspired to see that I never got my favorite meal:

chicken fried steak with cream gravy, French fries and fried okra. Now they even had a new menu item named The Milt. It was half a chicken breast, roasted and smothered with picante sauce, served with roasted new potatoes (two of 'em – which hardly seems worth the effort of cooking 'em *or* eating 'em), fresh green beans and a side of fresh fruit of the day. Needless to say, I hardly went there anymore. Anyway, Jean was in agreement with me that we needed to do something about my sister's cooking. Killing her seemed a bit drastic, so I asked Jean if she knew of a drug that might put her in a coma until their house was rebuilt. She said no.

Jean compromised by telling Jewel that since I needed to be on a special diet she would need to take over the cooking. Jewel, of course, just asked her what she needed her to cook, and that she'd be as happy as a clam to do it.

Jean told her, and on day four that's where we stood. Jewel had recipes from Jean's heart healthy cookbook and fresh fruit and veggies from the supermarket. And I wasn't looking forward to going home.

So I was sitting there on that fourth day after all the shit had gone down with Emmett in my office, telling him about my theory regarding Drew Gleeson.

'Yeah, OK,' Emmett said, 'but why?'

I shrugged. 'Motive schmotive,' I said. 'We got means and opportunity. That's good enough for me.'

'To arrest him?' Emmett said, somewhat surprised.

'Well, maybe not arrest him,' I amended, 'but, you know, have a nice long chat with him.'

Emmett nodded. 'Works for me.'

So we called up the hospital and told 'em we needed to see Drew Gleeson at the sheriff's department for details on the tornado victims. He obviously bought it, because he showed up.

In the eight years that Jean and Paula went to school together, Jean had never met Paula's family or gone home with her for a weekend. Paula did accompany Jean to her home on occasion – three Thanksgivings, an Easter and two New Year's Eves – but the invitations were never reciprocated. Paula rarely talked about her family – Jean knew her parents were still married and that she had an older sister, but that was about all. Except for Paula's trips to Chicago with Jean she rarely left their dorm room as an undergraduate, at least, not for more than a sleepover with the boy *du jour* – and the same had applied to her own apartment in med school.

Again, Jean chided herself for ignoring another sign of something deeply wrong in Paula's life – the obvious estrangement from her family on top her sexual acting out, even though she was probably too young and naive to be able to draw the conclusions she was reaching now at the time. In Jean's adult and professional experience, this all suggested one thing – sexual abuse by a family member. Jean was accompanying Paula's body to Kansas City and, once there, she hoped she'd finally be able to help her friend. She wanted to find out whether she had been abused and, if she had, bring that person or persons to some sort of justice. The statute of limitations was long passed but she would do something, even if that only meant outing them to their family and friends.

Drew Gleeson was a nice enough looking fella, with cropped blond hair, amber-colored eyes and dimples when he smiled, which I'm sure we all know makes for a definite chick-magnet. He was tall and well-built, and looked a hell of a lot better in his uniform than I ever did in mine. He came strutting into the station and Holly called me right up. I told her to send him through to my office, which she did.

He walked in, I introduced him to Emmett and we all shook hands. Well, Emmett and I didn't, but I suppose you get the drift.

Drew took a seat in the extra visitors' chair that comes with being the sheriff and asked, 'What is it that I can do for you, Sheriff?'

'First, I want to thank you for coming down, Drew. I understand you did a hell of a job up there in Bishop, and since my boy and my sister were caught up in that mess, all I can say is a heartfelt thanks.'

'It's the job, Sheriff. You know that,' Drew said, aw-shucking it all over the place.

'That was some hairy storm,' Emmett said.

'Yes, sir, it sure was,' Drew said.

'What happened with that teenaged boy y'all took out of here earlier in the day?' I asked, eyebrows raised like I was interested.

'They pumped his stomach and he went home the next day. Grounded for life, as I understand it,' he said, and all three of us laughed like it was funny.

'Did you notice anything while you were back there? You know that the other prisoner, Darrell Blanton, died soon after?'

'Really? I knew he'd died, but I didn't know it was right after that!' He shook his head. 'Damn. But no, sir, I don't remember seeing anything out of the ordinary. That pizza boy was there but that was all.'

'Yeah, Darrell ordered a pizza,' I said. 'How about when you went back for your bag?' I asked, all innocent like.

'Went back?' Drew asked, puzzled. 'Oh, yeah, wait! I did go back for the bag. We were in such an all-fired rush to get that kid to the bus that I almost left it.' He grinned at me and Emmett.

'Notice anything out of the ordinary when you went back?' Emmett asked.

Drew shook his head. 'No. I just grabbed the bag and ran out.'

'Did you talk to Darrell?' I asked.

Drew shook his head again then narrowed his eyes. 'What's going on here?'

'How well did you know Darrell Blanton?' Emmett asked.

Drew stood up. 'I didn't know him from Jack-shit! And if you wanna talk to me about this crap again you'll need to talk to my lawyer!' he said and walked out of the room. What's that old line? I think he doth protest too much? I was thinking of it as Drew left the room.

That night, in the confines of our bedroom, Jean told me about Paula's mother's request that Jean accompany Paula's body to Kansas City.

'Would that be a problem for you?' she asked.

'Well, yeah,' I had to admit. 'I'd miss you. Johnny Mac would miss you. And I'd be stuck here all alone with my sister.'

Jean laughed. 'No, you'll just be stuck eating her food – and not alone. John and Harmon will be here as a buffer.'

'Johnny Mac's a kid and he'll eat anything. And Harmon, well, he's either got a cast-iron stomach or he's just plain used to it,' I said in a sulk. Then I brightened. 'I know! Take Jewel with you! She's got manners, she's bored, you could use the company—'

Jean shook her head. 'I have other plans, Milt.'

I frowned. 'What other plans?' I asked.

'I came to this conclusion pretty late – only yesterday – when I should have seen the signs years ago. But Paula was very promiscuous sexually, and estranged from her family. I think she might have been sexually abused as a child, possibly by a family member,' my wife the doctor said.

'I'm sorry to hear that, honey,' I said. 'But I'm not following here.'

'I'm going to find out who abused her, and I'm going to out them to one and all—' she started, her voice steely and determined, but I quickly interrupted.

'Oh, no you're not!' I said, sitting up in the bed and looking down on her. 'I almost just lost you and now you wanna go stirring up a mess of snakes—'

'I have to do this, Milt. I have to,' she said, not looking at me.

'Call the police—'

'Even if I knew who to tell them did it, the statute of limitations on child abuse is way past. They couldn't and wouldn't do a thing.'

I just kept shaking my head. 'I won't allow it!'

My wife finally looked at me. 'You what?' she demanded.

I had to rethink my words fast. 'I'd rather you didn't,' I said.

'I can't believe you said you wouldn't *allow* me! Who are you to *allow* me anything?' She sat up in bed and stared daggers at me.

'Dammit, I'm your husband, that's who. The one who's gonna be left alone to raise our child when you go gallivanting off on your high horse to piss off some baby-raper in Yankee-land!'

'Could you *be* more insulting?'

'Sure. Do we have time?'

My wife just looked at me, then burst out laughing and threw her pillow at me.

I pulled her close. 'Honey, I'm serious. I'm so sorry this happened to Paula, and I know how upset you are, but just let the body go up there on its own. You don't have to go with it. Paula's gone. You finding out who messed with her when she was a kid won't change anything—'

'What if that person is still abusing children?'

I just shook my head and held her tight. She was right. Once a child sexual abuser, always a child sexual abuser. And if that's what happened to Paula, then the chances were good it was still going on. 'OK,' I said, 'on one condition—'

She pulled away. 'I don't do conditions!'

'OK, one favor then. Take Jasmine with you. She's a deputy and she can have your back—'

'Oh, for crying out loud, Milt! I don't need back-up!' she said.

'You don't know that!' I insisted.

'Shit, can you imagine Jasmine tangling with Vivian Carmichael?' said my wife, who rarely swears. 'I'd rather take your sister.'

I thought about it for a split second. 'Deal,' I said.

ELEVEN

Jean made all the necessary arrangements to ship the body to Kansas City and on Friday, nearly a week after the incident in suite 214, she and Jewel boarded an American Airlines flight, accompanying Paula's body home.

Jewel, who was still somewhat shaken up from her experiences during the tornado, was more than happy to take a vacation. 'They have a great shopping center – Village West – in Kansas City!' she told Jean. 'Wonderful little boutiques, and God knows I need new everything!'

Jean didn't mention that there wouldn't be a lot of time for shopping. As a matter of fact, she thought having Jewel off at the stores would be a good way for Jean to get done what she was going there to do – namely to find out whether Paula had been victim to an abuser; if she had then Jean wanted to know whether they were still active and have them arrested if they were or out them if they weren't. Jean didn't tell Jewel what she planned on doing; she felt it was safer for Jewel if she had no idea of Jean's real mission.

They were a curious couple, these two women of a certain age. Jean was tall at five feet ten inches, a healthy one hundred and fifty pounds, dark hair – that which hadn't already turned gray – freckled skin and always accompanied by her crutches and the one brace on her left leg. And then there was Jewel: petite at five feet two inches, weighing in at one-twenty at the most, with blonde hair (helped along lately), blue eyes like her mama's and a cute little overbite that still made Harmon swoon.

A hearse from the funeral home came to pick up the remains from the airport, and one of their limos had been assigned by Mrs Carmichael to bring Jean and her guest to her home. Although Jean had already secured two rooms at a nearby hotel, Mrs Carmichael had taken the liberty of canceling them and insisting that the two women stay with the family. Knowing what she intended to do, Jean wasn't pleased with the arrangement, nor was she pleased with Mrs Carmichael's controlling nature. Even without the abuse, Jean felt Paula would have had a rough upbringing.

The limo driver took them to one of the older, statelier sections of the city, on the Kansas side, where the rich derived their wealth from granddaddies who made a killing off Kansas City beef – by the hoof. When the driver finally made a left into a driveway, both women were somewhat taken aback.

'I thought Harmon's house was big when I first saw it,' Jewel said, 'but this is amazing.'

'I had no idea,' Jean said. Paula had never said, implied or acted like she came from serious money, but the house before them was definitely what one would call a mansion, with large and beautifully cultivated grounds.

The driver took the limo through a break in the tall evergreens that faced the street and then wound through large trees and beautiful gardens until it reached the circle in front of the entry to the home. The house itself looked for all the world like an English country manor house. It appeared to spread over at least a couple of acres, the grounds – in front, anyway – adding another three to four acres.

The limo driver stopped the car and opened the doors for the two women. Jean and Jewel headed up the steps while the driver brought their bags. When Jean attempted to tip him, he said, 'No, thank you, ma'am – Mrs Carmichael has been more than generous.' He tipped his hat as the front door opened and headed down the steps to the waiting car.

The woman standing at the door was obviously not Mrs Carmichael. She was way too young, and Jean doubted that Mrs Carmichael would be caught dead in a polyester maid's uniform.

'Doctor McDonnell?' the young woman asked.

'Yes, and this is Mrs Monk,' Jean said.

The young woman smiled and bowed ever so slightly. 'This way please. I'll have someone bring your bags.'

They followed her into an enormous foyer with a mosaic tile floor in a bursting star pattern, at the center of which sat a large brass filigreed table, upon which was an old Asian-style vase filled with freshly cut flowers. Could it be Ming? Jean wondered. Then she wondered what Paula must have thought about Jean's parents' home with its Norman Rockwell framed prints, it's early American furniture and the plain brown carpet that had been in the house when they'd bought it shortly after Jean was born.

The foyer was lit by a large skylight in the domed ceiling. There were four doors, two on each side of the foyer. At the back was a carved mahogany staircase and there were two sets of stairs on either end of the foyer, meeting halfway up at a convex railing where Jean could easily see someone standing and belting out, 'Don't Cry for Me, Argentina.' A wide single staircase went up from there to the higher floor or floors. She wasn't sure, but from the outside it looked as if the place was at least three stories.

Two of the four doors in the foyer were open, the first on both sides. The one on the right appeared to be a living room, or lounge, salon, parlor – whatever someone in this tax bracket called such a room – and on the left she could see an enormous room with a dining table that could seat at least fifty comfortably. The young woman dressed in the maid's uniform passed both these rooms and stopped in front of the second door on the right. She opened it, stepped inside and announced them.

'Ma'am, Doctor McDonnell and her guest, Mrs Monk, are here.' With that she stepped out of the room, closing the door behind her.

The room was obviously a library, with a large fireplace burning brightly – although it was already fairly warm in the house. It was two stories with a catwalk around the second floor which could be reached by a spiral staircase. The entire second floor was filled with wall-to-wall bookcases. The fireplace wall was flanked on both sides by tall bookcases. Two other walls of the room were also covered with bookcases, while the outside wall consisted of two sets of French windows that looked out on a veranda separating the library and the room on the other side – whatever that might be. Jean couldn't help hoping it was the guest room, because as beautiful as the staircase was she wasn't looking forward to traversing it several times a day.

There were three occupants in the room. An older man, an older woman and a younger woman, at least Jean's age if not a little bit older. She was the one who stood up first.

'Doctor McDonnell,' she said, offering her hand. 'I'm Constance Carmichael Mills, Paula's sister.' She turned, her hand languidly posed toward the older woman. 'This is my mother, Vivian. I believe you met by phone.'

'Yes, of course,' Jean said, stepping closer to the sofa on which the older couple sat and extending her hand. The older woman, Mrs Carmichael, touched Jean's hand briefly then pulled hers away.

Jean knew Constance was older than Paula, but didn't know by how much. Whatever her age, Constance Carmichael Mills was trying desperately to hide it. Slightly overweight, her Laura Ashley-style dress clung a little too tightly, her blonde hair was a little too yellow and her makeup a smidge overdone. Even as bad as Paula had looked when Jean first saw her at the airport, it was still obvious that she had been the 'pretty' sister.

Their mother, on the other hand, was the epitomy of a well-heeled dowager. White hair touched her ears in a smart but mature fashion, her dress had a high neck, reducing the risk of seeing a waddle, and she wore expensive but flat shoes. Her makeup was understated.

'And I'd like all of you to meet my sister-in-law, Jewel Monk,' Jean said as Jewel simply nodded her head at the two women.

'And this is my father, Walter Carmichael,' Constance said, indicating the older man who sat hunched over, his eyes never leaving the leaping flames in the fireplace.

Jean extended her hand, but the old lady said, 'Don't bother. He wouldn't know what to do with it. Alzheimer's, you know.'

'Oh, I'm so sorry,' Jean said.

'Don't be,' Vivian Carmichael said. 'He's much more pleasant now than he's ever been. Wouldn't you agree, Constance?'

'Mother's kidding,' Constance said. 'Please, won't you both have a seat.'

Jean and Jewel sat down on the brocade love seat Constance had indicated.

'Penny will be bringing in some refreshments shortly,' Constance said, taking a seat in a matching brocade armchair.

'Has Nicholas taken their things upstairs?' Vivian asked her daughter.

'I'm sure he has, Mother,' Constance said.

Turning to Jean, Vivian said, 'Don't worry. That staircase is just for show. There's an elevator behind it that we use to get up and down. You look like you'd have as much trouble as me.'

For the first time Jean noticed that there was a wheelchair next to the sofa. 'That's good,' Jean said and smiled.

'I talked to the person you call a coroner in your little town,' Vivian said. 'He told me Paula was shot in the back, so I saw no reason to have a closed casket. We'll also have a viewing tonight. The funeral director has assured me his people will have her ready in plenty of time.'

Jean nodded, wondering if all of Paula's acting out could be laid at the feet of this cold mother of hers.

'Please don't think harsh thoughts of me,' Vivian said as if reading Jean's mind. 'I just see no reason to pussyfoot around. Paula is dead and it is my duty to see that she is properly sent on her way to the hereafter – whatever the hell that might be—'

'Mother,' Constance said, giving her a chastising look.

Vivian Carmichael laughed. 'Don't mind her!' she said, waving a dismissive hand toward her daughter. 'She used to be married to a preacher man and unfortunately some of that rubbed off on her, right, darling?'

'He was the bishop of the Anglican church of Kansas City, Mother, not a "preacher man," as you are so fond of calling him!' Constance said, with just a little heat.

'Where did he go?' Walter Carmichael broke in.

Vivian patted his hand. 'He died, Walter. Remember? And he left poor Constance with that brood of rug rats.'

'Who?' Walter said, then proceeded to pick his nose.

'Oh, for God's sake! Constance, call Ingrid!' Vivian said, shying away from her husband.

Constance stood up and pulled a bell by the fireplace. There were several there, each labeled. Jean craned her neck as inconspicuously as possible and thought she read 'nurse' in big, black, bold handwriting.

A woman appeared almost immediately, dressed in – *ta-da* – a nurse's scrubs.

'Get him out!' Vivian said, enraged. 'He's doing it again! Can't you get him to stop that? It's disgusting!'

'Yes, ma'am,' the nurse, Ingrid, said. 'Please, Mr Walter, you come with me, now. We go upstairs, OK? We watch a show, OK?'

After the nurse had walked Walter Carmichael out of the library, Vivian said, 'He may have been hard to live with before but this nose picking of his is purely disgusting! I may have to have him confined!'

'Mother!' Constance said, still standing by the fireplace.

'Well,' Vivian said, obviously beginning to back down. 'Maybe we could put a muzzle on his nose?'

Constance looked at her mother for a moment, then both women burst out laughing.

OK, so maybe motive *was* an issue. Why would a guy who'd just moved to Longbranch less than six months ago kill a guy who lived all the way out in Blantonville? Nobody went to Blantonville if they could help it. Maybe Drew Gleeson just tripped and fell in, or didn't know where he was going and stumbled in. And Darrell Blanton saw him and didn't like a stranger intruding in his little township, and beat him up. The killing was payback.

Yeah, I know. Probably not.

So why did Drew kill Darrell? Why do people kill? Love or money, the two biggies. Darrell had a double-wide with a mortgage, a ten-year-old pick-up truck and part ownership in his sister Marge's dead husband's car repair shop. I figured they'd done an OK business these last couple of years as a lot of high-end cars had gone missing in the county and the Blantonville Car Repair had had its lights burning way into the night. It's just a theory I hadn't yet been able to prove. But even if it was true, seven Blanton cousins owned the place so how much money would the newest partner be entitled to? I just wasn't sure how liquid Darrell's assets might be at a given moment.

That left love. OK, I thought. Darrell said Joynell had been messing around on him – that's why he killed her. Who was she messing with? Drew Gleeson? Could be, I thought. Why not? Drew was a good-looking dude, a hell of a lot more interesting in looks, personality and potential than Darrell Blanton. But how did Darrell find out Joynell was doing the dirty on him? Did he know it was with Drew? So why didn't he shoot Drew instead of his wife? Because he was a Blanton, and Blantons didn't hold much stock in their womenfolk. And, I figured, Darrell was apt to figure killing Joynell, a tiny woman who was already kowtowed by her husband, would be a hell of a lot easier than killing a big old guy like Drew.

Well, that settled it, I thought. Pretty damn obvious: Drew Gleeson and Joynell Blanton were having an affair; Darrell found out and shot his wife. When Drew found out Darrell shot Joynell he went back in the cells and used that digitalis stuff to kill Darrell.

I called Emmett into my office and explained all this to him in vivid detail. 'Hum,' he said.

'Hum hell!' I said back. 'That's what happened!'

'And you're going to prove this how?' Emmett asked.

I blustered for a minute, then said, 'We'll check that bag the EMT guys carry and see how much digitalis is gone. Then we'll canvas Blantonville and the hospital to see if anyone knew they were having an affair.'

'Why the hospital?' Emmett asked.

The man is getting stupid in his old age, I swear to God. 'Because,' I said, slowly and succinctly like I was talking to Johnny Mac when he was four years old, 'Drew works for the hospital. He and Joynell had to meet somewhere, right? Why not the hospital? She was visiting a relative, or maybe she was a patient in the ER. God knows I wouldn't put it past Darrell Blanton to have roughed up his wife.' I smiled. 'Hell, maybe he beat her up bad one time and the ambulance had to come out. I can just see it,' I said, my mind conjuring up the scene. 'Pretty little Joynell, all beat to hell, lying in a pool of blood. The big, good-looking EMT comes to her rescue.' I continued to smile. 'This is good!' I said.

'If you're writing a romance novel,' my second-in-command, soon to be unemployed deputy said.

The door to the library opened and Penny the maid came in, carrying a tray.

'Oh, goody!' Vivian said, clapping her hands. 'Scones!'

The tray was silver, the tea service on the tray was silver and the silverware was silver, while the teacups and saucers, the serving plate the scones resided on and the small plates for service appeared to Jean to be Wedgwood – as were the two matching little pots that held butter and jam. Penny the maid set the tray on the delicate rosewood table in front of the sofa and backed out of the room.

Constance poured and handed a cup of tea to her mother first, then to both guests, along with a monogrammed linen napkin, a plate on which she had placed a scone, a small spoonful of butter and another of jam. A silver butter knife rested serenely on the small plate.

Jean glanced at Jewel but her sister-in-law appeared to be enthralled with the entire ceremony.

'You know,' Vivian said, after a sip of tea, 'we normally, under such circumstances, would have the bishop of the Anglican church preside at the funeral, but he died in another woman's bed several years ago—'

'Mother,' Constance said for the umpteenth time, having obviously had this bit of family dirty laundry brought up before.

'Oh, Constance, darling, don't be so childish. Men stray. It's their nature. God only knows how many women your father bedded over the years. I lost count when I lost interest. I believe that was in the early seventies.'

'I hope the tea is to your liking,' Constance asked her two guests, swiftly changing the subject.

'Perfect,' Jewel said. 'Although I have to disagree with you, Mrs Carmichael—'

Jean, who was sitting to the left of Jewel, used her good right leg to kick her sister-in-law. Jewel stopped talking.

'About what, my dear?' Vivian asked, raising the Wedgwood teacup to her lips.

'Nothing,' Jewel said, then smiled brightly.

'I think she believes you might be wrong in your statement that all men stray,' Constance said. 'There are honest, loving men out there, Mother.'

Vivian made a derisive sound. 'And they're not worth the powder to blow them up,' she said. 'A real man is insatiable. A real man needs more than one woman to satisfy him.'

Jean noticed that Jewel's smile was looking a bit ragged. She put her hand on Jewel's and squeezed. Jewel squeezed back.

Jean stood up. 'Thank you so much for your hospitality and the wonderful scones—'

'Aren't they divine?' Vivian said.

'Definitely,' Jean said, trying on her best smile. 'But the flight was crowded and we really need to rest for a bit—'

'For God's sake, Constance, get these girls upstairs to their rooms! Call Penny!' Vivian said.

Constance got up and rang another bell, this time with 'maid' written in the same bold, black handwriting.

Penny arrived, was told to escort the women to their rooms and led them off.

I had Anthony Dobbins check the hospital records for any indication that Joynell Blanton had ever been a patient there. But he came back empty handed.

'They need a warrant, Milt,' he told me when he entered my office.

I sighed. 'So go get one,' I told him.

'Well, I tried that, Milt. I went to Judge Schnell with what we've got and he said it wasn't enough.'

I sighed again. This was gonna be harder than I'd thought. 'OK,' I finally said. 'Just go to the ER and ask around. See if anyone there knew Joynell or if they'd seen Drew Gleeson in the company of a woman of Joynell's description.'

Anthony pushed himself up from one of my visitors' chairs. 'Will do,' he said, and headed back out the side door to his squad car.

Although it wasn't a productive day as far as catching Darrell Blanton's killer, it worked out well in other ways. Like, Dalton got to a wreck on Highway Five faster than anybody else and was able to pull a guy out of a car that was on fire only seconds before the gas tank blew. Score one for the good guys. Jasmine, although off-duty, was going into the Stop 'N Shop just as two guys wearing ski masks and carrying a sack of cash came rushing out. She tripped one, kneed the other in the nuts and had her side arm out and the boys under arrest in less than two minutes. Score two for the good guys.

Then all hell broke loose – yet again. The rescue team of Longbranch volunteer firefighters was still working up in Bishop, trying to recover, if not people, then at least bodies. It appears they were excavating one site when four of the five fell into a hole a story deep. In Oklahoma we don't do basements much, which is why we have to build storm cellars out in the backyards. But this particular house *did* have a basement, and that's what they fell into. I had to call all my guys and gals in to rescue the rescue team, and by the time we got them all to the hospital with another team of EMTs – not Drew Gleeson and his partner this time, thank God – the ER was much too busy for Anthony to interview anybody about whether they'd seen Drew Gleeson with Joynell Blanton.

All of which put us back another day. I just wanted to wrap this business up. Get Drew Gleeson behind bars with the mama and brother of the man he killed and see what transpired. Personally, I didn't think he'd survive anywhere near Eunice Blanton.

Who, by the way, was being treated like a queen. Breakfast, lunch and dinner were being provided by one of many Blanton women who'd come in, shoot dagger stares at me then sit in the cell with Eunice while she'd eat and shoot the shit. Sometimes they brought knitting or crocheting with them, sometimes a deck of cards, dice or dominoes to keep the old lady busy. The only Blanton women who didn't show up were Eunice's daughter, Marge, and her granddaughter, Chandra. Eunice never mentioned their names.

I wasn't happy. None of my people seemed all that fired up to find Darrell Blanton's killer, and I think I knew why. They just didn't give a shit. Because of Darrell Blanton's own stupidity, my people and/or their loved ones were held hostage for many hours, and one of the party had been shot in the back. Who cared who killed Darrell Blanton? That was what I was thinking my people were thinking. And I sort of understood that. Hell, even I hadn't cared much at the time. My wife had been one of those hostages, and her friend had been murdered by Earl Blanton. It had been a horrible ordeal for everyone involved, and it was all Darrell Blanton's fault. If he hadn't killed his wife I wouldn't have had to arrest him, and if I hadn't arrested him, his mama wouldn't have thought it wise to invade Holly's bachelorette party and hold everybody hostage. And if she hadn't done that, all of our women-folk wouldn't be experiencing nightmares and trauma, and Paula would still be alive and at my house, insulting me and my redneck ways.

But the law was the law and as sheriff of Prophesy County, Oklahoma, it was my duty to find, arrest and deliver to trial the person who took Darrell Blanton's life, for whatever reason. Now, if a jury of his peers decided that Drew Gleeson did the only responsible thing, then so be it. I'd live with it. But until that time

I was responsible for finding enough evidence to at least arrest the sucker.

It's my job, like it or not.

The elevator they took up to the third floor of the mansion was as smooth a ride as any Jean had experienced in high-rise buildings. But the walk was a bit strenuous. The center building of the large home had wings coming off it and each of those wings had a wing. Penny the maid led them to the left, down a long hall, turned right, down a longer hall, then another left.

'The forest room,' Penny announced as she opened the door of the first room on the right and indicated to Jean that she should enter.

It was aptly named. There was a mural on the east wall of a beautiful green forest with sunlight pouring through an opening in the treetops. The bed, a gigantic king, was a four-poster with posts carved to look like tree trunks that reached to the ceiling, where leaves and birds had been painted at all four points. The duvet was a brilliant green silk. The five-drawer-tall chest was painted with forest scenes that included pixies and fairies, and the lamps on either side of the bed were made of branches and covered in shades that resembled birch bark. There was a chaise lounge in the same brilliant green silk as the duvet, and a small claw-foot table with two delicate rosewood chairs. This arrangement was set by the French doors that opened to a small balcony that overlooked the estate's backyard – if one should call such an expanse merely a yard.

The whole thing was so over the top that Jean had to put her hand over her mouth to stop herself from laughing out loud. Penny the maid indicated to Jewel to follow her out of Jean's room, but Jewel turned for one last look at her sister-in-law and rolled her eyes, which made Jean cough to cover the laugh that escaped her lips.

When the door closed behind them, Jean noted her bags were on a stand near one of the two doors in the room. She opened it to find a closet as big as her office back at the house, empty except for a fluffy white terry robe – just like one you'd find at certain high-class hotels but without the price tag. She moved to the second door to find an opulent bathroom with a large glass brick enclosed shower, the largest claw-foot tub she'd ever seen and a double sink with bowls above the counter. The forest theme had been carried through to the bathroom. The sink bowls were a coppery green resting on a brown marble counter top. The floor was a mosaic tile depicting both flora and fauna – the fauna being mostly birds. The outside of the claw-foot tub was painted with another mural of forest life, and the walls were covered in a moss-like substance. As large as the room was, Jean felt instantly claustrophobic. Stepping back into the bedroom, she opened her suitcase with the intention of unpacking but her cell phone rang. Picking it up, she saw it was Jewel.

'The bedroom was bad,' she said, 'but you've got to see the bathroom.'

'After you see my room,' Jewel said. 'It looks like a decorator threw up in here.'

Jean giggled. 'Open your door and stand outside so I can find you,' she said. She hung up her phone and stepped out into the hall. She saw Jewel standing about three doors down on the opposite side of the hall, and headed in that direction.

'I'd say shut your eyes then I'd drag you in, but I'm afraid seeing all of it at once might give you a heart attack,' Jewel said, 'so just go in. Penny called it the rose room.'

Jean stepped over the threshold into Jewel's quarters. The walls were covered in Pepto-Bismol-colored silk, with a pink-on-pink embossed design of small roses. The four-poster bed was painted white and draped with white velvet swatches with rosebuds adorning them. The duvet was a matching white velvet with rosebuds, and the bed-skirt matched the Pepto-Bismol pink of the walls. The bedside lamps were tall and had skinny green 'stems' with shades made to look like a bouquet of white roses. There were vases upon vases of roses sitting atop anything that didn't move. The floor was white-painted hardwood with a large rug adorned with – guess what? – roses. The furniture was basically the same as that in Jean's room: a five-drawer tall chest painted with leaves and roses, a chaise lounge covered in the same white velvet/rosebud design as the duvet and bed drapes, and a small claw-foot table painted white with two white-painted Louis-the-whatever chairs. The vase of roses on top of the table was the only receptacle with real roses in the room, and there were so many in the large pink vessel that dwarfed the small table that the scent was nearly overpowering. French windows led out to a balcony overlooking the front of the estate.

'I'm afraid you might asphyxiate from the smell of those roses,' Jean said, backing away from the small table.

'I'd rather have the forest room. You wanna trade?' Jewel asked.

'No, thank you. I'm beginning to see the merits of my little slice of forest,' Jean said. 'How about the bathroom?'

'I haven't found it yet. Should be one of these two doors,' she said.

The bedroom was a mirror image of Jean's, so Jean pointed to the door that matched the location of her own bathroom entry. 'There,' she said.

Jewel opened the door. Unlike Jean's bathroom, this one did not carry on the rose theme – as much. It was just blazingly white. Everything – the tiles covering the floor and the walls, the marble counter top, the two white basins, the claw-foot tub, the shower surround, towels, shower mat, everything – was white, including the white vase filled with white roses, their green leaves the only hint of color in the room.

'Now you've got to trade with me,' Jewel said. 'As pale as I am, I'll get lost in here!'

Jean laughed. 'Take your cell phone with you and call if you need help.'

Jewel turned quickly to her sister-in-law, a big smile on her face. 'You think the rest of these rooms are themed? Maybe we should look!'

Jean grinned back. 'We've got time,' she said.

TWELVE

That night I got my first call from my wife up in Kansas City. 'So how's it going?' I asked, after we exchanged all the 'I love yous' and 'I miss yous' the moment required.

'Well, little did I know, but Paula came from serious money. This place is a mansion,' she said.

'You still at her mama's house?' I asked.

'Hum . . .' She started, then stopped. 'Here's the thing, honey,' my wife said in that tone of voice she uses to placate me. I'm not fond of that tone of voice. 'Mrs Carmichael – Vivian – canceled our hotel reservations and insisted that Jewel and I stay here.'

I felt my heart skip a beat. My wife planned on outing a pedophile while probably staying in the same house as him. Not good. Not good at all. 'Thank her kindly,' I said, somewhat stiffly, 'and go back to your hotel.'

'She canceled the rooms, Milt. And there's a big festival in town through the weekend – there's not another hotel room to be had,' she said.

'Then come home. Now.'

Jean sighed on the other end of the phone. 'I'll tread carefully, honey, I promise. But I can't leave right now. The viewing is tonight, with a catered buffet afterward, then the funeral is tomorrow. I'm obligated, Milt.'

'Bullshit!' I said. 'You're not obligated to get yourself killed! And my sister, too—'

'You're the one who insisted I bring her—'

'I wanted you to bring Jasmine – with a loaded gun! Now you've got a barely five-foot-tall housewife as back-up!'

'Milton, don't make me hang up on you!' Jean said. Not very productive for a debonaire psychiatrist, I thought.

I sighed, trying to calm down. 'Honey,' I finally said, 'just don't out this person if you find him. Not there anyway, not now. Come home, then call someone back there and tell them. It can all come out while you're safely here with me.'

'I'll think about it,' she said.

And that was just about the gist of the conversation. We were at a stand-off, with her probably deciding not to keep me abreast of her situation, and me wanting to run up to KC and drag her ass back home.

Jean and Jewel rode in the family's chauffeur-driven limousine to the funeral home with Vivian and Constance. Mr Carmichael remained in his rooms as he could not comprehend the fact that one of his daughters was gone, nor did Vivian require or even want his nose-picking presence. As she said, 'God only knows what he'd pick in front of a roomful of Kansas City's elite. Probably his ass.' Which, of course, made Constance respond with her usual, 'Mother!'

Jean was afraid that Paula's abuser would be the most likely suspect – her father. If that was the case, there would be nothing Jean could do, even if she could find evidence of it. The man was beyond caring and it would be more than cruel to out an Alzheimer's patient. But she was determined to check out possible suspects at tonight's viewing – other family members, long-time family friends, business partners . . . anyone who would have had access to Paula as a child.

As the first ones to the funeral home – a beautiful turn-of-the-twentieth-century Victorian – the Carmichael women and their guests were allowed access to the viewing chamber for a private few minutes with the deceased. Vivian, being pushed in her wheel-chair by the chauffeur, had him park her at the back of the room, far away from her daughter's current resting place. Jewel sat in a chair near the old woman as Constance and Jean went up to the casket.

'Doesn't she look natural?' Constance said, quietly touching the back of her hand to her sister's cheek.

No, she didn't look natural. Jean had never seen a body at a funeral that did. She looked like a wax dummy, ready for Madame Tussaud's. The clothes were obviously ones her mother had sent to the funeral home as they weren't the ones Jean had given the coroner in Longbranch to dress her in. She'd found a business suit Paula had obviously brought for her interview in Houston in her suitcase. It still had tags on it and Jean had removed those before sending the clothing on. But now Paula was dressed in a fussy pink Laura

Ashley-type dress, complete with buckled white shoes, which made her seem even more dummy-like. Jean thought righteously that Paula wouldn't be caught dead in such an outfit – then had to amend her thought. She'd been caught. Paula's short gray hair had been replaced with a longer blonde wig, and the make-up that adorned her face was out of character for the bare-faced woman who had died in suite 214.

Jean hadn't noticed much of a resemblance between the two sisters until now. Like the body in the casket, Constance's hair was a little too blonde, her face a little too made up, and her dress, although the proper black, was a little too feminine and frilly. Jean had to wonder at Constance's ability to consider that she and her sister *both* looked 'natural.'

Jean simply nodded her head at Constance, unable to verbally agree. She moved to the chair next to Jewel, who took her hand in hers and squeezed it. Jean smiled at her sister-in-law, thankful to have their little adventure with the rest of the third-floor wing to think about, rather than the caricature of Paula now lying in a casket in front of them.

And it had been fun, their little adventure. Starting with the room next to Jean's, they'd opened each door and peered inside, giggling like schoolgirls and coming up with an 'appropriate' name for each room. For a room sporting fake palm trees and Adirondack chairs, they assigned the name 'Beach Blanket Bingo.' For the room that was several different shades of blue with celestial bodies covering the ceiling and walls, they decided on 'Blue Monday.' 'Cabin Fever' was their vote for a room decorated in early American chic, and 'Pasta Primavera' for the room decked out like a Tuscany villa. Some of the rooms were empty, sporting only stepladders and paint cans. These they dubbed 'Visions of a Horrible Future.'

They'd clambered to their rooms when they heard the elevator stopping on the third floor. Penny had been sent up to check on them, she'd said, and had brought bottled water and bags of nuts – like you'd get on a plane. Jean had begun to feel like she was in an over-the-top hotel with a really, really bad decorator.

The four women were alone for about ten minutes before the doors were opened by the funeral director and people began to parade in. Their voices were hushed, which was appropriate, their attire subdued, which was appropriate, and the curiosity and expectancy on their faces, Jean admitted to herself, might be appropriate at the viewing of a murder victim. Only Jewel and Constance stood to welcome the arrivals, but all four were greeted, hands shaken, an occasional hug for Vivian and more for Constance. Jean studied their faces.

A man was introduced as Walter Carmichael's business partner for over forty years – Mitchell Sewell and his wife, Lana, a big woman who towered over her husband. The man was much shorter than Jean and had a weak handshake. He had the look of a man who might feel a need to overcompensate for his size. Could that overcompensation include the abuse of someone even smaller and more vulnerable than himself?

Then there was Uncle Max, Walter Carmichael's younger brother, with a woman at least thirty years his junior. Although well into his sixties, Uncle Max was strikingly handsome and obviously enjoyed the company of younger women. Could that have included a very young niece? His handshake was firm, and Jean couldn't help noticing how he lingered over Jewel's hand, giving every indication he was about to kiss it, before the woman with him yanked him onward.

'That's his fourth wife – Serene,' Constance whispered to Jewel and Jean. 'Looks like he's eyeing Jewel as a replacement.'

'Humph,' Jewel said, as more people came down the line.

Two young women were next and Constance left her station to hug them both. Turning to Jean and Jewel, she said, 'These are my daughters, Megan and Dru—'

'Stepdaughters,' the one named Dru said as she shook Jean's hand.

'Nice to meet you,' Jean said.

'Aunt Paula talked about you,' Dru said. 'She said you were the only friend she ever had. She said she was really looking forward to seeing you on her trip to Houston. Too bad you got her killed.'

'Dru!' Constance said, taking her stepdaughter by the arm. 'I believe you need to sit down.'

'Come on, Dru,' the other stepdaughter, Megan, joined in. 'Just hush.'

'Yeah,' Dru said, 'don't let Drusilla talk – God only knows what truths might escape!'

The man behind the two stepdaughters was shaking his head and laughing. 'I know they aren't actually blood relations, Constance, but that Dru reminds me so much of Paula!' He leaned down to hug Vivian and then in turn hug Constance.

'Yes,' Constance replied, smiling stiffly at the man, 'sometimes there is quite a resemblance.' Turning to her house guests, she said, 'Jewel, Jean, this is our next-door neighbor since forever, Neil Davenport.'

Jean shook his hand. A firm handshake from a large, beefy man. Probably an athlete in his younger days, age had caught up with him, sagging his jowls, dropping his gut over his belt and thinning his hair. Jean's thoughts went something like this: right next door. Easy access. Probably good-looking when Paula was a child. Possible abuser?

'This is my wife, Emily,' he said, indicating a small woman Jean had not noticed until Davenport had pointed her out. And still, she was almost invisible. Pasty skin topped by fading blonde hair, eyes the color of fog, and decked out entirely in beige. Straight away, Jean's instinct told her that she was surely the type of woman who'd be easy to cheat on, because even if she knew she'd do nothing about it. Not even if it was a child.

Jean knew she was making snap judgments about these people, but that was all she had time for. She needed to sum these people up quickly and try to see who could be a possible candidate for the abuse Paula had suffered as a child. Because it was no longer just a theory, as far as Jean was concerned. It was fact. The more she thought about it, the more she studied Paula's family situation then added to that what Jean already knew about Paula's promiscuity, she was sure that her diagnosis of child sexual abuse was on the nose. Now all she had to do was figure out which one of these assholes had hurt her friend.

Saturday I awoke to a downpour, although it wasn't attached to another tornado, thank God. And speaking of tornadoes, the reason I woke up in the first place was because the dog, Tornado – or Nado – was standing with his front feet on either side of my head, one of his hind feet next to my hip and the other on my balls. He was also licking my face like it was smeared with kibble.

'Get!' I said, shoving at him as I doubled over in pain. 'Get off, you brute!'

'Hey, Dad,' Johnny Mac said from the doorway from Jean's and my bedroom to the kitchen. He had a spoonful of peanut butter that he was licking like a lollypop. I had to assume that Johnny Mac had opened my door, allowing the giant dog inside. Otherwise, I'd have to believe that the beast had learned to open the door, with no (visible) imposable thumbs. And that just put the fear of God into me.

'Get. This. Dog. Off. Me,' I said succinctly.

'Hey, Nado,' Johnny Mac said, 'come on.'

The dog jumped off my bed and followed Johnny Mac into the kitchen. I got up gingerly and went into the kitchen, finding a dish towel and some ice before going back into the bedroom to tend to my balls. Come on, that dog's gotta way a hundred pounds easy!

After the pain had subsided I went into the bathroom, took a shower, shaved, brushed my teeth and did all those things one does upon rising, even on a Saturday. My job being what it was, just because it was Saturday didn't mean I wouldn't wind up at the shop taking care of business. I went back out to the kitchen to find Johnny Mac alone in the breakfast nook. I looked out of the sliding glass door that led to the backyard and saw Tornado dancing in the rain like he was on LSD or some other hallucinogen. I'm telling you, that was one strange dog.

'Started the coffee for you, Dad,' Johnny Mac said.

I looked at my son and grinned. 'You're trying hard to make up for that stunt you pulled last Saturday, huh, boy?' I smiled and nodded my head. 'You keep this up,' I said as I grabbed a cup and poured myself some coffee, 'and you should be out of the doghouse by the time you're ready for college!'

I ruffled his hair as I sat down at the table. My brother-in-law, Harmon, wandered into the room. He obviously didn't do the same things I did upon rising on a Saturday. He was wearing a white T-shirt, plaid boxer shorts and a robe I happened to know belonged to my wife since it was a gift from me last Christmas. It was blue silk with a dragon on the back. His hair was suffering from extreme bed-head, his beard had what looked more like two weeks' growth rather than just overnight, he was barefoot and, as he passed the breakfast nook on his way to the coffeepot, I could smell him – it wasn't pleasant. I figured I'd have to get Jean's silk robe to the dry cleaners before she got back – and then lock it away somewhere where Harmon couldn't find it.

I'd been up half the night, alternately worrying about my wife and trying to figure out a way to catch Drew Gleeson. I'd gone to sleep with several ideas in my head. Gotta get somebody back to the hospital to see if anyone saw Drew and Joynell together, for one. But mainly, I needed to talk to Jasper Thorne, Drew's EMT partner, and the teenager we had in the cells when we brought in Darrell Blanton. I know he'd been mostly out of it, but he might possibly remember something. Maybe he saw something go down between Darrell and Drew when the EMTs first got there. Maybe Darrell said something Darrell-like, such as, 'Hey, you can't hump my wife no more, I done kilt her.' That would be good. We'd gotten all the boy's vital stats from the hospital – things we didn't already know, like his name, address, phone number, etc. All we'd known before that – when he was dumped in the cell – was that his name was Larry and he was seventeen. So I was planning on heading to the shop, before I got called in on some emergency, to try to find out where Larry lived and head my ass on over there. Anthony was on half-day duty this Saturday so I thought I'd send him back to the ER to check if anyone had seen Drew and Joynell together, and also to see if he could set up an interview with Jasper Thorne. Figuring I'd done a quality job of thinking that morning, I rewarded myself with a second cup of coffee.

The viewing was long and tedious. Over one hundred people came through the line, spent a moment staring at Paula's remains then filed out into the next room where refreshments were being served. Constance had hired a caterer for the event, and the room was filled with tables holding platters of boiled shrimp, Kansas City beef on a stick, mushrooms stuffed with crab, vegetable and fruit crudités, and chafing dishes with hot hors d'oeuvre. When the line had finally stopped and the last people had left the viewing, Jean, Jewel and the Carmichael women – Constance pushing her mother's wheelchair – went into the crowded reception room. Constance parked her mother near a small seating arrangement and Jean sat down next to her.

'Mother, what do you want to eat? There's seafood, steak, all sorts of wonderful things,' Constance said.

Vivian Carmichael sighed. 'Just some fruit, I think. Thank you, dear.'

'Jean, how about you?' Jewel asked. 'What can I bring you?'

'Whatever you're having, and thanks,' Jean said.

As they left, Vivian turned to Jean. 'I know you must think I'm a terrible mother,' she said. 'I can't imagine the things Paula must have told you.'

Jean patted Vivian on the hand. 'Honestly, Mrs Carmichael, Paula never said anything derogatory about you,' she said, omitting the fact that Paula never said *anything at all* about her family.

Vivian stiffened. 'I hardly think that could be true,' she said, removing her hand from Jean's touch.

'It is. In all the years I knew her, we pretty much stayed in the here and now. What was happening on campus, how our classes were going – that sort of thing.'

'She was so smart,' Vivian said. 'Smart as a whip, the saying goes. I'm not sure how smart a whip is, but my Paula could have been anything she wanted to be. I wasn't surprised at all when she chose medical school.' Her face had perked up a bit when she said this, but then a very sad look spread across it. 'But she could never keep a job. She had to have three internships before she was certified.' She shook her head. 'I just never understood that. She was a very pretty girl, don't you think?' She didn't wait for Jean's answer, but continued, 'She looked a lot like I did when I was younger. Constance, now she was never that pretty. I think she may have resented Paula a little bit because she got so much more attention.'

'Sibling rivalry is quite common,' Jean said.

Vivian snorted a laugh. 'I keep forgetting you're a psychiatrist. I was happy Paula went into *real* medicine – cardiac surgery! Now there's a field! She could have made millions. But—' She stopped talking and shook her head again. 'I don't know if you know this, but Paula had been at home again these past few years. She hadn't been able to find a job. And she was a board-certified cardiac surgeon!' The headshake again. 'She was so hopeful about the interview with the hospital in Houston. If she hadn't stopped to see you . . .' Again, her voice trailed off.

'I'm so sorry, Mrs Carmichael,' Jean said.

'Vivian,' the older woman said brightly, making Jean wonder about her mental health. 'You promised you'd call me Vivian!'

I got to the shop, leaving Johnny Mac in the care of a finally cleaned-up Harmon, and found the information for Larry the teenage lush. His name was Larry Pottz and he lived just outside of Longbranch in a subdivision that never really happened. Some enterprising yahoo built three model homes on spec back in the early1960s but nobody bought them, so the county took them over and sold them at auction for pennies on the dollar. Larry Pottz's grandmother had grabbed one, raised her daughter in it, and still lived there with her daughter and her daughter's son, Larry. The house was a gray brick single-story ranch, with fresh white trim and a freshly painted red front door. The lawn was well-tended and still mostly green, although some of the trees in the yard were turning colors. There was a Honda Civic in the driveway, next to a classic Volvo. I knew who the Volvo belonged to: Lois Dunlap, a very nice lady from my church who taught Johnny Mac's Sunday school class. Too bad I never knew that Larry the lush was her grandson. I woulda called her right away.

I rang the bell and waited on the small front porch. By the look of the place I would guess it to be a three bedroom, possibly two bathroom house. There was a two-car garage, but noting the cars sitting in the driveway, I assumed the garage – like so many others – was filled to the brim with junk.

Lois Dunlap, the grandmother, opened the door. When she saw me, her face fell. 'Milton,' she said. 'Are you here to arrest my grandson?'

'No, ma'am, not at all. He didn't get caught breaking any law. He was definitely under the influence, but he wasn't driving and he wasn't particularly disorderly. He just couldn't walk too well.'

'I'm very embarrassed about this, Milt,' she said, opening the door wider and inviting me in.

'You shouldn't be, Miz Dunlap. I was a kid once and I gotta say I did a lot more damage than he did the other night. I do need to talk to him, however, if he's around,' I said.

'Just let me go get him,' she said, and left the room.

She left me standing in a small foyer. To my right was a wall, beyond which was, I'm sure, the garage. To my left was a living room with a dining area attached. The room was furnished just the way I would think Miz Dunlap's home would be furnished – if I ever were to think on something like that. The furniture was traditional, in muted shades of blue, while the walls were white with a few reproductions hanging on the walls. Not many doo-dads. Miz Dunlap just wasn't the doo-dad type.

Miz Dunlap came back into the foyer. 'Would you mind sitting in the kitchen?' she asked. 'We do all our best work there.'

'Of course,' I said, and followed her to the other side of the living-room wall. The kitchen had obviously been renovated since its original early 1960s design. It was huge with an obvious add-on to make it so. Part of the add-on was a glass wall, the top of which curved over about three feet to join the roof so that the sun streamed in, brightening the whole room. A picnic-style table sat under the sun roof, and the rest of the room was filled with appliances, counters, two sink locations, a wall of ovens and an island stove top with a rack holding shiny copper-bottomed pots and pans. If I could figure out how to do it, I'd have our own kitchen redone just like it.

There were already two people sitting at the picnic table – Larry the lush and his mother. They both stood when I entered.

'Milt, this is my daughter, Charlotte Pottz—' The daughter leaned over the table and we shook hands. 'And I believe you've already met my grandson, Larry – although he may not remember you.'

The boy blushed. 'Grams,' he said in that way children everywhere say your name and make it sound like an indictment. He held out his hand, not having to lean like his mama. His arms were long, which befitted a boy his height. As I'd never seen him actually standing, I was surprised at how tall he was. Well over six feet, but not weighing, I'd bet, much more than Johnny Mac. He was a skinny kid with a huge Adam's apple and bony arms that ended with gigantic hands. I'd bet good money he wore at least a size thirteen shoe, but I couldn't see his feet. I shook his hand and Miz Dunlap and I sat down opposite the boy and his mother.

I had a feeling I wasn't about to speak to this kid without one or both of these women present. And that was OK. I thought I'd get the truth out of him, as it wasn't going to get him in any trouble.

'Hope you're feeling better, Larry,' was my opening gambit.

'Yes, sir,' he said. 'Thanks for asking.'

'I'm not sure if you're aware of this, but right after you were taken off to the hospital the man in the cell next to yours was murdered,' I said.

Larry's eyes got big, his mother gasped and Miz Dunlap said, 'Oh my God!'

'I know you were pretty much out of it that evening, but I wonder if you remember anything at all about your time in the cell,' I said.

Larry shook his head. 'No, sir. Not much. I know I got sick and threw up 'cause of the smell.'

'What smell?' I asked him.

He shook his head again. 'I dunno. Like food. Pizza, maybe?'

I nodded. 'A pizza was delivered to the other man in the cells.'

'I couldn't help puking and I'm real sorry about that, Sheriff.'

'It happens. You remember anything else?'

'Well, when I puked somebody said something funny, like "how appetizing" and both guys laughed.'

'By both guys, you mean the man in the cell and the pizza delivery guy?' I asked.

He nodded. 'Yeah – I mean, yes, sir. I guess that's who they were.'

'Did you see anything?' I asked.

'I looked up at the guys – there were two of 'em – and then one of 'em opened the pizza box and I think I sorta passed out.'

'Do you remember the EMTs coming in?' I asked.

Larry shook his head. 'No, sir. I don't remember anything else until I woke up in the hospital.'

I sighed inwardly and stood up. 'Thanks, Larry. You were a big help,' I lied.

Miz Dunlap rose too, as did her daughter and grandson. 'Won't you have a cup of coffee before you leave, Sheriff?' Miz Dunlap asked.

I patted my stomach. 'Thanks, but I've already had my quota for today.'

I shook hands all around and left through the front door, thinking that had been a big old waste of time.

THIRTEEN

The ride back to the Carmichael mansion was quiet, none of the women speaking more than to say what was necessary to be polite. The family had left the funeral home and gone to a nearby restaurant that had a private room. Since everyone had eaten at the catered buffet served at the funeral home, most just ordered drinks or coffee and dessert. Besides the four women, all the key players had been there – Uncle Max and his fourth wife, partner Mitchell and his wife, and neighbor Neil and his wife, but Jean found out little from their small talk.

It was after eleven before the chauffeur pulled up to the front doors. As had been explained to Jean and Jewel earlier when they left for the viewing, Mrs Carmichael refused to have a ramp built on the front of the house ('Ruins the lines, you know'), and instead came in and out via a ramp built at the back. Constance got out with Jean and Jewel and Constance's two stepdaughters, Megan and Dru, who were going to spend a couple of days with their stepmother, while the chauffeur, with Vivian in the back, continued on to the back of the mansion. Luckily the two girls were staying on the second floor – the family floor – leaving Jean and Jewel alone on the third. They went into the forest room to discuss the events.

'There were certainly a lot of people,' Jewel said, sitting on the chaise lounge while Jean stretched out on the bed to rest her left leg, which was beginning to hurt. 'Paula had a lot of friends.'

Jean shook her head. 'None of those people were Paula's friends,' she said. 'They were all Vivian's and-slash-or Constance's friends.' She was silent for a moment, then said, 'What did you think about Uncle Max?'

Jewel shuttered. 'Creepy. I couldn't believe he almost kissed my hand. If he had I'd have had to dunk it in bleach.'

Jean laughed, then quickly sobered. 'Jewel, I have to tell you something,' she said.

'Sure,' Jewel said.

Jean sighed. 'I haven't been exactly truthful with you.'

'About what?'

'Our reason for being here.'

'You're not here to bury your friend?' Jewel asked.

'Of course, that's the main reason.' Jean stopped for a moment then corrected herself. 'Well, maybe not the main reason, but the perceived main reason.'

'You're losing me,' Jewel said.

'I didn't figure this out until after Paula died. I'm not sure why – I was just in denial, I suppose. And back when Paula and I were good friends, in our younger days, I wasn't able to pick up on or understand the signs properly. But I've come to the conclusion – one I'm now positive of – that Paula was sexually abused as a child.'

'What?' Jewel exclaimed. 'Oh my God! Are you serious?'

'Yes, of course I'm serious. There are several reasons I came to this conclusion, none of which I need to burden you with. I just think you should know that, while I'm here to pay my respects to my friend, I'm also here to find out who abused her and out him.'

Jewel was quiet for a moment, then said, 'Oh, shit.'

Jean looked up at her. 'What?'

'That creepy Uncle Max! I bet he did it!'

'At this point it would only be speculation,' Jean said.

Jewel grimaced. 'Jeez, you and Milt and your gotta-have-proof bullshit! That guy obviously did it!'

'The most obvious suspect would be her father—' Jean started, but Jewel interrupted.

'He has Alzheimer's!'

'Now, but he didn't always. Remember what Vivian said? How he's so much easier to get along with now? Vivian is very controlling so I have to wonder what Walter was like before the onset of his illness. And she indicated that he had plenty of sexual relationships outside the marriage.' Jean shrugged. 'In my opinion, that makes him a suspect. Besides, he was in closer proximity to her than anyone else.'

'Yeah, but he's not creepy and that Uncle Max is. Then again, so's that neighbor. What was his name?'

'Neil Davenport. And yes, he's creepy. Did you notice how his wife seemed to disappear into the woodwork?' Jean said.

'Oh, right. I forgot he had a wife.'

'Exactly. And then there's Walter's old business partner.'

'That weasel-faced little guy with the Amazonian wife?' Jewel asked.

'Yep.'

'But he hardly seems the type—'

'Bullied by a wife bigger, stronger and more assertive than he, and finding a child more pliable—'

Jewel shuddered. 'Oh, stop! I can't stand it! If anyone had done that to any of my children, I'd, I'd—'

'Be really upset?' Jean supplied.

'I'd rip their bellies out with a garden hoe!'

'Wow, you country folk really know your way around revenge!' Jean said.

Jewel threw a cushion off the chaise lounge at her sister-in-law. 'I'll have you know I spent fifteen years in the big city of Houston – where revenge is a sport played on the freeways because somebody's not going fast enough!'

Jean laughed. 'True.' Sobering, she said, 'I'm sorry I brought this up—'

'God, no! Don't be sorry. I'm glad you shared it with me. Now I can be on guard, too.' Jewel got up and walked to the bed, where she leaned down and hugged Jean. 'I'm so sorry this happened to Paula – her past and her present. The poor thing – no wonder she was rude. I would be too just from having a mother like hers, not to mention the other stuff.' She straightened and said, 'I'm heading to bed. You get some rest.' As Jean started to rise, Jewel motioned her back down. 'Don't get up! I'll let myself out. You want me to lock your door?'

'Sure,' Jean said. 'That might be a good idea. And you might want to do the same.'

'Ha!' Jewel said. 'I'm not only going to lock it, I'm going to put a chair under it like you see in the movies!'

I went back to the shop only to find it all locked up. I opened it, went in and checked to make sure the phone system had been forwarded to our on-call deputy, which today was Jasmine Bodine Hopkins. I know she hates it when I put the 'Bodine' in there, as that was the name of her ex-husband who was a philandering shit and who also happened to be a total idiot. I guess I could substitute her maiden name, Flowers, but I always thought that was so damn cute it made me want to puke. Jasmine has three sisters: Iris, Rose, and Daisy. Mr and Mrs Flowers either had a weird sense of humor or were just plain cruel.

I called Jasmine on her house phone and Emmett picked up.

'Hey,' I said when I heard his voice. 'Jasmine getting any calls?'

'Got a cat up a tree. She told the old lady to call the fire department.'

'Ah, they're mostly still in the hospital,' I said.

'Yeah, should take her a while to figure that out. By then, the damn cat will have crawled down, if he hasn't already,' Emmett said.

'Anything else?' I asked.

'Not a peep. You working?'

'Went by and interviewed Larry Pottz, our drunk teenager in the cell next to Darrell's.'

'And?'

'Not so much. He smelled the pizza, puked, heard Darrell and the pizza guy laughing about him puking, saw one of 'em open the box, saw the pizza and passed out. He thinks.'

'You're right. Not so much. Any more keen ideas?' Emmett asked.

'I need to check with Anthony. He was supposed to go by the ER this morning and see if anyone saw Drew and Joynell together, and set up a time to have a talk with Drew's partner, Jasper. Other than that I'm gonna stick my hand up my ass and wait for you to come up with something.'

'Hope you're constipated, 'cause I don't have diddly squat.'

'Like I didn't already know that.' I said bye and hung up. Then I locked the shop back up and headed home. I thought it might be fun to get my son and go do something. *What* I didn't know. He was grounded, sure, but from his friends, his iPad, his Xbox and his Wii, not from adventures with his dad. As I stepped outside it hit me. The sun was bright and warm, there was a cool breeze, and as I was the sheriff I figured it didn't really matter that my license was twenty years out of date. I was gonna take my boy fishing.

* * *

Saturday at the mansion started with a modest breakfast in the family dining room, four newspapers for those who wanted to read – *The New York Times, The Kansas City Star, The Washington Post* and *The Wall Street Journal.* Jean and Jewel were alone in the room. Food was in chafing dishes on the large buffet and consisted of two types of scrambled eggs, bacon, sausage, biscuits, croissants and bowls of fruit. Before either of them had time to choose, the cook came out of the kitchen and asked, 'Is there anything in particular you would like? A poached egg? Fried egg? Waffles? Hot cakes? I can do anything you want.'

'No,' Jean answered. 'Thank you, but this is just fine.'

Jewel nodded her head in agreement. 'Looks wonderful,' she said.

'I want eggs Benedict, Martha,' said a voice entering the room. Jean turned to see one of the stepdaughters, Dru, going up to the table. 'And some of that chi tea I brought with me. With half and half. Is that fruit fresh?'

'Of course, Miss Dru,' the cook said.

'How fresh?' Dru asked. 'I mean, did you buy it at the store yesterday or what?'

'It was brought in this morning from the farmer's market,' Martha the cook said.

'Humph,' Dru said, then sighed. 'I guess that will have to do. Bring me the tea now.'

'Of course, Miss Dru,' Martha said, and backed out of the room.

Jean had the overwhelming urge to stick a bar of soap in the girl's mouth. That had been her own mother's choice of punishment for everything from foul language to skipping school to being rude. Instead she just said, 'Good morning.'

The girl looked up like she'd just noticed the presence of the other women. 'Oh. Right. Morning. Whatever.'

'Did you sleep well?' Jewel asked in what Jean had come to know as Jewel's sweetly insincere voice. She used it on officious, rude and other sweetly insincere people.

'What?' Dru said, taking her eyes off the empty space she'd been staring into. 'I guess. Whatever.'

Jewel laughed as she took her loaded plate back to the table. 'You are so charming, Dru! Did you go to a special school to learn that?'

Dru stared at Jewel for a full minute, her face showing utter confusion. Finally she gave up trying to figure out what Jewel had said, uttered, 'Whatever,' and got up to go to the buffet for the almost adequately fresh fruit.

At that point the other stepdaughter, Megan, came into the room. The girls were negatives of each other. Megan was blonde and blue-eyed with a honey-colored complexion. Dru had very dark brown hair, brown eyes and a pale, freckled complexion. Other than that, they looked exactly the same. Square-jawed faces with pert noses and high cheekbones, both perfect size twos and almost exactly the same height. The only difference in the height, Jean figured, could very easily be the difference in shoes. Where Dru was wearing a Vanderbilt T-shirt, cut-offs and flip-flops, her sister was dressed more appropriate to her surroundings in gray trousers, a white long-sleeved blouse and flats with just a bit more heel than Dru's flip-flops.

'What are you having?' Megan asked her sister as she entered the room.

Dru brought her fruit bowl back to the table. 'I told Martha to fix me eggs Benedict,' she said. 'And she's taking her own sweet time about it.'

'Good morning, Doctor McDonnell, Mrs Monk,' Megan said as she walked to the buffet. 'How are these eggs with the red stuff?'

'A little spicy,' Jewel said, 'but quite good.'

'Oh, goody, I love spicy,' Megan said and spooned a huge amount onto a plate, along with several rashers of bacon, some sausage links, a heaping scoopful of hash browns, then covered it all with cream gravy. She popped a grape into her mouth but that was it for the fruit. She sat down next to her sister.

'Oh my God, how can you eat that crap?' Dru demanded.

'You just don't know what's good!' Megan said, sticking a napkin in the front of her blouse to keep it clean.

'I do know this – when I turn thirty I'll still look great, while you're going to be a freakish blob!' Dru countered.

'Uh uh,' Megan said, her mouth full.

'Uh huh!' Dru said, taking a bite of fruit.

The cook came in with a tray which she handed to Dru. 'Your eggs Benedict and your chi tea, Miss Dru.'

'About time,' Dru said, never looking at the cook, who glanced at Jean and Jewel, rolled her eyes and walked out.

Megan laughed. 'I saw that!'

'Saw what?' Dru demanded as she cut up her food.

'Never mind. It's not for you to know.'

'What's not?'

'What I'm not telling you!'

'What aren't you telling me?' Dru demanded, having abandoned her attempt to cut her food in order to glare at her sister properly.

'Oh my God! Where do I start? What am I not telling you?' Megan shook her head and went for another forkful of scrambled eggs and gravy. 'Let's see, I failed, I'm sure, to mention that your half of our rent is due – or did I already tell you that? Oh, and you haven't paid your share of the phone bill.'

'Fuck off,' Dru said and dove into her food.

Jean's good right leg was going numb from the kicks she'd been receiving under the table from Jewel, and she was quite in awe of Megan's ability to thwart her sister's questioning and turn it around on her. When the two girls finally stopped their bickering, Jean asked, 'Do you know what time we'll be leaving for the funeral?'

Neither girl answered for a minute, then Megan looked up. 'Oh, are you talking to us?' Jean nodded and Megan nudged her sister, causing Dru to stick her forkful of eggs Benedict in her cheek rather than her mouth.

'Watch it, for Christ's sake!' she said, elbowing Megan in the ribs.

Deflecting the blow, Megan said, 'Doctor McDonnell wants to know what time we're leaving for the funeral.'

'Good for her,' Dru said.

'Do. You. Know!' Megan bellowed.

'No, I don't fucking know! Jeez! Leave me alone so I can eat in peace!' Dru said.

'So the two of you live together?' Jean asked.

'Umm,' Megan said, her mouth full of food. Swallowing, she said, 'Yes, we do. We have an apartment off campus at KU.'

'Oh!' Jewel said. 'I thought Dru went to Vanderbilt, what with the T-shirt and all.'

'Ha!' Megan said. 'She couldn't get into Vanderbilt even if Daddy hadn't lost all his money. No, we both go to KU in Lawrence. Constance helps us with a small monthly stipend, but we both work so we don't have to get student loans. I work at the campus bookstore and Dru works—'

'Dru works,' Dru said. 'That's all that matters.'

'At a bar off campus. She waits tables. Unfortunately, with her personality, the tips aren't that great,' Megan continued.

'Shut the fuck up,' Dru said, bending further over her plate. Jean could see some color come to Dru's face. So the girl could get embarrassed, Jean thought. Nice to know.

'Which one of you is older?' Jewel asked.

'Me,' Dru said.

'By two minutes,' Megan said. 'We're fraternal twins.'

'Oh!' Jewel said. 'I didn't realize that. What year are you at KU? My son's at OU in his last year.'

'Bully for him,' Dru said under her breath.

'We just started our junior year,' Megan said.

'And you're majoring in . . .' Jean left the sentence open-ended.

'I'm in electrical engineering,' Megan said. 'Dru is studying . . . Hum. Dru?' she said, turning to her sister. 'What is it you're studying this semester?'

'Fuck off,' Dru said, sinking even further into her plate.

Megan laughed. 'Dru has changed her major every semester so far. I think possibly basket-weaving is her future.'

Jean was beginning to re-evaluate her first impression of the sisters. Although Dru definitely had an attitude problem, Megan was certainly showing signs of advanced mean-girl syndrome. Jean smiled to herself, thinking about the possibility of getting such a diagnosis past the board and onto the DSM – the Diagnostic and Statistical Manual for mental disorders.

Dru reached out her free hand and began to paw through the newspapers on the table. 'Why the hell isn't there a *People* mag around here?' she muttered. 'This is all crap.'

'Dru's the intellectual one of the two of us,' Megan said, then laughed out loud.

Yes, that diagnosis certainly needed to be in the DSM, Jean thought.

Constance came through the door to the family dining room. 'Good morning, ladies,' she said, smiling at one and all. 'Lovely morning for a funeral. The sun is bright and the temperature is supposed to rise to at least the high seventies. A nice day to be outside, even if it is a cemetery,' she said as she graced the buffet with her presence. She was wearing a floor-length dressing gown of raw silk – pale pink with pink fur-topped mules. Her hair and makeup had already been artfully arranged.

'What time will we be leaving for the service?' Jean asked.

'The service will be at the funeral home at one p.m., then we'll go from there to the cemetery where the Carmichael family plot is located. It's fairly old and no longer in the best part of town, but Mother insists on the tradition,' Constance said as she sat down with her plate. 'So we'll probably need to leave here a little after noon.'

Martha, the cook, stuck her head out. 'Would you care for anything from the kitchen, Mrs Mills? Or you, Miss Megan?'

Both women shook their heads. 'I'm fine, thank you, Martha,' Constance said as the cook retracted her head and shut the door. Looking at Jean and Jewel, she said, 'Mother insists on the ancient rituals, like having the servants come to the funeral, as if they thought of my sister as the little lady of the house. Most of the people now employed here weren't with us when Paula and I were growing up and they only know her from the past three years, since she's been back.' She took a bite of scrambled eggs, chewed, swallowed and leaned closer to Jean and Jewel. 'And these past three years have been a total disaster. Drunken binges, bringing strange men home at all hours of the night! Hung-over mornings when she'd lambast the servants for God only knows what reason!' Constance shook her head. 'I see no reason why these people should be dragged to the funeral.'

'Maybe so they can have some time off from waiting on you hand and foot?' Dru said.

Constance laughed. 'Dru, darling, you are such a cut-up. Isn't she, Megan?'

'A cut-up?' Megan repeated, appearing to savor the word for a moment. 'I'm not sure, Constance. Of the three phrases that come quickly to mind with the word "cut," cut-up, cut-above, or cut-out, the one I find most germane would have to be the latter.'

Constance laughed again, although it seemed strained. 'You two!' she said.

Jean balanced herself with one hand on the table as she stood up and found her crutches. 'It's been lovely, but I need to head back upstairs. I've a million things to do before the service,' she said.

Jewel instantly followed suit. 'So nice having this time with all of you,' she said in her sweetly insincere voice. Then she followed Jean out of the room and away from Constance and her not-so-loving stepdaughters.

Harmon had to go to his car parts store outside Bishop, the one that had been hit by the tornado, so he took off right after I got back to the house. Johnny Mac was sitting in front of the TV in the living room, watching a PG-13 movie. I let it slide since he was eleven, even knowing his mother would have objected. Let's face it, Mom wasn't here and us guys needed to bond over *something*! I sat down with him and watched it through to the end. I don't know the name of it but there were soldiers, robots and a lot of things getting blown up – even a few body parts. When it was over I took the remote and shut off the TV.

'Thought maybe you and me could go do something today,' I said.

'Like what?' he asked, not looking at me.

'I don't know. Fishing?'

He shrugged. 'I don't know how,' he said.

'I can teach you,' I said.

Again, the shrug. 'Whatever.'

'OK,' I said, 'fishing doesn't appeal to you. What would *you* like to do today? Other than play video games or be with your friends?'

I swear, if he shrugged one more time I was gonna make him lose a shoulder. He did – I didn't. 'I dunno.'

I sighed. 'Well, you think about it. And I'll go fix lunch—'

'Can we go eat lunch somewhere?'

I stopped in my tracks. It was a start. 'Sure, I guess,' I said evenly. 'Where were you thinking?'

'Definitely not the Longbranch Inn,' he said.

'Definitely not,' I agreed.

Johnny Mac grinned real big. 'You got gas in the Jeep?' he asked.

'Full tank.'

'How 'bout we go to that Mexican restaurant you like in Tulsa?'

'That's a drive for lunch, all right,' I said.

'Well, you know, while we're there, maybe we could go see that Lego display that's going on.'

I nodded. 'Sounds like a plan. Go get dressed.'

And he was off.

Jean's usual wardrobe did not lend itself to upper-class funerals, so she'd gone to Tulsa before she'd left Oklahoma to find something appropriate for her trip to Kansas City. Jewel, of course, had accompanied her. Although Jewel's wardrobe could lend itself to almost any occasion – including a White House ball – her wardrobe was no longer available, being sucked up in the tornado and hopefully let loose on appropriately clothing-deprived women in some third-world country, or maybe Dallas. They could use some ingenuity in their wardrobes there, Jewel thought, that was for sure.

So Jean had picked out a navy-blue suit for the viewing and a black three-quarter-length sleeve wrap dress for the funeral. She wore her grandmother's pearls and her black orthopedic shoes with both. Jewel had gone with a gray silk dress for the viewing and a black raw silk suit for the funeral. As the party met in the foyer for the trip to the funeral home, Jean and Jewel both looked appropriately lovely.

They were the first ones there and Jean found a bench in the foyer on which to sit while they waited for Constance and her stepdaughters to arrive. Ten minutes later they heard the slight pitter-pat of Constance's kitten heels on the grand staircase, followed by the clomping of Dru's hiking boots. Constance, of course, was lovely in a black and white Chanel suit a half-size too small, with black patent kitten heels with red soles that could only signify one designer. Immediately behind her was Megan in a short black lace minidress with long sleeves and lacy cuffs that practically covered her hands. She looked like a refugee from a 1960s English rocker movie. Although Megan's attire might have seemed a touch inappropriate, she was Lady Di in comparison to her sister. The hiking boots were just the beginning of her

thumbing-her-nose-at-the-world attire. She was wearing khaki
cargo pants and a concert T-shirt from a band Jean had never heard
of called 'The Dead Kennedys,' which was not just inappropriate,
in Jean's estimation, but downright disgusting – under these or
any other circumstances.

Seeing Jean look at Dru, Constance said, 'Don't worry about
her. She's staying in the car.'

'Why don't I just stay home? That's what I want to do!' Dru said.

'Because I'm not going to reward you for being a bitch!'
Constance spat at her stepdaughter. 'If you don't have the decency
to dress respectfully for my sister's funeral then you can sit in the
car and twiddle your thumbs, but you *are going with us!*'

'God, you suck!' Dru said, then rushed past everyone and out
the front door.

When Jean got to the front of the house she half expected Dru
to be long gone, but the girl was leaning against one of the balus-
trades, arms crossed over her chest, her lower lip sticking out like
the spoiled brat she was. The car came around the corner of the
house, Vivian seated in the back.

She took one look at Dru and said, 'I will not have this!'

Constance crawled into the car, taking the seat next to her
mother. 'She's staying in the car.'

Vivian gave Dru a strongly disapproving look. 'You hate us,
don't you, girl? That's why you're doing this. But what did your
aunt Paula ever do to you to make you disrespect her so?'

Dru snorted. 'I'm only here in the first place because that old
bat,' she said, indicating Constance, 'threatened to cut off my
allowance and not pay for my tuition if I didn't come. She didn't
say anything about *dressing appropriately*,' she said, attempting
to mimic her stepmother's voice but failing miserably.

'I can see my mistake,' Constance said in a deadly cold voice.
'Next time I'll have a list of rules for you to follow.'

'Oh?' Dru said. 'Do you have another sister who's going to get
shot in a hostage situation while drunk on her ass?'

'No, dear,' Vivian said, her voice as icy cold as her daughter's.
'I believe she might have been referring to me.'

'Mother!' Constance said.

Dru snorted and looked away, while Jean and Jewel kept their
eyes peeled out the windows as Kansas City flew by.

They stopped at a red light near a trendy-looking shopping center and Jean spied a dress shop with junior clothing on a window display. 'Please ask the driver to turn into that driveway,' she asked Constance.

'Why on earth—'

'Just do it, please,' Jean said, not smiling.

Constance snorted but clicked on the intercom and asked the driver to turn in.

As the light turned green, he took the turn and Jean said, 'Have him stop right here. Jewel and I will get out.'

They left the car and headed into the dress shop, returning in little more than fifteen minutes. As Jean crawled back into the car, she threw the bag at Dru.

'Dress, shoes and appropriate underwear. Change your clothes now!'

FOURTEEN

OK, La Margarita in Tulsa is the best Mexican food restaurant I've ever been to. It's greasy and dark, and instead of tortilla chips they serve saltine crackers with the salsa, but the enchiladas are so good the grease runs down your arm and you're like I don't care 'cause this is so damn good.

I gotta say my boy did the place proud – he rolled up his sleeves, ate three tacos, beans and rice, and was ready for *sopapillas* at the end. We filled them with honey, which dripped and drooled all over the both of us. We ended up in the bathroom practically taking baths to get ourselves clean enough to be seen in public.

Then we went to the Lego thingy. It was terrific. I thought Johnny Mac was gonna pee his pants he was so excited. He rushed me through the entire place then went back to the start and we had to go slowly, checking out every display, figuring out how each was built, marveling at the giant things and the teeny-tiniest of things. As we were leaving I laid down about fifty bucks for crap he didn't need. But I figured putting those Lego toys together would keep him off all of his electronic crap.

By the time we got home, he'd built a Lego Starship and lost half the pieces for the Lego dragon he just had to have. So we cleaned out the car, finding most of them and headed inside. I needed a Tums, but the meal had been worth it.

I was on my third Tums when the house phone rang. It was Jasmine. 'Milt?'

'Yeah, Jasmine?'

'We got a possible attempted suicide at the hospital,' she said.

'Excuse me?'

'Yeah, I know. Hell of a place to do it, but that EMT? The one from Tulsa? Drew something—'

'Gleeson,' I said, perking up in spite of the circumstances.

'Yeah, well, the nurses caught him downing a whole punch of OxyContin he was stealing from their drug supply cabinet. So I guess we need to do something? He was stealing, and that's a crime. And isn't suicide still a crime?'

'I think so. Where is he now?'

'He's having his stomach pumped. Should be good to go in a couple of hours.'

'Call me when you're on your way to the shop with him,' I told her. 'I'll meet you there.'

'Over and out,' she said. Jasmine liked to do that kinda shit. I think it came from watching too much TV as a child.

Harmon still hadn't returned by the time Jasmine called to say she and the prisoner (I liked the sound of that!) were on their way, so I packed up Johnny Mac and what was left of his Lego booty and we headed to the sheriff's department.

I realized I needn't have bothered bringing the Lego booty along as Petal, Jasmine's daughter who's just a year behind Johnny Mac, was already sitting in the bullpen doing something creative at one of the desks. Johnny Mac ran over to her as Jasmine said, 'Well, I was gonna apologize for bringing my daughter to work, but now I guess I don't have to.' She smiled. That's the thing about Jasmine. The first six or eight years I'd known her – all the time she was married to that no-good Lester Bodine – I never saw her smile. It first appeared shortly after the divorce – not a big smile, just a quirking of the lips. When she and Emmett got together, it turned into a grin, and when her daughter was born – well, now that smile was just something to behold.

'Emmett tired of babysitting?' I said, displaying my own grin.

Hers disappeared. I think I'd said something inappropriate. 'It's not "babysitting" when it's your own child, Sheriff,' she said.

'I was just kidding,' I tried, but she was back to business.

'Another call came in just after I got the one about Gleeson. A wreck out in the far north of the county – dead bodies all over the place. We decided it would be best if he took that by himself and I took Petal with me to the hospital call.'

'Well, that makes sense,' I said, still trying to make up for my inappropriate statement. Come on, I'm old and I'm male. We're not good at political correctness, or whatever the hell that was. 'So where's Gleeson?' I asked.

'Lying down in the cells.'

I went down the hall to the cell block and went in. I almost lost my shit when I saw that Drew Gleeson was in the same cell as the man I was pretty damn sure he'd murdered. Poetic justice, I thought, but then the chances were fifty-fifty that he'd end up in that cell. It was just pure dumb luck that both cells were empty. Eunice Blanton and her son, Earl, who had been our guests for several days, had been moved to the regional facilities near Tulsa to await hearings. It wouldn't have been pretty if we'd had to put Drew Gleeson in with either one of the Blantons – more'n likely Earl, them both being men and all. But still, although I do believe Eunice might have inflicted more damage on her son's suspected killer than her older son, I still think Earl coulda done some too.

'So, hey, Drew,' I said as I walked in.

He was lying on the bunk, his left arm over his eyes, his right at his side. He had his shoes off. He removed his arm from his eyes, raised his head and looked at me. Then he lowered his head, put the arm back over his eyes and said, 'Hey, Sheriff.'

'How you feeling?' I asked, leaning against the bars.

'Like dog shit. Ever had your stomach pumped?'

'Nope. Never had the pleasure.'

'It's no pleasure,' he said.

'I'm thinking you and me need to have a sit-down, Drew. Work some things out.'

'What things?' he asked, still not looking at me or anything else but the inside of his arm.

'I'm gonna have Jasmine come in here and take you to the facilities so you can wash your face, maybe rinse out your mouth. Hey, how about a Coke? Would you like a Coke? Or a Dr Pepper? Could even get you a Sprite if you're so inclined.'

'Coke sounds good. As long as it's really cold,' he said, taking his arm down and beginning to sit up.

'Coke it is!' I said and grinned. I reached through the bars and patted him on the back. 'We're gonna work this all out. Don't you worry.'

I went back outside and waved my deputy away from the kids.

Once we were in our little lobby area, I gave Jasmine her instructions and went back to my office to review the notes I'd written down on why I thought Drew Gleeson was a killer. It didn't take more than two minutes for me to remember all my theories, suppositions and bullshit. When I came back out I saw that the kids were loaded down with soft drinks, chips and chocolate, and that Jasmine was in the break room with the door partially closed. There was a TV mounted in the corner next to the two-way mirror that looked into the interrogation room where Drew was sitting at the table with a Coca-Cola in front of him – the same view that was on the TV screen. His hands were clasped on the table in front of him, uncuffed, like I'd instructed Jasmine.

'So, hey, Drew,' I said again as I came in, shutting the door behind me. I took a seat opposite him. 'Sorry, but I gotta ask – what made you do such a crazy thing?'

He shrugged and looked away.

'You got some big problems, huh? Financial?'

He shook his head.

'You into drugs, gambling, any of those things?'

Again, he shook his head.

'Then it must be your love life. Always room for that to go bad, don't ya think?'

No response. Not a shake of the head or shrug of the shoulders. But then, after almost a full minute, Drew Gleeson broke into great big, less-than-manly sobs, complete with tears and snot everywhere.

I stood up and walked around to him, leaned down and put my arm across his shoulders. 'I'm real sorry, Drew,' I said. I squeezed his shoulders then went back to my seat. 'It must have been real awful finding out about Joynell the way you did, huh?'

His head popped up and he looked me in the eye. 'I don't know what you're talking about,' he said.

It was time for me to shake my head. 'Aw, come on, Drew. Why pretend? I know you were bonking Darrell's wife. Everybody knows that – including, I'm sure, Darrell himself. Did he say something to you when you were in the cell alone with him? Something that provoked you? Darrell was a real asshole and God knows he didn't know when to keep his mouth shut. And you, just finding out he killed Joynell, the love of your life, you just couldn't take his nastiness, isn't that right, Drew? What did he say? Did he talk about Joynell being a great lay? Or maybe he said she was a lousy lay? That's the kind of crap that would come out of Darrell's mouth. And who could blame you, Drew? The guy was asking for it.'

I stopped talking. Let the silence build. Finally, as the tears again began to slide down Drew's face, he hiccuped and said, 'She *was* the love of my life. And she loved me, too. We were going to run away together.' He tried to catch a sob but it came out anyway. 'And that son-of-a-bitch killed her!' He sighed, paused for a second and looked up at me. 'I didn't kill him but I wish I had. I'd like to shake the hand of whoever did.'

'It's real easy to say you didn't kill him, but you were alone with him when you went back in for your medical bag. Easy enough to slip him something lethal.'

It only took a minute, maybe a minute and a half, for Drew Gleeson to say, 'I want a lawyer.'

The service was being held in the largest room of the funeral home, which still wasn't big enough. The usual suspects – the people from the viewing – were there, plus about a hundred others. It was standing room only.

Dru had grudgingly changed clothes in the back of the limo. Jean had guessed right that the girl wasn't wearing a bra, and had bought one for her. This had led to Dru exposing herself to all as she pulled off her Dead Kennedys T-shirt. She didn't seem to care. But she was in the family box now with the rest of them, dressed in a sedate navy-blue skirt and matching blouse and navy-blue flats. Unfortunately, the family box included Uncle Max and his wife, Serene.

The service was given by a clergyman who obviously had never even heard of Paula until that day, much less known her. Each time he spoke her name it was preceded by a quick glance at his notes as he was obviously unable to remember it. There were eulogies – too many to keep count. Uncle Max was the first and talked about Paula as a young girl. This piqued Jean's interest, especially when he made statements about 'what a beautiful child she was,' along with her being 'so obliging and helpful.'

After the last statement, Jewel leaned closer to Jean and whispered in her ear, 'Did he just confess?'

Jean squeezed her hand and tuned back in.

'I remember once when I took Paula and Constance camping with my own kids, how she loved the outdoors and kept asking me what the name of this tree or that tree was. She was so smart, so inquisitive, so ready to take on the world.' Then Uncle Max choked up and his wife Serene went up to the podium and brought him back to the family box.

There were many more eulogies, but Jean only fixated on the ones given by those closest to Paula – like the long-time neighbor Neil Davenport.

'My wife and I were not blessed with children of our own, so we opened our home to the two Carmichael girls. They loved to come over and eat the cookies that Emily baked for them, and sometimes helped her make more. They'd follow me out to my workshop where I played around with woodworking. Paula always wanted to use the circular saw, but I'd never let her. She was too small for that.' He gulped in some air to steady himself, and went on: 'When they were teenagers, the girls would come swimming in our pool, sometimes spending the entire day at our house. They were like our own children. But I have to disagree with what Max said. Paula wasn't smart – she was brilliant. She had a mind like a steel trap. I don't think anyone was surprised when she became a cardiac surgeon. It had been a joy, these last three years, having her back home.' He stopped and looked over at the family box. 'Vivian, I can hardly express how sorry I am that this has happened to your family. I will love and miss sweet Paula for all of my life.'

Then he went back to his seat, and Jean had an overwhelming urge to take a bath.

Jasmine took Drew Gleeson back to his cell after his phone call to his lawyer. He knew the number right off the bat, which made me wonder why. Did Drew have the need of a lawyer often enough to have memorized the phone number? When he hung up, Drew turned to me. 'He's driving in now from Tulsa. He has advised me not to cooperate with you in any way, which is just fine with me.' He turned to Jasmine. 'Will you take me to my cell, please, Deputy?'

Both kids were watching all this as Drew had had to use the phone on Holly's desk. After he'd been taken back to the cells by Jasmine, Johnny Mac asked, 'What'd he do, Dad?'

He does that now. Calls me 'dad' instead of 'daddy'. I don't know what to do about it. I'd prefer he kept calling me 'daddy'. Hell, my own has been dead now for close to thirty years and I still refer to him as 'daddy.' What's so wrong with that? Doesn't make *me* any less manly. Just means I respected my father and still do.

'Don't worry about it, kiddos,' I said. 'How about I take the two of you over to the Longbranch Inn for some ice cream?'

'Ah, Dad,' Johnny Mac said as I looked up and saw the dubious expressions on both their faces. 'Maybe the Dairy Queen? We don't really wanna go to the Longbranch Inn any time soon.'

'Oh, right. I forgot,' I said. I hoped for the sake of Loretta and the other employees of the Longbranch Inn that everybody involved with the hostage situation there would get past it all and go back for at least lunch, if not a roll in the hay in the upstairs rooms.

When Jasmine returned I told her I was taking the kids for ice cream at the Dairy Queen and asked her if she wanted us to bring her something.

'A Blizzard. An Oreo cookie Blizzard.' She grabbed her purse but I stopped her.

'It's on me,' I said. 'Least I can do to make up for that dumb remark earlier.'

She gave me the good smile. 'Yeah, the least you could do.'

I grinned back. 'What's the best?' I asked.

She thought for a moment then said, 'A raise.'

'Ha!' I said and ushered the kids out the back door to my Jeep.

The sun was shining as the family took seats under the awning at the cemetery. Constance's comment about the cemetery no longer being in 'a good part of town,' seemed to mean that the area, which housed students and low-income families of varying ethnicities, was *not* good – i.e., bad. Driving slowly through the area in the funeral procession, Jean noted an active, lively community.

The cemetery was large enough, and the Carmichael plot far enough in it that sounds of that lively community went unheard. Nothing extraordinary happened at the graveside; nothing out of the way, nothing dramatic. They just buried Paula six feet down, and each person present planted a shovel full of dirt on her casket. Each person – except Jean. She kept her seat, even though Vivian had been rolled up in her wheelchair to do her honors. Jean stayed back.

They were beginning to get to her – this self-indulgent family with their need to hurt one another as cruelly as possible; this family that didn't shed a tear for the lost Paula; this family who thought the whole thing was an ordeal they must go through for the sake of appearances.

Paula deserved something better than this. No wonder she'd rarely, if ever, spoken about this family, hadn't had any pictures of them on her side of the dorm room, and had only gone home to them when life had kicked her to the gutter and she had nowhere else to go. Was this it? Was this the reason her friend had shunned her family and been so promiscuous? Had there been no sexual abuse, just hatefulness and neglect? Jean was beginning to wonder about her diagnosis. Had she wanted a quantifiable excuse for Paula's behavior? Something she could point at and say, 'That's it! It wasn't her fault! Someone abused her!' Hatefulness and neglect are also considered abuse, but not in a family this rich, who could make sure there was someone other than parents to look after the children's basic needs.

Jean wished she'd stayed in better contact with Paula. She would have known when she'd hit rock bottom and offered her solace in her own home, away from the Carmichael clan and their many issues.

The crowd had begun to file out of the shade of the awning when Jean felt a hand on her shoulder. She looked up to see Jewel standing there. 'You OK?' she asked gently.

Jean shook her head. 'Not really.'

Jewel handed Jean her crutches and helped her stand and navigate the lumpy lawn of the cemetery. Before they got to the limo, Jean turned to Jewel. 'Do you think we can call a taxi?' she asked. 'I really don't want to get back in that car.'

'No problem,' Jewel said, guiding Jean to a bench as she took out her cell phone. She found the number for a taxi service and called.

We'd had a lively time at the Dairy Queen – me and my two young'uns. They told jokes to each other then started gossiping about people at school. Petal hadn't gone to school with Johnny Mac until this year. She'd been going to a private Christian school that got itself in trouble last year, so Emmett was bound and determined that his daughter went to a public school where he figured she'd belonged in the first place. Jasmine was the one with the grand idea of private school. But even Jasmine had to admit that Petal was happier now in public school, and I could tell, just by listening to Petal and Johnny Mac gossiping, that that was the case.

We walked in the back door of the shop just as Drew Gleeson's attorney was walking in the front. Jasmine gave me the eye and I deposited the kids in my office with a go ahead to play on my computer (as I rarely used it, I doubted they could do it any harm), and headed into the foyer.

The guy was Drew's age, tall and slender, wearing blue jeans and a western-style shirt, his feet clad in Tony Lama snakeskin. We shook hands and he said, 'Harry Joyner. I'm Drew Gleeson's brother-in-law – and his attorney of record.'

Well, I thought, that explained Drew knowing the phone number right off the bat and all.

'Sheriff Milt Kovak,' I said. I turned to Jasmine and said, 'Deputy, please get the prisoner and put him in the interview room. And make sure the equipment is off in the observation room.'

'Certainly, Sheriff,' Jasmine said, trying to repress a smile at my new-naming of the break room and the interrogation room. But I figured one sounded classier and the other a whole lot less offensive.

As Jasmine walked off to the cells, Harry Joyner said, 'What are the charges against my client?'

I walked him over to a bench in the foyer and we both sat down. 'Well, now, we're gonna start with him stealing that Oxy to try to kill himself. If he'd succeeded we probably wouldn't be pressing charges, but as he didn't, well . . .' I shrugged my shoulders.

'This is ludicrous, Sheriff. My client was obviously in an irrational state of mind or he wouldn't have attempted suicide in the first place, and taking the Oxy was only a means to that end. He'll repay the hospital for that and go to treatment, but I'll make sure he retains his job and his status as chief EMT,' the lawyer said.

'Well, that's all well and good,' I said, 'but there might be another matter.'

'What other matter?' Joyner demanded.

'Ah, here's my deputy now. You get Mr Gleeson all settled in the interview room?' I asked Jasmine as I stood up. I've noticed that standing up is easier now I've lost thirty-five pounds. But I still miss chicken fried steak. Just saying.

'Snug as a bug,' she said. Turning to the lawyer, she said, 'If you'll follow me, Mr Joyner, I'll take you to your client.'

He looked at me, I guess half-expecting me to continue with that 'other matter.' I didn't, so he followed Jasmine into the interrogation room. I really wanted to be a fly on the wall in that room, but that's not allowed. Attorney/client privilege and all that bullshit. I know, I know, I sound like a right-wing small town sheriff, huh? Well, I *am* a small town sheriff. And I figured I could probably wind this whole thing up if I could just hear what Gleeson was telling his brother-in-law.

But that was a no-no, so I pushed that thought out of my head and went back to the office to see if I still had a computer. Personally I'd have been as happy as a clam if the kids broke the damn thing, because the county commissioners had us on a real tight budget and replacing it wouldn't be an option – which meant I could turn all the damn paperwork that I had to fill out in the hunt and peck system over to Emmett. He actually *liked* computer stuff.

Emmett came in the back door right about then and we conferred in my office with our kids. The upshot of that was that Johnny Mac was going home with Petal and Emmett until I was finished here. Worked for me.

Once Emmett and the kids were gone, I sat down at my desk and put on my thinking cap. I really needed to interview Drew Gleeson's partner, Jasper Thorne. I still needed to check with Anthony to see if he'd made a date with Jasper and if he'd interviewed the ER employees about Drew and Joynell. And maybe I should interview that pizza delivery guy. Not about the girlfriend so much as about what might have gone on back in the cells when he was there. Maybe he didn't realize he saw something, but my astute questioning skills could bring that out. Maybe. If I had astute questioning skills. All I could do was consider the two of 'em possible witnesses and interview 'em both.

Just as I was thinking about sending Jasmine out to get one or both of 'em, Drew Gleeson's brother-in-law/attorney rapped on my door jamb. 'I want Drew out on bail.'

'Well, I guess you do,' I said. 'But it's Saturday and the court's closed. Judge Schnell usually goes fishing on a Saturday. And he doesn't believe in cell phones, more's the pity.' I said this last part with a tiny bit of sarcasm. I'm not proud of it.

Harry Joyner gave me a look. It wasn't a pleasant one. 'When will this judge be back from' – and here he used finger quotes – 'fishing?'

'Oh, he really is fishing. And on Sunday – tomorrow – he's got church and family dinner and probably a football game. He's got cable, you know.'

Mr Joyner's jaw looked tight, like maybe his teeth were clenched. 'I'll put up the bail for Drew right now, Sheriff.'

'Well, you know, the bail hasn't been set, Mr Joyner, or may I call you Harry?' He didn't answer. 'But if you're saying you wanna give me money so you can get your client out of jail now,' I started shaking my head, 'I'm afraid I'll have to arrest you for trying to bribe a law official.'

Joyner squared his shoulders. 'Of course, I wasn't implying anything of the sort,' he said. 'May I go back to the cells and speak to my client briefly?'

'Sure,' I said with a big old grin. 'Deputy!' I called out.

I gotta say Jasmine took her own sweet time getting to my office. I'm not sure who she was trying to piss off – Harry Joyner or me. 'Yes, sir?' she said, practically saluting. OK, me. She was trying to piss *me* off. She was succeeding.

'Please allow Mr Joyner a brief second visit with his client. He can see him in the cell.'

'Yes, sir,' she said, doing an about-face like she was an army recruit.

I looked at my watch. It was close to six o'clock in the evening and if I didn't get home quick, Harmon, my brother-in-law, was going to start supper and, as I've discovered since our womenfolk left, the only food worse than what my sister served was the food served by her husband. I called Dalton and told him we had a guest and he needed to relieve Jasmine in an hour or two, then told Jasmine I was off and headed to my Jeep. I figured me and my boy could pick up a bucket of chicken on our way home.

FIFTEEN

K nowing there was to be a reception back at the Carmichael mansion, and assuming that at least half, if not all, the people at the funeral would be in attendance, Jean and Jewel took the taxi to the Village West shopping area, ate an early dinner and perused the shops. Jewel managed to find several things she couldn't live without, some too bulky to transport herself. These she had Fed-Ex'ed to Jean and Milt's home.

'Don't you think that credenza will look lovely in my new foyer?' Jewel asked Jean, who only nodded in response.

Jean's mind was too busy dealing with the possibilities the ride to the funeral had provided. Had her entire theory been wrong? Was Paula only rebelling from a neglectful, unloving mother by her promiscuity? It was certainly possible. It was also certainly possible that Paula's psyche wasn't strong enough to bounce back from that early neglect, and it had colored her entire life with promiscuity and alcohol. Those two ingredients alone worked hand in hand. Get drunk and get laid. The old reliable. Scratch an itch, get back at your mother and drown the memory in booze.

Had Jean overreacted? It was certainly possible, Jean thought, considering her own culpability. She'd been ready to write off her old friend, to get her a room at the inn rather than take her home to abuse Milt and Johnny Mac. Then she'd been shot dead. And the only way to counter her own guilt was by giving Paula a good reason for her behavior: it wasn't her fault she was a mean-spirited bitch – she'd been sexually abused as a child. There was no doubt in Jean's mind that Paula had had an awful child-hood. But what about Constance? She'd grown up in the same household and she'd apparently had some modicum of success in life. A husband, stepchildren, a role in her family of origin. But she too was living in her family home, not on her own, as a woman in her fifties should be doing.

It was possible, Jean considered, that Paula's superior intellect went hand in hand with a more acute awareness of her place in

the family hierarchy. That is, dead last. After eighteen years of
this kind of neglect, she began acting out in a way that would
most embarrass her parents.

She tuned back in when she realized Jewel was asking her a
question. 'I'm sorry, what?' Jean asked.

'This top! What do you think?'

'It's nice,' Jean said, barely glancing at it. 'It would look lovely
on you.'

'Ah, it would fall off me! I'm talking for you, Jean! It's your
size!'

'Oh,' Jean said, looking again at the top. It was definitely
something out of Jean's comfort zone. Sheer white organza with
tiny pleats, long sleeves and a black collar and cuffs. 'Well, I don't
know where I'd wear it to.'

'To work, silly!' Jewel said. 'With a white cami – ooo, or red! A
pair of high-waist black trousers and it would look very professional.
Maybe save the red cami for night time.' She wiggled her eyebrows
at Jean.

Jean laughed. 'I'm fine with my button-downs and blazers,' she
assured her.

Jewel snorted in a most un-lady-like fashion. 'I'm buying it for
you. As a gift. And it would be insulting to me if you refused to
wear it.' Still with the top in her hands, she went to the counter
of the boutique and slapped down her American Express. Jean just
shook her head and smiled inwardly. She'd bought a lot of new
clothes lately – the stuff for the bachelorette party, the two outfits
for the viewing and the funeral, and now she had this. Maybe, she
thought, it was time to give some thought to changing her wardrobe. Maybe she'd been plain Jean for long enough. Maybe it was
time to try strutting her stuff. Hard to do in crutches, she thought
to herself, but not impossible.

Shortly thereafter they made another call for another taxi and
headed back to the Carmichael's home. It was after nine when
they got there but the party was in full swing. And a party it was.
There was loud music and raucous laughter, the clinking of glasses,
a couple making out in the foyer and two couples in the grand
salon dancing. Jean and Jewel headed straight to the elevator behind
the grand staircase. They punched in the third floor but the elevator
began slowing as it neared the second.

There were voices, loud voices, that could be heard over the noise of the elevator.

'I said no, goddammit! I'm through with that shit! You can do what you want with your fucking money! I don't want it! I don't!'

'We've got a good thing going here! Don't fuck it up!'

There was the sound of hurried thumping footsteps, followed by the sound of hurried high-heeled footsteps and the exclamation, 'Come back here!'

The elevator stopped and the doors opened to an empty hall.

Along with the chicken, me and Johnny Mac went to the video store and rented a bunch of old scary movies – *The House on Haunted Hill*, *The Blob* and *The Tingler*. Can't go wrong with two Vincent Price movies and a Steve McQueen. We were lucky: Harmon was just pulling in the driveway when we signaled to turn. We followed him up to the house, me happy in the thought that he hadn't started his idea of dinner.

'Fried chicken and scary movies!' I said to my brother-in-law as me and Johnny Mac got out of the car.

'Not some of those slasher flicks, I hope,' Harmon said as he unlocked the door to my home.

'Nope, older than that. Vincent Price.'

Harmon grinned. 'Now those are scary movies!'

So we set about getting TV trays, paper plates and sodas out of the fridge, and piled our plates with fried chicken, French fries and coleslaw. In case my son or my brother-in-law was prone to ratting me out, I stayed away from the fries and gave myself extra coleslaw. And we had a blast.

The next day was Sunday and, although it was Jean's turn to pick the church (she's Catholic and I'm Baptist so we alternate), since she was out of town we – that is, me, Johnny Mac and our new shadow, Harmon – headed for the Baptist church. According to some of the people at the church, our new pastor was a raving liberal. He wasn't exactly pro-gay marriage, but he actually said in the pulpit how it wouldn't do a thing to hurt a happy 'regular' marriage. On top of that, he hinted at thinking it might be all right to legalize the use of hemp. He was a young guy, married with two small girls, and he seemed OK to me. Of course, there are those in my community who have called me a 'knee-jerk pinko commie' due to the fact that I voted for an African-American president. Of course, my deputies Anthony Dobbins and Nita Skitteridge both worked on the president's campaign, and the whole department voted for him – at least they said they did.

So that Sunday we went to church and later, at my insistence, met up with Emmett, Jasmine and Petal at the Longbranch Inn for dinner – which is at the noon hour on a Sunday. I figured it was time the kids got over the madness that had happened in the Longbranch Inn's upper story, and Jasmine was ready to get back on that particular horse.

We had a good time, shooting the shit, telling tales. I wasn't allowed anything good to eat, of course, so had to be satisfied with The Milt. My brother-in-law got the chicken fried steak and was kind enough to slip me a couple of bites under the table. He tried it with the mashed potatoes and cream gravy, too, but that just kept slipping off the fork and onto the floor.

When we got back to the house and Johnny Mac had gone upstairs to do his homework, me and Harmon had the same idea and called our ladies up in Kansas City. Jean answered on the second ring.

'Who is this stranger calling me from the great state of Oklahoma?' she said upon answering the phone.

I grinned. 'I just heard there was a real pretty woman on the other end of this line, and thought I might see if she was a bit randy.'

My wife sighed. 'You have no idea,' she said.

I grinned wider. 'That's what I like to hear.'

'Any progress on your murder case?' she asked.

'Yeah, I got Drew Gleeson, the EMT who was in the cells that night, back in the cells – but not as an EMT this time. I'm pretty sure he's the one who done it,' I said.

I could hear my wife settling down. She loved to talk shop with me. And sometimes, having a real-life psychiatrist hear out my theories kinda helped.

'So what makes you think this EMT is responsible?' she asked.

'OK,' I said. 'Here's my reasoning. One, Darrell's wife was cheating on him, right?'

'Right.'

'So he shot her, right?'

'Right.'

'So who was she cheating on him with?'

'I don't know,' she said.

'Drew Gleeson confessed it was him,' I said. 'Said she was the love of his life and they were gonna run away together. Number two: Drew was alone in the cells with Darrell after everybody left – he said he left his bag in there. Three, Darrell was killed with some kind of digitalis stuff, which was probably in Drew's medical bag—'

'EMTs don't carry pharmaceuticals, Milt. That would be perimetics.'

I stopped. I didn't like that one bit. I hadn't been able to check out said bag yet, as I couldn't get a warrant to do so with the little evidence I had so far. But, even so, I started up again. 'And then, out of the blue, Gleeson tries to commit suicide by stealing Oxy from the hospital and taking it. They had to pump his stomach.'

'Why did he do that?' Jean asked.

'It boils down to his love life but he lawyered-up and I didn't get any further than that.' Then I had a thought. 'But if he could figure out how to break into the drug room at the hospital to kill himself, why couldn't he have broken into the drug room before that and stolen some digitalis?'

'So you believe he went in the cells, found out Darrell had killed his wife, who was Drew's lover, then went back in on the pretense that he'd left his bag in there, took out the digitalis he had conveniently stolen *before* he knew his girlfriend was dead, and what, forced it down Darrell's throat that quickly?'

'I don't think I want to talk to you anymore,' I said, and I'm pretty sure I sounded petulant.

'Why? Because I busted holes in your theory?' she asked.

'Yes.'

'Well, better me now than Drew's lawyer later, right?'

'I think I'm going to hang up now,' I said.

'You're such a baby,' my wife said with a laugh.

'And you're a big ol' buzz kill,' I said. It was all quiet for a moment, then I asked reluctantly, 'How's it going up there? Find out who diddled Paula yet?'

'Please don't use that word ever again when talking about child

sexual abuse,' my wife said in that 'I'm the doctor and I know
more than you' tone of voice she puts on sometimes.

'Sorry,' I said. 'Meant no offense.'

Jean sighed. 'I know you didn't, honey. I'm just frustrated. I
was almost convinced I had it all wrong, that she'd been neglected,
sure, but not necessarily sexually abused. But then . . .' Her voice
trailed off.

'But then what?' I asked, almost afraid of what I was going to
hear.

'I don't know. Things are just off here. Off kilter. Not right.'
She sighed again. 'I don't know how to explain it, but there *is*
something wrong here. I just don't know yet what it is.'

'You still coming home tomorrow?' I asked.

'I'm thinking of changing my ticket to Tuesday, Milt. I know
that's putting an undue burden on you, but I just can't leave
tomorrow morning without some sort of closure on this.'

I nodded my head. Much as I hated it, I understood. When
something's not right, well, it's just not right. And you needed to
find out why. At least, if you had a mind like me and my wife
both had.

Jean said goodbye and hung up the phone. She wasn't sure why
she didn't tell Milt what she and Jewel had overheard on the
elevator. Considering it with an open mind, though, she did know
why: Milt would have been afraid for her and he would have tried
demanding she come home, which would have led to a fight. Jean
had never, ever, in her whole life bent to a demand – not even
from her parents.

There was a knock on her door. 'Come in,' she said, hoping it
was Jewel. It was.

'Harmon just called,' Jewel said as she walked in and took her
place on the chaise lounge.

'So did Milt. What did yours have to say?'

Jewel shrugged but her expressive lips were in a downward
position. 'Not much. He's having a great time.'

'Missing you?'

Jewel sighed. 'Not so you'd notice.'

Jean used one crutch to lever herself up from the bed and hobble
to the chaise. She pushed Jewel's legs down and sat at the end of

the lounge. 'You're right. He doesn't care that you're not there. He's probably planning a divorce,' she said, looking directly at her sister-in-law, her eyebrows raised and a grin playing across her lips.

Jewel missed those cues; instead, her eyes got big and tears quickly brimmed in them.

Jean patted Jewel on the leg. 'See how silly that sounds?' Jean laughed. 'I've never seen a man so in love with his wife after this many years of marriage. You doofus!'

'Did you just call me a doofus?' Jewel said.

'Why, yes, I believe I did.'

Jewel leaned forward and hit Jean on the arm. Jean laughed. 'I'll call you more than that if you don't snap out of it! Be thankful he's having a good male bonding experience. It's time Harmon and Milt got better acquainted. Just the two of them.'

Jewel shook her head. 'Well, I hope that's what's happening. Milt never did like Harmon. Ever since I was a kid.'

'He's been over that for years. And he has regrets, you know that.'

'His one real regret,' Jewel said, 'was insisting I marry Henry when I got pregnant with Leonard, but I don't regret that. I wouldn't have my two other children if he hadn't insisted.' She shook her head. 'I can't imagine how different my life would have been if I hadn't married Henry. No, Milt should never regret that. I don't.'

'Listen,' Jean said, her head bent, 'I was thinking that I probably won't go home tomorrow. I'll go to the airport with you but then take a taxi back to town and find a hotel.'

'That conversation outside the elevator yesterday, right?'

Jean shrugged. 'I guess.'

'No. I'm not going home either and neither of us can get much done if we're in a hotel downtown instead of here in the house.'

Jean laughed. 'I think we might have outstayed our welcome.'

'How?' Jewel demanded. 'We're hardly ever around the family! I think that's been our first mistake! We need to interact with them more. And, by the way, you were right the first time. I'm sure Paula was sexually abused. And I think it's still going on.'

We were watching Sunday night TV when the phone rang. I left the living room to answer it in the kitchen. 'Hello?' I said cleverly.

'Sheriff, what in the hell kind of a place are you running down there?' came an irate voice.

'May I ask who's calling?' I said pleasantly.

'This is Harry Joyner! I just talked to your clerk and I have a big question, *Sheriff.* Why isn't my client on suicide watch?'

'Pardon me?' I asked, somewhat confused.

'Suicide watch, you ignoramus!' he shouted.

Now I'm not sure if 'ignoramus' is the same as calling me a bastard or a son-of-a-bitch, but it felt kinda like it. It's against the law in this county to call an officer by anything other than a G-rated name. I wondered what the judge would say about 'ignoramus'?

'Why would we have him on suicide watch?' I asked.

'Because, you idiot' – he said, just as I was thinking, yeah, maybe I should call the judge – 'he just tried to commit suicide!'

'Again?'

'No!' There was a deep sigh on the other end of the line. 'Earlier. With the OxyContin. At the hospital.'

'Hum. Well, we don't keep Oxy-whatever in the cells – or at the station at all, truth be known. We took his shoelaces and he wasn't wearing a tie. The cheap linens the county gives us don't actually tear – they don't burn either, just let off a toxic gas – so I don't see how he can hang himself. Nothing in there to stab himself with. If you're thinking he should be having someone in there watching him twenty-four/seven—'

'That's exactly what I'm thinking!' Harry Joyner yelled at me.

'Well, OK, then, I'll let my deputy know you're on your way down and to put some extra linens in the adjoining cell. Sound reasonable?' I asked.

There was silence on his end of the line for about a full minute before he said, 'You're a real piece of work, Sheriff.'

'Thank you. I've been told that before,' I said.

Then he hung up on me. I didn't call Dalton. I didn't expect Drew Gleeson's brother-in-law was headed our way.

Next morning, when I got to the shop, I was glad to see that Gleeson was still alive – not that I thought he wouldn't be, but a little part of me wondered if he had a lighter or matches and if the fumes from the bed linens really did give off a toxic gas. Be just my luck.

Anthony and Nita were on day duty and I sent Anthony out to get the pizza delivery guy who had been in the cells with Darrell, and Nita out to get Jasper Thorne, Drew Gleeson's EMT partner. I wasn't expecting a whole lot, but you just never know. That's why we law enforcement professionals keep plugging away – interview anybody who coulda seen anything; follow down every possible lead. Question everything.

Nita and Jasper Thorne got to the office first. I had Nita set up the equipment in the break room, get Jasper the soda of his choice and take him into the interrogation room – which this time really was just an interview room. But I wanted it all on tape, just in case I missed something – or Nita, watching from the break room, missed the same thing. Always have back-up. It's in the handbook.

I went in and Jasper stood, a Dr Pepper in his left hand. We shook. 'Thanks for coming in, Jasper. I appreciate it,' I said, taking a seat as Jasper resumed his. 'I suppose you heard about Drew?'

'Yes, sir,' he said. 'I heard.' No editorializing on Jasper's part. This was gonna be a long interview.

'Why do you think he did that?' I asked.

'I wouldn't rightly know.' And, as an afterthought, 'Sir.'

'He into gambling, drugs, alcohol?' I asked.

Jasper shrugged. 'I have no idea,' he said.

'Did you know he was having an affair with Joynell Blanton?'

'Who?'

'Joynell Blanton. You know, the wife of the dead guy,' I said, trying not to grit my teeth. 'And please stop fucking around.'

The use of the 'F' bomb got his attention. 'We aren't exactly close, me and Drew,' Jasper said. 'I don't know about any girlfriends or anything.'

'But did you suspect?' He didn't respond. 'Surely something he said or did over the past month or so led you to believe something was up one way or the other?'

Again, he shrugged. I decided to change the subject. 'Do y'all carry digitalis in that bag y'all tote around all the time?'

He shook his head, a look of confusion on his face. That's the way I like to do it – keep 'em on their toes. 'Digitalis? No, sir. We don't carry prescription drugs of any kind. If somebody needed that they'd get it at the ER, not from us.'

Well, shit, I thought. Score one for my wife. 'You know of any reason why Drew would have digitalis on him?'

He shook his head again. 'No, sir. Can't imagine why.'

'So he hasn't been out of sorts since the time around the tornado last weekend?'

'What do you mean, out of sorts?' Jasper asked, obviously stalling. I know he knew exactly what 'out of sorts' meant.

'Depressed? Moody?'

Jasper straightened up in his seat. 'I'm not sure what you're going for here, Sheriff. What exactly are you accusing my partner of?'

'Right now he's been arrested for stealing OxyContin from the hospital to try to kill himself.'

'You think he didn't try to kill himself? You think he wasn't depressed? You think he was gonna try to sell that shit or something?' His voice was getting louder and louder, and then he stood up. I stood up too, in case he took a swing at me. 'I'll tell you something! Yeah, the boy was depressed! So depressed he busted out crying, and yeah, it was over some woman! Coulda been that Joynell. He wasn't stealing those drugs for any other reason than to off himself, Sheriff, and you and I both know it!'

'Please have a seat, Jasper,' I said, pointing at his vacated chair. He sat. I sat. 'When exactly did he bust out crying?' I asked.

'When we were on our way to Bishop right after the tornado struck,' Jasper said. 'He had to pull over he was so upset. He just sobbed and sobbed and I didn't do diddly squat to help him,' he said, hanging his head. 'I shoulda done something.'

I patted his hand. 'There was probably nothing you could have done, Jasper. Did he ever mention Joynell or any other woman?'

He shook his head. 'Naw, and I never saw him with anybody. Hell, it coulda been a guy for all I know.'

I raised an eyebrow. 'Drew's gay?' I asked.

Jasper shrugged. 'Hell if I know. Who can tell nowadays? I'm just saying, I didn't know diddly squat about his love life, except it obviously wasn't going too well.'

It was my turn to stand up. I held out my hand and Jasper stood and shook it. 'Thanks for coming in, Jasper. You've been a big help.'

'I don't see how I could be. Hey, can I go back and see Drew?'
he asked.

I shook my head. 'Not right now. He's on suicide watch,' I said,
thinking that sounded good.

It obviously did. Jasper nodded. 'I understand,' he said, and
headed out the door. Nita was out there to meet him and drive
him back to the hospital.

SIXTEEN

Jean and Jewel came down to breakfast on Monday morning to find Vivian already there, tea and a croissant in front of her. Dru was slouched in a chair, her dirty, bare feet ruining the silk upholstery, a cup of her chi tea in both hands. Constance was at the buffet getting scrambled eggs and fruit. Jean propped one crutch against the wall and headed to the buffet on the other, leaving a hand free.

'Don't do that, my dear,' Vivian Carmichael said. 'Constance, ring for someone to help her.'

'Thank you, Vivian,' Jean said, 'but I'm fine.'

Vivian sighed. 'Well, if you don't mind looking like an idiot, who am I to say otherwise?'

Jewel swung around, her face set to tell the older woman off, but Jean grabbed her arm, shaking her head slightly. Jewel frowned and turned back around.

'Mother, you really know how to piss people off, don't you?' Constance said as she headed to the table.

'What? I was just stating the obvious,' Vivian said.

'Oh, wow!' Dru said, her tone sarcastic. 'We can state the obvious now? That's great! OK, here goes—'

'Drusilla!' Constance scolded.

Dru put down her tea and yelled, 'Hey, Martha! Where's my food?'

Jean and Jewel, plates loaded, headed to seats at the table just as Megan came in the room. True to form, Megan was immaculately dressed in crease-pressed khakis and a pink Polo shirt, with a white cardigan tied around her neck. Her blonde hair gleamed under the lights and her make-up was so perfect it almost looked as if she wore none – almost. In contrast to her twin, Dru was wearing baggy cut-offs, a torn sweatshirt a la the eighties movie *Flash Dance*, no makeup, was barefooted and still suffering from bed-head.

'Good morning, darling,' Constance said to Megan.

'Morning all,' Megan said, smiling at each person individually. Each person except her sister, whom she totally ignored. 'I'm surprised you two are still here,' she said, addressing Jean and Jewel. 'I thought your plane left this morning.'

Jean sighed in preparation for the deceit she was about to perpetrate. 'I got a call on my cell late last night. They've canceled our flight – not enough people. And there's not another one until tomorrow.'

'Not enough people?' Constance said, frowning. 'On a Monday? Monday flights are usually SRO for the business types. Oh! Do they have business in Tulsa?'

'Of course,' Jean said with a forced laugh. 'But we don't want to overstay our welcome. If we could get a ride into downtown, Jewel and I can try to find a hotel.'

Vivian slammed down her tea cup. 'I won't have it! I won't!'

'Mother?' Constance asked.

'You actually questioned the validity of our guest's statement and I will not have it!' Turning to Jean and Jewel, she smiled, but it never reached her eyes. 'You will of course stay here. When is your flight tomorrow?'

'Not until six in the evening, but we can't continue to impose—' Jean started.

'No imposition at all, my dear. None at all. We've loved having you here. It's brought a part of Paula home that I never got to know well. Her college and medical school years are a mystery to me. I hope we'll have time to sit and chat about my darling Paula as she was when you knew her,' Vivian said.

'I'd enjoy that, Vivian,' Jean said, the smile not as forced as she'd thought it would be.

Martha the cook came in with Dru's breakfast – eggs Benedict again – and all conversation dimmed as they turned to their food.

Jean and Jewel had talked long into the night confirming the identities of the two voices they'd heard outside the elevator. The protester was obviously Dru – Jean would recognize that shriek of hers anywhere – and the other they both agreed had to be Constance. What the fight was about was still a mystery. But the sisters-in-law had worked up a plan. Jean would follow Dru out of the breakfast room and attempt to get her alone for a chat, while Jewel did the same with Constance. They'd rehearsed the night before, coming up with potential scenes, questions and responses. They only had a day and half left, and they both knew they should have been doing this from the beginning, but the business of burying her old friend had taken Jean's mind away from her true mission.

Now she was ready. She was going to find out the truth if it killed her.

As I walked Jasper Thorne out of the interrogation room, Nita came out of the break room to drive him back to the hospital. They were walking to the side door, where Nita's cruiser was parked, when it opened and Anthony came in with the pizza guy – whatever his name was.

'Sheriff,' Anthony said, 'this is Ronnie Jacobs who works for Bubba's Pizza and Pasta. He's the one who made the delivery the night Darrell Blanton was killed.'

We were close enough to the break room that the recorder, which was still on, got that nice introduction. I held out my hand to Ronnie. 'Nice to see you again, Ronnie. We didn't get to talk much last week, what with all the commotion.'

'Yeah,' Ronnie said, shaking my hand with a vengeance. 'Y'all heard about the boy? That teenager who puked? How's he doing?' He looked from me to Anthony as he asked his questions.

'He's fine. Bet he won't be going on any more benders any time soon,' I said with a smile.

'Yeah, he's not very good at it,' Ronnie said seriously.

'Come on in here to our interview room so you and I can have a chat, OK with you, Ronnie?' I said, my hand on his back as I ushered him in.

'Yeah, sure, Sheriff. I don't know whether I got any info for you, but I'll do what I can.'

'And I appreciate that,' I said, indicating he sit while I took my own chair. 'The thing is we do have someone in custody, but not necessarily for Darrell's murder. It could be related, though.'

'No shit?' he said, his eyes big as saucers. 'Who is it?'

'I'm not at liberty to say at the moment, Ronnie, but I would like to ask you some questions about that night, things you might have seen without realizing it, you know, stuff like that.'

'Sure. I don't think I saw anything but ask away.'

'Let's start at the beginning. When did you get the call from Darrell about his pizza order?'

He shrugged. 'I dunno. The dispatcher takes those calls. I got the order, I guess, at around five-thirty or six, or thereabouts. Sometimes Bubba's stays open all night. Specially on the weekends. So delivering a pizza that early in the morning was no biggie. It was one extra-large pizza with Italian sausage and extra cheese. I brought it right on over here.'

'While you were in the cells with Darrell, did y'all talk about anything?'

'Naw, not really. I mean, I said, "Here's your pizza," and he said, "Here's your money," and that was about it, until the kid puked and then we said how gross it was and I think we both kinda laughed at him. You know, 'cause the kid couldn't hold his liquor.'

'Right,' I said. 'So when he started convulsing – the kid – what did you do?'

'I yelled for that girl who brought me back there – Holly?' I nodded my agreement that Holly surely was her name. 'And she came running back, then back out. And then you came in, and then those ambulance guys came in, and then you threw me out.'

'Right,' I said. I stood up and held out my hand. 'Thanks for your time, Ronnie. You did a great job. OK if I check back with you if we have any more questions?'

'Sure, Sheriff,' he said, again pumping away on my outstretched hand. 'Just call me and I'll drive on over here. No reason to have your deputy come and get me. He *is* gonna take me back, right?'

'Absolutely,' I said, rescuing my hand, which I used to slap the boy on the back. We walked out the door. 'Anthony, can you see that Ronnie here gets wherever he wants to go?'

'Yes, sir,' Anthony said and ushered the boy out.

Two interviews in maybe thirty minutes and I still didn't have much to make my case against Drew Gleeson. I was just gonna hafta get busy.

Jean followed Dru out of the breakfast room to the solarium on the east side of the house. It was a long walk and Dru was doing a good job of out-distancing Jean, but Jean thought the solarium was the most likely place Dru would be headed. The other rooms in that direction were Constance's office, a lady's sitting room – very feminine and not a place Jean figured Dru would find comfortable – and the smoking room, which was a large room with leather sofas, pool tables and a bar, left over from the days when the men would leave the dinner party and adjourn to the smoking room, while the ladies would adjourn to the grand salon. Jean did glance in there, but, not seeing Dru, she continued on to the solarium.

Jean saw through the windows that the sky had darkened and she saw lightning strike, heard the boom of the thunder. This only increased her urge to get to the solarium. This room ran almost the full length of the mansion on the east side and was lush with hot house flowers, exotic plants and large cages housing parrots, flamingos, peacocks and other large birds. There were several sitting areas of white wicker scattered about the room's length. Dru was in one of those, a yellow-and-blue plumed parrot on her shoulder, her nose burrowed in her iPad.

'Oh, hi, Dru, I didn't know you were here,' Jean said, trying to put on an innocent smile.

Dru snorted, not taking her eyes off her iPad. 'Following me didn't give you a clue?'

Jean sat down on the white wicker love seat across from the sofa-sized piece Dru was sprawled on. 'We need to talk,' she said.

Dru finally looked up. 'I doubt it,' she said, and went back to her iPad.

'I heard you at the party after the funeral. You and Constance, on the second floor by the elevator. I was in the elevator. I heard every word.'

Dru looked up again. 'And just what do you think you heard, *Doctor* McDonnell?'

Jean didn't miss the emphasis on the word 'doctor.' 'I heard you say you were through with that shit. That Constance could do what she wanted with her money. And you said rather emphatically that you didn't want it. And then Constance responded with, and I quote, "We've got a good thing going here! Don't fuck it up!" Does any of this sound familiar?'

'Not in the least,' Dru said, but she was staring at Jean, not back down at her iPad. Jean thought that was progress.

'Oh, maybe you were sleep-walking,' Jean suggested, letting sarcasm color her statement.

'Wasn't me,' Dru said.

'Then maybe it was your sister. Does she screech like you?'

Dru jumped up from her sofa, dislodging the parrot on her shoulder. 'You wanna hear screeching, lady? I'll give you screeching!' And she ran around the sofa to the cage of flamingos and began banging on the bars, then ran on to the next one full of parrots and banged on those bars. The yellow-and-blue plumed parrot that had appeared to be Dru's pet was flying in little short bursts all around the room, though with its clipped wings it couldn't get very far off the ground. But he – and the rest of the avian inhabitants – could certainly be heard. With Dru's behavior and the storm now raging outside the windows of the solarium, the birds were hysterical.

Jean jumped up from the wicker love seat and made a fast swinging flight of her own to where Dru now stood in front of the peacock cage. Jean grabbed the girl's arm away from the cage and pulled her around to face her.

'Stop it, you spoiled little brat!' Jean hissed. 'Why terrify these animals? What is the matter with you?'

Dru tried to grab her arm back, but Jean's hold was tight. 'I'm not letting go of you,' Jean said, her voice soft but menacing. 'You're to calm down this minute or I'll take you to Vivian and tell her what you did. Or would you rather I discuss it with Constance?'

Dru's entire body slumped. 'No,' she said. Jean let go of her arm. 'I don't know what you want from me.'

'The truth,' Jean said. 'That's all. Let's sit down. I'll tell you my truth, and then you'll tell me yours.'

'I don't know anything about truth,' Dru said, 'but I sure can tell you a story that will curl your hair.'

It was a typical Monday. There was a three-car collision on Highway Five, not far from Mountain Falls Road – the road I live on. It took two deputies to handle that one as two of the cars were filled with older teenage boys who'd been racing, and the skinny from the occupant of the third car was that the guys appeared to be squaring off. So Dalton and Anthony took that. Nita got busy on a possible sexual assault out in the country on the way to Bishop. Emmett was at the VFW Hall giving a talk to the fellas there. And I was holed up in my office, busy trying to come up with ways to prove Drew Gleeson killed Darrell Blanton. Just before I was getting ready to stand up and go to lunch, I got a call from Holly at the front desk.

'Sheriff, Mr Joyner, Mr Gleeson's attorney, is here to see you.'

'Oh, joy,' I said, sarcastically. 'Send him on back.'

I sat back down, trying to ignore the rumble in my belly. I stood back up when Harry Joyner knocked on my door jamb and came in. We shook hands and I said, 'Please, have a seat.'

'Thanks, Sheriff. Have you set up a hearing time with the judge to release my client on bail?'

'And how was your weekend?' I countered.

He smirked at me. 'Not good. My wife spent the entire time yelling at me for not getting her brother out of jail. So when is the hearing?'

'I haven't called about that yet – it's been a busy day. But I'll put in a call to the county clerk's office and we should have a hearing set up in, I don't know, a couple of days?' I said, all innocent-like.

Joyner's smirk was back. 'I thought that might be the case, so I took the liberty of calling the clerk's office myself. The judge will see us at two o'clock this afternoon.' He stood up. 'I'd like to see my client now. And I'd rather see him in his cell as I'm not one hundred percent certain that you don't break the law by taping our interviews!'

'Sir, I never break the law,' I said, although I might bend it occasionally – I didn't tell him that, though. 'But it seems to me that if your client is so all-fired innocent, there'd be no reason for us not to hear your conversations. Just saying.' I shrugged and smiled.

He smiled back. 'Oh, my client is innocent all right – and I have no problem with you hearing him say so. It's the other stuff, you know, personal stuff – family stuff.'

'You're charging him by the hour and talking about family business?'

His smile disappeared and he glared at me. 'I don't charge family,' he said emphatically.

'Wow, no shit? You are a credit to your profession,' I said as he turned and walked out of the office. I picked up my phone and

buzzed through to Holly. 'Let Mr Joyner meet with his client in
the cell, OK?'

'Sure, Milt. Whatever you say,' she answered. That's the thing
about Holly – why she's so much better than our former civilian
clerk who was with us for almost twenty years. Gladys, the
former, would have been all, 'Why in the cell and not in
the interrogation room? Do you really think that's a good idea?
Sheriff Blankenship never would have let a lawyer meet with
his client in his cell. This is highly inappropriate, Milton,' and
on and on and on. I was never so happy to see someone retire
as I was to see Gladys do so. Holly, on the other hand, for all
her oddity in attire, hair and makeup is a real professional at
her job, and the only untoward thing I've ever caught her doing
is sneaking a smooch with Dalton now and then. Personally, I
can handle that.

I got up and headed out the side door, with a whole new scenario
on how to talk Loretta at the Longbranch Inn into serving me a
chicken fried steak. None of my carefully thought-out scenarios
had worked as of yet, but I had high hopes.

'You tell yours first,' Dru said.

Jean nodded. 'OK. I'm pretty sure Paula was sexually abused
as a child. And I want to find out who did it and if they are still
doing it.'

'Sexually abused,' Dru said, as if rolling the words around on
her tongue. 'You mean raped or, you know, just doing it?'

'If it was a child with an adult, it doesn't matter. It's all rape,'
Jean said.

'No shit? Even if the kid is sorta OK with it?'

'How can a child be "sorta OK" with something like that? They
don't have the ability to make a decision like that, and even if
they did, any adult who has sex with a child is a degenerate and
needs to go to jail.'

Dru laughed. 'Wow, and you're a shrink? Where's your compas-
sion for these poor people who are just mentally unbalanced?'

'It's more than that. Pedophilia is a disease, of course, but it
has no cure. The recidivism rate for pedophiles is the highest of
any crime. Even castration doesn't work. It's the power, not so
much the actual sexual experience.'

Dru was nodding her head. 'That way even a woman can do it.'

'Do what?' Jean said, holding her breath.

'Have sex with a kid. Or, like you said, rape a kid.'

'Why would a woman want to do that?' Jean asked.

Dru shrugged. 'Mainly 'cause some man wants to watch.'

'Did a woman do that with you?' Jean asked, her fists clenched by her side.

Dru shrugged again. 'I didn't say that,' she said.

'I told you my story, about Paula,' Jean said. 'It's your turn to tell me yours.'

'Huh. Well, this is a story, right, so maybe it's not true? Maybe I'm just making it up.' She smiled at Jean. 'Like, what's that word, hypothetically?'

'Yes,' Jean said. 'So tell me your hypothetical story.'

'So maybe there was this woman who married this man whose wife had just died, and this man had two daughters. And this man and this woman had been knocking boots since the woman was real young, like maybe a child herself, and so she thought it was OK to do what she wanted to do. And maybe the man liked to watch this stuff.' She stopped talking.

A sick feeling washed over Jean. 'Are you implying that Con— this woman used . . . something to . . .'

Dru cocked her head. 'Maybe. Could be. And then the man dies and doesn't leave anything to his wife or his daughters, and the woman knows that the dead man had friends who liked this stuff, too, so she contacts them and gets this whole thing started. And when the girls are old enough to realize she's getting paid, maybe they demand that she pay them too.'

'Is this still going on?' Jean asked, damping down her need to jump up and confront Constance.

'Maybe, maybe not.'

'Maybe one of the girls wants out,' Jean suggested.

'Maybe,' Dru said.

'Maybe the woman is giving one of the girls a hard time about it,' Jean suggested.

'Maybe,' Dru said.

'Maybe if this girl had someone to stand beside her, someone she could trust, she could expose the woman for what she is,' Jean said.

'And that would be you, right?' Dru said with a sneer. 'No thanks, Doc. This was all just hypothetical. None of it really happened. It was just a joke.'

She got up and left the solarium, leaving Jean sitting there alone, too shook up to even move.

My new thought-out scenario didn't work. I ended up with a spinach salad and one small piece of garlic bread. And iced tea with sweetener, not the good sweet tea they serve at the Longbranch Inn. None of it was particularly satisfying.

I got back to the shop and heard voices and laughter coming from the bullpen area, so I walked that way. Holly was holding a baby and I saw the two – and I use this term loosely – adults watching her were Chandra Blanton and Mike Reynolds.

'Well, hey there, you two! Is this your baby?' I said, which was a stupid question, but no one gave me a look so I figured no one noticed.

'Michael Nelson Reynolds, Jr,' Chandra said, smiling at me. As young as the girl was, she seemed to have gotten her figure back real quick, although her breasts were probably bigger than they would be when she stopped nursing.

I moved closer to Holly and looked down at the baby. Thank God he looked like his daddy and not a male Blanton. Although the women tended to be pretty – or maybe it's just me – the men tended toward butt ugly. I coogie-cooed a bit then asked them why we were so honored by their presence.

'My mee-maw's lawyer said I should pick up Uncle Darrell's person effects,' Chandra said. 'Is that OK?'

'Sure!' I said. 'Can Holly care for Junior while the three of us go back and see what we've got?'

'Please!' Holly said.

Chandra smiled. 'OK. But holler if you need me.'

Leaving her extra-large diaper bag with Holly, Chandra and Mike followed me down the hall toward my office. We have a room across the hall from Emmett's office that we used for all kinds of storage, including evidence. This is where Darrell Blanton's personal effects would be.

I went to the right shelf, found the right box and opened it. The first thing I noticed was Darrell Blanton's cell phone. And I just

stared at it. It took maybe a full minute for my brain to unfreeze
and the ramification of what I was seeing to register. If Darrell's
cell phone had been confiscated when he came in, how in the hell
had he called for a pizza?

SEVENTEEN

Jean heard voices in the hall outside the solarium. They were quiet at first, then raised in anger. She got up and moved to the half-open door to the hallway. Peering around, she saw the twins, their faces scrunched in anger and their fists clenched, spewing harsh words at each other.

'I told her I was out!' Dru said.

'You're going to screw up the whole thing!' Megan said.

'Like I give a flying fuck!' Dru shot back.

'Well, you'd better!' Megan almost screamed. Then she turned her head slightly and saw Jean. She stopped and stared at her, then turned and stared at her sister. 'Did you tell?' she hissed. 'Did you?'

Dru shrugged. 'Not exactly,' she said.

Megan flew at Dru, hands grabbing Dru's hair. Dru fought back, kicking and screaming.

Jean moved in and with one crutch managed to persuade the girls to stop what they were doing.

'She told you!' Megan managed to get out between clenched teeth.

'I think the three of us should have a chat,' Jean said.

'Fuck you, you interfering gimp!' Megan shouted and ran away from them.

Meanwhile, at the other end of the house, Jewel was in quiet conversation with Constance as they lounged in the library, an attractive two-story affair with generations of books and furniture adorning it.

'So the whole thing was just about her not wanting to stay here over the winter holiday?' Jewel said.

'I know it sounds trivial, but it's important. I'm trying to get my mother to see that the girls are part of the family. That they deserve a share of the Carmichael fortune. And the best way to do that is to have them near her, for her to get to know them.'

Constance laughed. 'I understand that getting to *know* Dru might not be the best strategy, but the girl has a good heart, she really does.'

'You seem very close to your stepdaughters,' Jewel said.

'I've been their mother since they were ten. They are so precious to me,' Constance said.

'I wish I had that kind of relationship with my husband's daughters, but their mother poisoned them against me – and their father. Now that they're grown up, he hardly ever gets to see them.'

Constance shook her head. 'That's such a shame. If only—'

The door to the library burst open and Megan rushed in. 'Dru told that bitch doctor everything!'

'What?' Constance said standing.

Megan seemed to notice Jewel for the first time, and backed up a few steps.

'Are you sure?' Constance asked.

Megan nodded.

'How much?' Constance asked.

'Everything.'

Constance turned to Jewel. Her demeanor had changed from charming to dangerous. 'And I'm sure you're also in the know, Mrs Monk.'

'In the know about what?' Jewel asked, at this point really confused. She'd almost accepted Constance's excuse for the fight between her and Dru the night of the funeral.

'Where are they?' Constance demanded.

'In the solarium,' Megan said.

'Bring her!' Constance said, and Megan went up to Jewel and grabbed her arm, and the three left the library on their way to the solarium.

Darrell Blanton's wallet was also full of cash. So he probably didn't have any money on him in the cell. How did he pay for the pizza he probably didn't order? I walked out in the hall and called for Holly. She came, carrying a sleeping Junior with her.

'Did you pay for the pizza when it was delivered to Darrell?' I asked her.

She shook her head. 'No, of course not. I knew you wouldn't want the county to pay for it, and I'm saving all my money for the honeymoon.'

'Call that pizza kid back and have him come in. Just tell him I've got a few more questions.'

'You're supposed to be at the hearing for Drew Gleeson in about a half hour,' Holly told me.

'Shit,' I said, then turned and apologized to the new mother. I knew calling Harry Joyner and asking to reschedule wasn't gonna fly. He'd think I was just stalling. And I could well be. At that point I had no idea what I was doing or why. Thinking fast, I said, 'Call the pizza kid now and tell him to come in ASAP. When's Emmett gonna be through at the VFW?'

'He should be leaving about now. They were gonna serve lunch—'

'Call him. Tell him to come back here and get the prisoner and take him to the courthouse. He knows just about as much as I do about the case.'

She handed the baby back to his mother and ran for her phones. And I went back into the storage room with Chandra Blanton and her new family.

'So,' I said, taking out the inventory typed up by Holly the morning after we'd brought Darrell Blanton in. I compared the inventory with the items in the box. 'One cell phone, Fonetastic brand; one wallet holding thirty-two dollars in cash, an out-of-date driver's license and a lapsed MasterCard; one Swiss Army knife – forty-seven blade variety; a half-eaten roll of Mentos; eighty-seven cents in loose change; and his Nikes, complete with shoelaces.'

'That looks to be it,' Chandra agreed.

'OK, let's go out front so you can sign about a hundred forms to pick this stuff up.'

'Do we really need any of that crap?' Mike asked his soon-to-be-wife.

'I can buy three boxes of newborn diapers with that thirty-two dollars!' she informed her soon-to-be-husband.

Mike shrugged. 'OK,' he said, which I agreed was the wisest choice of an answer.

We went back out to the bullpen where Holly was just hanging up the phone. 'That was Emmett. He's on his way. He said he should be here in no time at all.'

'Did you get hold of that pizza kid?' I asked her.

'Ronnie Jacobs,' my clerk said succinctly, obviously not impressed with my memory. 'Yes,' she said. 'He said he was close and he'd be right here.'

'Good,' I said. 'Chandra's got papers to sign?'

'Right here,' Holly said with a smile. 'I've got them all sorted out for you.'

'Thanks,' Chandra said. 'And if I haven't said it enough, I just want to tell you how sorry I am about what my family did to your bachelorette party. And about that lady who got killed.'

Holly reached out a hand and cupped Chandra's elbow. 'You've already said it plenty and you really don't need to keep saying it. No one blames you. We all know you were as much a hostage as the rest of us.' Holly grinned widely. 'And if it wasn't for this little one,' she said, gently rubbing Junior's back, 'we'd probably still be there!'

Chandra laughed but still hung her head. That was some heavy guilt that girl was carrying, I thought. I hoped she could work through it. Maybe with my wife's help.

The front door of the shop opened and the pizza kid – Ronnie Jacobs – came in with a tall, striking blonde hanging on his arm. The blonde stopped upon seeing all of us standing there, but she seemed to be looking at someone in particular. I glanced at Chandra, who was staring right back at the blonde.

'Cousin Lucinda,' she said. 'What are you doing here?'

No phone to order a pizza, no money to pay for a pizza, and the pizza kid was involved with a Blanton woman.

Light was beginning to dawn.

Dru looked around the solarium, her eyes darting back and forth. 'We need to get out of here,' she told Jean.

'Why?' Jean asked.

Dru looked at her as if she found her slow. 'Because Megan went to get Constance. And God only knows what Constance will do to keep this whole mess from getting out.'

'So the story's true?'

Dru rolled her eyes. 'Of course it is, stupid. And yeah, she's the one who got Aunt Paula involved, too, with my dear old dad. He started with her when she was like a kid. Way before Megan and I were born. But one child – Constance – wasn't enough for him. When she got "too old", he told her to bring in Paula. According to Constance, though, Paula was a bad girl and didn't play the games like she should.'

'Jesus,' Jean said, dropping down on one of the wicker chairs.

Dru leaned down and grabbed her arm. 'Get up! We've got to get out of here.'

Jean stood and pointed to the double doors that led to the hall they'd both come down. 'Out there?'

'No! Of course not!' Dru said, again shaking her head at Jean's obvious stupidity. 'That's the way they'll be coming. We need to go outside. Come on!' she said, and took Jean by the arm, almost dragging her to the French doors that led to a veranda.

But the storm was still in full swing. Beyond the veranda there was nothing but grass, trees and flowerbeds. There were no walkways, nothing that would keep Jean's crutches from sinking into the softened earth and sending her tumbling to the ground.

'I can't!' Jean shouted to be heard over the deluge. She pointed to her crutches.

'Fuck!' Dru said, looking back into the room they'd just left. Jean followed her gaze and saw Constance entering the solarium, followed by Megan, who had a tight grip on Jewel's arm.

'I can't leave my sister-in-law,' Jean said.

'I couldn't give a shit about her – or you, for that matter. Lady, you are not my hero!' Dru said and took off into the rain, leaving Jean standing alone.

Cousin Lucinda, the tall blonde, grabbed Ronnie Jacobs' arm and said, 'Let's get out of here—'

She said this just as I walked up to Ronnie with a big old smile and, taking his free arm, said, 'Ronnie! Thanks for coming by so quick! Just a few questions, then you can be on your way.' Turning to my clerk, I said, 'Holly, why don't you take Mike into the break room so he can get some refreshments for everyone?'

Holly gave me a quick nod to indicate she got the message, then said brightly, 'Sure, Sheriff! What a good idea!'

I ushered Ronnie into the interrogation room – now aptly named for what was about to transpire.

'So, Ronnie,' I said, still smiling, 'you said Darrell Blanton called in his order to your dispatcher?'

'Yeah, I guess,' he said.

'Ronnie, we'd confiscated Darrell's cell phone. He didn't have any way to call for a pizza.'

'Oh. Well, maybe someone else called it in for him?' he suggested. 'You'd have to check with our dispatcher about that.'

'Oh, I will, don't worry about that,' I said, still smiling. 'And one other thing: you said you gave him the pizza and he gave you money, is that right?'

'Uh huh,' Ronnie said, turning a little green around the gills.

'But we'd also confiscated all his belongings – including his cash.'

Ronnie shrugged. 'Maybe you didn't get all of it?' he suggested.

'Hum,' I said, as if thinking that over. 'Maybe he had a hidden stash, is that what you're thinking?'

'Sure,' Ronnie said, his face coming back pink as he smiled and nodded.

'You said he took it out of his pocket, right?'

'Ah, I don't know. Did I say that? Ah, I don't remember. I mean if I said that or if he did that.'

'Surely you'd remember if he took off his boot and pulled money out of there?'

'Ah, yeah, maybe—'

'Or if he opened his shirt and he had a money belt taped to his chest,' I offered.

'Yeah, sure, I guess—'

'So more than likely he would have to take his money out of his pocket, right?'

'Ah, well, yeah, sure, I guess.'

'Thing is, I checked with the ME's office and he said there was nothing in his pockets at all. Not even lint. We cleaned him out when we took his crap and put it away.'

'Huh,' Ronnie said. 'Well.'

'Well, what?' I asked him.

He was silent. Then the door burst open and Cousin Lucinda, Ronnie's girlfriend, came barging in. 'Honey-bunch, tell him you want a lawyer! They do that on *Law and Order* all the time!'

Well, she had me there. Maybe Harry Joyner wouldn't mind taking on a paying client.

Jean moved back into the solarium just as Constance pulled a very ladylike, pearl-handled pistol out of the pocket of her full skirt. Jean mused to herself that a straight skirt or pants would have shown the bulge of the pistol – good fashion choice to go with a full skirt if you needed to go armed.

'Thank you for coming back in, Doctor McDonnell,' Constance said, leveling the gun at Jean's heart. 'Why don't you and your sister-in-law have a seat?'

Megan pushed Jewel to the nearest white wicker sofa. Jean sat down next to her.

'Where is Drusilla?' Constance asked.

Jean shrugged. 'Off to tell the world about you, I hope.'

Constance laughed. 'You're giving her far too much credit, Doctor. Dru bitches and moans a lot, but when she can't pay her rent or buy booze she'll come back.'

'So you're making another alcoholic, are you?' Jean said.

Constance sat down on the love seat opposite the two other women. 'Now you're going to blame me for Paula's drinking problems?'

'Dru told me about what you did to Paula.' She shook her head. 'You truly are a sick woman, Constance.'

Constance laughed. 'Thanks for the diagnosis. But you won't be sharing it with anyone else.'

'You're just going to shoot us? Right here? That sounds complicated.'

'No, I'll think of something less complicated and more apt. Maybe an accident – or rather, two.' She turned to Megan. 'What kind of accident can two people have, dear?'

'A car accident,' Megan said, smiling at her stepmother.

'Of course! Why didn't I think of that?' She patted Megan on the arm. 'You always come through for me, darling!'

Constance and Megan both were sitting on the love seat, their backs to the door from the hall. They didn't see or hear Vivian come through the doors in her silent automatic wheelchair, but Jean did.

'So you gave your little sister to your pedophile boyfriend, and then later his own daughters . . . You've been pimping them out for how long?'

'Don't give me that holier than thou bullshit! Paula enjoyed it! Just like my girls did, and don't let Dru make you think she didn't! Because she'd be lying! And what else was I supposed to do after their father left me with nothing?'

'Get a job?' Jewel suggested.

Constance was about to respond but never got the chance. Her mother took that opportunity to hit her only surviving daughter over the head with a very expensive vase.

The next day I met my wife and sister at the airport in Tulsa, both me and Harmon loaded down with flowers to greet our women and Johnny Mac loaded down with Godiva chocolates for both his mom and his aunt. We don't do things half-assed in Oklahoma, folks.

It was all over. When I called Emmett and told him to tell the judge and Harry Joyner – oh, and Drew Gleeson, too, I suppose – that Drew was no longer a suspect, I asked if he could see whether Harry would like to sit in on an interview with the new suspect. Harry said sure. Since I doubted Ronnie Jacobs made much more than the minimum wage at the pizza joint, I figured I'd hit up the judge to pay Joyner as a court-appointed attorney.

Joyner advised Ronnie to tell the truth, and when he started to do so, his girlfriend, Lucinda Blanton, tried an easy stroll out of the building. Holly, bless her, saw her going for the door and she and Chandra Blanton managed to grab both the girl's arms and bring her back in. Holly knocked on the door to the interrogation room where me and Joyner and Ronnie Jacobs were sitting, and said, 'This one was taking a hike, Milt. I think you might want her in here?'

I nodded. 'Swell idea,' I told Holly, and grinned like an idiot. She pushed the girl in and I stood and offered her a seat. 'So good of you to join us, Ms Blanton,' I said.

She looked at Ronnie, whose head was down, hands clasped in front of him. 'Baby?' she said.

Slowly, Ronnie's head came up. 'I gotta tell it all, honey-bunch.'

Lucinda jumped up and ran to the door, but my wise clerk had locked it. I encouraged the girl to sit back down.

So it went like this: Ronnie and Lucinda fell in love, which was a no-no for a Blanton girl. When Darrell and his cousins found out about it, they accosted Ronnie, beating the ever-loving crap out of him. And Darrell told him that if he saw Ronnie with Lucinda again he'd kill him. So after enough time for Ronnie to heal up, he and Lucinda decided the only way they could get out of Prophesy County with both of 'em alive and kicking was to do something about Darrell, the ring leader.

Ronnie was on his way home from the pizza joint that Saturday night, having stayed late to clean up, and carrying a nice hot pepperoni with him, when he saw my Jeep going by with Darrell Blanton all snug in the back seat. He ran back to his apartment where Lucinda was waiting for him and the pizza, and told her what he'd seen. And then the girl took over.

Seems Blanton women know a lot about herbs and flowers and stuff, and Lucinda knew that the oleander bush in Ronnie's side yard was poisonous. So she blended the petals up with some oregano and garlic and olive oil, poured her concoction over the pizza, added extra cheese, stuffed it in the oven long enough to melt the new cheese, and they were ready to do the deed. The girl had no idea that the oleander mimicked digitalis, she just knew it was poisonous. It wasn't the first time Ronnie had delivered a pizza to the sheriff's office, to the deputies or to prisoners, and he didn't think anyone would think anything about it.

At that point in his recitation, Ronnie looked up at me with big watery blue eyes and said, 'And it worked like a charm!'

'Just shut up, Ronnie, for God's sake!' Lucinda said.

'But, honey, I have to tell the truth!'

'Why?' she demanded.

Obviously she had him there, because Ronnie failed to reply.

I stood up, knocked on the door and Holly unlocked it. 'I need the keys to the lock-up,' I told her. She handed me her ring of keys and I took the lovebirds back to the cells – one for each.

When I came back out, I told Harry Joyner, 'You might want to find another attorney for the girl. I don't think you're gonna want to defend them together.'

'She pissed?' he asked.

I shrugged. Looking over at Holly, I said, 'You might wanna get the first aid kit and go back to Ronnie's cell. He needs to get cleaned up.'

Holly didn't say anything, just grabbed the first aid kit and headed back. Joyner raised an eyebrow at me. 'Fingernails,' I said. 'Before I could get them locked up, she went for his face.'

'Separate attorneys for sure,' Joyner said.

That Monday night I got a phone call from Jean telling me she'd finished up her business. 'You know who it was?' I asked her.

'Long story, babe, but I'll give you all the gory details tomorrow night. Can we go to La Margarita when Jewel and I get in? We'll be starving,' she said.

'La Margarita? You sure? I thought you said it was too greasy for your taste.'

There was a silence on the other end of the phone for about thirty seconds, then she said, 'I could use a little grease right now.'

And it wasn't until the ladies deplaned, we ate dinner, sampled some Godiva chocolates, drove all the way back to Prophesy County and got Johnny Mac to bed that the four of us sat down and discussed the situation in Kansas City.

And I gotta say I was shocked. A child doing that to her own sister, not to mention the crazy father of those two girls. It was sickening and personally I wanted to exhume the old man's body and shoot it a couple of times.

'And the old lady cold-cocked Paula's sister?' I asked.

'Knocked her right out!' my sister Jewel said with a big grin.

'But then we had to talk Vivian into calling the police,' Jean said. '"That is not something we do!" she told us. I just looked at her for I don't know how long, then I told her she had to. That's when Megan jumped up—'

'She tried running to the door to the hall,' Jewel said, still grinning, 'but I tackled her!'

Jean looked at Jewel and grinned herself. 'It was beautiful!' she said. 'Jewel was like the best linebacker I've ever seen! Made a dive right for Megan's knees and took her down in about two seconds!'

Jewel shrugged and tried to look modest. 'I think it might have been more like ten or fifteen seconds, but,' again she shrugged, 'it was cool!'

My wife and my sister high-fived each other.

'So what did you do after that?' Harmon asked.

'I dragged her ass back to the love seat!' Jewel said.

'And I used my cell phone to call the Kansas City cops, while Vivian used hers to call the family attorney,' Jean said.

'And I sat on Megan so she wouldn't try to leave again,' Jewel cut in.

'What about Dru?' I asked.

'She called Vivian about an hour later and Vivian told her the police were there and were arresting Constance, but that she and Megan were in the clear and she could come home.'

'But Megan dragged you into the solarium!' Harmon said to his wife. 'She should go to jail for that!'

Jean looked at Jewel, who took a deep breath and said, 'I decided not to press charges. Earlier today Jean got the name of a colleague in Kansas City who works with adult victims of child abuse. Vivian said she would make sure the girls went twice a week as scheduled.'

'But—' Harmon started.

'Honey,' Jewel said, 'Megan is a victim, too. So is Constance, for that matter. But she turned her own victimization into a family business and she needs to be punished for that.' Jewel looked at Jean, as if to confirm her own statement, and I had a pretty good idea where my sister's psychobabble had come from. Sorry, I'm not supposed to use that word.

'Megan was doing it for the money,' Jean explained. 'She'd tamped down her feelings so deep that she could only see the goal of finishing school without student loans.'

Jewel shook her head. 'I don't know, Jean. Megan was pretty loyal to Constance, enough so to think about killing the two of us! And she sure didn't stick by her twin!'

'I think Megan had developed tunnel-vision,' Jean said. 'All she could see was finishing college, then she could get away from Constance and the life she'd created for her and Dru.'

'And what about Dru?' I asked.

Jean shook her head. 'Dru's a lot like Paula. More sensitive than her sister, with a higher intellect. Unlike Paula, who masked her pain with alcohol and promiscuity, Dru masked hers with bitchiness – and alcohol.'

'You think those girls are gonna be OK?' Harmon asked.

Jean shrugged. 'They'll get better with help – their own and Vivian's and the therapist's, but I can't say they'll ever be OK. They've lived through something that will color their lives forever. But with help they'll be able to see beyond that and hopefully both of them will find a real life for themselves.'

'From your lips to God's ear,' Jewel said softly.

EPILOGUE

I t was yet another Saturday, two weeks to the day from that awful Saturday at the Longbranch Inn. But this one was different. Great big chunks of different. We were at the Holy Trinity Church of Christ in Longbranch at the wedding of my deputy, Dalton Pettigrew, and my clerk, Holly Humphries. I was all decked out in a tux and looking good. I had two roles to play at this shindig – one, walking the bride down the aisle and giving her away, and two, standing up as the groom's best man. Anthony and Emmett were the other groomsmen and Jasmine was the matron of honor. Nita and my wife Jean were the bridesmaids.

The bride was wearing her mother-in-law's wedding dress, a beautiful whitish (my wife called it eggshell, who knew?) thing from the fifties, satin with little pearls around the top – a bodice, my wife insists I call it. She said if I was describing what women were wearing I should have a woman's input. Whatever. The bridesmaids were in pink – excuse me, *rose*-colored taffeta. We guys were all wearing tuxes we rented from Big Jim's Men's Store on the square. They matched.

The preacher talked too much, as preachers do, but he got the job done. After, we went into the church's fellowship hall where the reception was to be held. The thing about that, though, is when you have a reception in a church building you can't have liquor, and, I'm sorry, but weddings are a time of rejoicing and who wants to rejoice without booze? So Jean and I had lined up an after-reception party at our house, after which we transported the soused newlyweds back to the Longbranch Inn for their wedding night.

As the weeks and months wore on, a few things happened: Drew Gleeson moved back to Tulsa and Jasper Thorne was promoted to head EMT; Chandra Blanton and Mike Reynolds got married, with their son and Jean and I in attendance; and my deputy, Anthony Dobbins and his wife, Maryanne, were expecting their first child in just a few months. She'd made it way past the eight-week mark that had ended her earlier pregnancies, and the doctor said that everything looked real good. We put an ad in the local paper about Tornado, the golden retriever/Shetland mix that had been abusing my testicles, but nobody claimed him. He now has his own dog house, one that Evinrude, my cat, occasionally visits, when the two aren't lying together in front of the fireplace. Go figure.

Eunice Blanton pleaded guilty and was sentenced to ten years with a possibility of parole; Earl Blanton pleaded guilty and was sentenced to life imprisonment; and Jean got monthly written reports from the therapist in Kansas City on the progress of the twins. She also got weekly phone calls from Vivian, which was probably a good thing for the old lady, but maybe not so good for my wife. She seemed to be bummed out after every call. During one call Jean found out that one of her earlier prime suspects – a guy named Neil Davenport, who lived next door to the Carmichael estate – had been using Constance's services: namely sleeping with both Dru and Megan from about the age of twelve onwards. He was being investigated.

But mostly life went on, as it does in Prophesy County. Shit happens, then we clean it up. That's just the way we roll.